The Weekend Break

The Weekend Break

RUTH O'LEARY

POOLBEG

Published 2024
by Poolbeg Press Ltd.
123 Grange Hill, Baldoyle,
Dublin 13, Ireland
Email: poolbeg@poolbeg.com

© Ruth O'Leary 2024

© Poolbeg Press Ltd. 2024, copyright for editing, typesetting, layout, design, ebook and cover image.

ISBN 978-1-78199-698-0

www.poolbeg.com

About the Author

Ruth O'Leary lives in Dublin with her family and Golden Retriever Rusky. She works as a freelance movie extra playing various roles from a nun to a Viking and everything in between.

Ruth's short stories have been published many times in two of Ireland's national publications, *Woman's Way* and *Ireland's Own* magazine. She has also had a memoir piece published in the online magazine *Childlike* and a poem and a short story published in a local regional paper. Her short story 'Memory Lane' was chosen to open the inaugural author live-reading event run by Shorter Stories. In 2021 she was awarded a bursary by the Irish Writers Centre.

Her work can be found on her website *www.rutholearywriter.com* where she writes a monthly blog called *Rambling Ruth* combining her passion for writing and travelling. She is also very active on social media, and you can chat with her about all things writing on *twitterhttps://twitter.com/rutholearywrite* and also on Instagram *https://www.instagram.com/rutholearywriter/*

Find out more:

www.rutholearywriter.com

Email: rutholearywriter@gmail.com

Acknowledgements

This book would never have been written without the advice and support of my online writers group Writers Ink. Bestselling author Vanessa Fox O'Loughlin aka Sam Blake and writing mentor and journalist Maria McHale joined forces to create a space for aspiring writers to learn and grow and show their work in a supportive and kind environment. The support of my fellow Inkers is a big part of my writing life and we have so much fun cheering each other on and celebrating everyone's achievements.

Thank you to my agent Kate Nash who, from the first time we met, has been a great support and guide to this newbie. My publishers Poolbeg have been nothing but supportive since the day I delivered my query letter. Paula Campbell has been so kind despite my many emails at all hours! Editor Gaye Shortland has been very patient even when I edited the wrong document and has helped me get this book to where it is today. It is a great privilege to get to work with these three amazing women.

The Weekend Break is a complete work of fiction, but I have had many fantastic weekends away with my FLG girlfriends. Thank you Ann M, Anne K, Annette, Dervil, Emily, Fiona, and Niamh for all the laughs and adventures we have had, some of which may or may not end up in future books!

I want to thank all the extras, background actors and AD's I work with. Being able to work in this field and watch dedicated creative people inspires and supports my own creativity.

Finally, thank you to everyone who has bought this book. It is a dream come true for me and I am grateful every single day. And to Hughy, Jack, Michael and Tim, let's keep the adventure going.

Dedication

For Hughy, Jack, Michael, Tim,
Barbra, Peter
Mum and Dad
Rusky
– My world –

FRIDAY

Chapter 1

MIRIAM

This is a bad idea, Miriam thought, as she wiped the sweat off her brow and the vomit from her lips. Her pale face looked back at her from the mirror in the toilets of the train station as she washed her hands. She reapplied her make-up, adding more concealer under her eyes, and pinched her cheeks as they did in old movies, to add some colour. Taking out a comb, she tried to backcomb her thin, brown, shoulder-length hair to put a bit of life into it. The blow-dry from the day before had been ruined by the tossing and turning of her disturbed sleep. She hadn't slept a wink last night, thinking about this trip. Arriving an hour before the others had been a mistake too. She had thought that she could relax and have some breakfast but hanging around just made her nerves worse. Her stomach rumbled. She was starving but she couldn't eat. She groped around the bottom of her bag for some mints to cover her vomit breath and hopefully settle her stomach for the journey ahead.

"*The next train for Galway will be departing from platform five at ten thirty.*"

That's our train coming in now, thought Miriam, as the muffled announcement came over the tannoy. She packed her make-up away in her clutch bag and smoothed down her blue cashmere jumper, pulling it down over her hips. The feel of the cashmere gave her comfort, but the colour drained her, she noticed, as she took a last look in the mirror.

Why oh why, am I going ahead with this trip, she asked herself. But she knew why. None of the girls would want to have anything to do with her if they found out what she had done. But, until then, she was going to try to enjoy this trip. After five years of going away for a Christmas break with the girls, Miriam knew this one could be her last.

VIVIENNE

Vivienne cut through the crowds of Dublin's Heuston Station, carrying her skinny flat white in one hand while pulling her matching designer cases behind her with the other. Her tall, thin frame was heightened by her 4-inch heels that clip-clopped across the tiled floor. Making her way to an empty table in the concourse, she perched on the edge of the uncomfortable metal seat and crossed her long, trousered legs while she waited for the girls to arrive. Taking a small mirror from her clutch bag, she puckered her lips, checking that her lipstick was still perfectly in place. Her Louis Vuitton handbag in taupe matched her suitcase and purse. It didn't come as a set, but Vivienne liked everything to match.

Vivienne had been counting down the days to this trip. The stress in the house was unbearable. She had hardly spoken to her husband in four weeks and her demanding children were grating on her nerves. Licking a finger, she flattened a loose blonde strand of hair over her ear, nervously pushing it back in place. Her scraped-back hair was tightly secured with a diamante hairclip and tons of hairspray. Organising this weekend away had been a very welcome distraction. As usual, once the women decided on the destination, Vivienne arranged everything else. Having worked in the travel business for over twenty years she relished the task, and the girls were delighted for her to do it all. It was like having their own private tour guide.

Using her contacts, she got great rates on hotels, usually boutique, always central. She loved to find unusual or quirky restaurants and made reservations months in advance. Private transfers were always included. She smiled to herself, remembering the look on the girls' faces when she organized a private speedboat from Positano to their hotel in Sorrento instead of taking the public ferry! Yes, it was triple the cost, but the memory was worth it. This year everyone was surprised when Vivienne suggested they stay in Ireland for their pre-Christmas break, but they very quickly agreed that supporting Irish hotels and businesses was a good idea and travelling by train would be a great laugh.

Vivienne liked to plan a surprise or treat for her friends and this time would be no different. The extra Louis Vuitton case contained savoury nibbles from the M&S luxury range, macaroons freshly made in Paris and collected from Brown Thomas this morning, and four bottles of Dom Perignon. She took the champagne from her husband's special collection in the temperature-controlled fridge in his office. Fuck him, she thought, the girls deserved a treat.

Vivienne wanted to make this trip special because her life was about to change forever and the fallout for her family was going to be painful and difficult – but it had to happen. She was determined to have a new life and it would start this weekend.

CLARA

A trickle of sweat rolled down the side of Clara's face as she jostled for space on the Luas. There was nothing she could do to wipe it away. One hand firmly gripped her weekend case, and the other was hanging on to the overhead bar as the public-transport tram snaked its way through the city streets. Clara clung to the bar desperately, trying not to sway into a group of tourists beside her. She tried to blow the bead of sweat away with her lower lip but to no avail.

She cursed herself for not getting up and leaving the house earlier, but she had been up half the night trying to settle Seán after his feeds. Although twelve months old now, Seán had been born with a cleft palate, so he was awfully slow to feed and even longer to wind. He had been particularly unsettled last night, as if he sensed she was going away. So, when the alarm went off this morning, Clara had hit the snooze button. She knew it was wrong but, with the exhaustion of the night feeds, that extra twenty minutes in bed was too much of a draw. That little lie-in meant that Clara had no time for a shower which she regretted now as the heat of the packed Luas made her sweat under her big, red, wool coat. She longed to open her coat and take her scarf off, but the fear that the winding Luas might send her flying into unsuspecting passengers was enough to make her leave her hands where they were.

Instead, she closed her eyes and tried to imagine herself floating in the hotel swimming pool this afternoon and relaxing on one of the poolside loungers. The thought of a pool and spa had been keeping Clara going for the past few months. Money was tight at home, but she had put a little aside in an old tea caddy like her mum used to do because she really needed this break. Although the mental image of being in a swimsuit in public, still carrying her post-baby weight, made her nauseous.

Damn! She felt beads of sweat on her upper lip now. Are we nearly there, she wondered as she strained to look past the tourists' heads to the outside. So much for doing my make-up and straightening my hair, she thought. No doubt the heat in here is expanding my bob into a fuzzball. Just for once, I would like to arrive cool and calm and not feel like the odd one out. No doubt Vivienne has had her hair and nails done and travelled in a taxi with her matching luggage. She looked down at her well-used case and sighed.

Pull yourself together, she said to herself, straightening up as the Luas pulled into Heuston Station. Think positive. You need this break. You deserve this break. She stepped off the crowded Luas, breathing in the cold December air, and marched towards the entrance.

Clara needed this weekend to be fabulous because, after five years of wonderful trips away with the girls, this was the one she needed the most. She didn't feel herself; she felt a bit lost and needed the headspace away from her family and home to try to find a way forward. Something needed to change in her life.

HELEN

"Jesus Christ!" Helen roared at the car in front of her as it stopped at a red light. *"Shit! I can't be late!"* Leaning on the steering wheel, she stared at the traffic lights, willing them to change. The traffic was always busy on the quays but, having lived in Dublin all her life, Helen knew the shortcuts and had been doing really well on time until the car in front stopped when the lights turned orange. Of course, you should prepare to stop when the lights turn orange

but today Helen would have driven through them. She tapped her fingers on the steering wheel impatiently. *Come on, come on! Oh no! Not a hot flush. Not now!*

"*For fuck's sake! That's all I need now!*" Helen shouted again as she grappled with the cold-air dial. Feeling the heat on the back of her neck, she grabbed one of the hair bobbins she kept on the gearstick and dragged her long black hair up into a high ponytail. That's better, she thought, taking some deep breaths to calm herself down.

"*Green light!*" she shouted and beeped her horn at the car in front. Once she saw an opening, she jumped lane and passed the car, glaring at the poor man, and accelerated up the quays. She could see Heuston Station now. The hot flush was still burning her up. She didn't need to look in the mirror to know her face was red, and she could feel a trickle of sweat at the base of her spine. They say stress can make hot flushes worse and I am certainly stressed, she thought.

She had put her suitcase into her car last night so that she could race away early this morning. Despite leaving lists for her husband, she knew she would still get at least five texts a day while she was away. Jerry would try his best. He wasn't happy about her going away with the girls and organising four boys was no easy task. Helen knew the boys' schedule off the top of her head but, even when she wrote it all out for Jerry, it looked exhausting.

"*Jesus Christ! You're blocking my lane!*" Helen shouted out her window to a taxi man dropping passengers at the station.

"Relax, love!" he said with a smirk.

"Don't call me 'love'!" Helen said under her breath as she tried to squeeze past his terrible parking.

Finally, she got to the car park and got a spot easily enough.

Jumping out of the car, she grabbed her keys and her weekend case and opened her boot to get her jacket.

"*Shit!*" she cursed. No jacket. "*I don't bloody believe it!*" It was a frosty December morning in Dublin and the forecast for Galway was for sleet and possibly snow. She slammed the boot and headed for the entrance, wearing only her black jeans and an AC/DC T-shirt. Well, at least my hot flushes will keep me warm, she thought, grinning.

Dragging her bag into the station, she finally let out a big breath. She could relax now.

Helen had been counting down the days to this trip. After five years of wonderful trips away with the girls, she needed this weekend to be great. Jerry hated her going away on her own and he always made it difficult for her. But Helen would be lost without the girls and their Christmas trips away. She needed to get away and breathe and have some space away from her controlling husband. Taking another deep breath, she could feel her whole body relax. She made it here and she was going to make every minute of the weekend count.

Chapter 2

The girls hugged excitedly when they met up in the concourse. It had been about two months since they had seen each other.

"Hey, everyone!" Helen said, throwing her arms around Miriam and Clara. "I cannot wait for this trip!"

"Me neither, I have literally been counting down the days," said Clara, smiling from ear to ear. "Have you no jacket? Are you not freezing?" She was looking at Helen's bare arms.

"I forgot the bloody thing in the rush to escape the house. I'm fine for the moment but I'll have to buy one when we get to Galway."

"I have a cardigan in my case if you want it?" offered Clara.

"Thanks so much. I'll take that off you when we get on the train." Helen shrugged. "My hot flushes are keeping warm at the moment."

"Now, ladies, the train is in, and here are your tickets," Vivienne said, handing out the tickets. "Let's get on the train and get settled." She gathered her things and marched ahead.

The others followed her down the platform until they arrived at the first-class carriage.

The first-class seats were a little more spacious than in the economy carriages. The girls spotted their names over their seats and, after securing their bags overhead, they settled into their reserved seats two opposite two with a big table between them.

"I hear the full Irish breakfast is top-notch," said Clara, scanning the menus that were placed on the table. She was starving. She had been attending the Slim4U slimming club for two months now, but despite measuring her portions, and giving up alcohol, cakes and biscuits, she had only lost 4lbs which really disappointed her. So, she was giving Slim4U a break for the weekend and planned on eating anything she wanted. She had been salivating on the Luas just thinking about the full Irish breakfast she was going to have on the train.

"No Full Irish for us, ladies," Vivienne said as she picked up the menus and put them to the side of the table. "Let me get my case down." She stood up to remove one of her cases from the overhead rack.

Her cream, tailored trousers and gold-trimmed, cream, short jacket fitted her perfectly, thought Clara, comparing Vivienne's style to her black leggings, oversized black tunic and long cardigan.

"Let me get that for you," said a suited businessman as he was passing by.

That would never happen to me, thought Helen as she looked at the handsome stranger showing off while smiling at Vivienne. Annoyed, she searched in her bag for her fan, feeling another hot flush coming on.

Vivienne shot the man a dashing, fake smile as she stood aside and let him lift the case down for her. She was used to this kind of attention from men.

"You are so kind!" she gushed and then quickly ignored him as he was about to continue talking.

He moved on.

"Now, ladies, I have packed a few treats for our breakfast this morning." Vivienne opened the case and produced the goods. Out came the beautifully packaged savoury bites, the brown Thomas macarons, and some miniature cucumber sandwiches.

"Oh, wow, this is fabulous!" said Helen.

Oh no, thought Clara as her stomach rumbled, realising she would not be getting her much longed-for fry-up.

"And to wash it all down, the best bubbly!" Vivienne said as she took out Tom's awfully expensive champagne and four glasses.

"Oh, yes, bring it on!" said a delighted Helen, determined to drink as much as possible this weekend.

Oh no, thought Miriam and she felt nauseous again.

As the train pulled out of Heuston Station, Vivienne popped the champagne cork with experienced ease and laid out matching paper plates and napkins.

"*To the weekend!*" she said, raising her glass.

The four ladies clinked their glasses.

"*To the weekend!*" they said together and let Tom's expensive bubbles kickstart their weekend.

They threw back the first glass and laughed, feeling delighted to be on their way.

Everyone, that is, except Miriam who was looking very pale and still holding her glass.

"Are you not drinking, Miriam?" Helen said.

"No ... I ... can't ... I ..." Miriam started to sweat now.

"Are you okay, love?" Clara said, putting her hand on Miriam's arm. "You don't look great."

"No ... I'm not sick ... I'm pregnant."

The faces of the three friends froze in shock and silence.

"Oh my God, Miriam, that's wonderful news!" Clara was first to find her voice.

"This is amazing news," said Vivienne, still looking shocked.

Helen jumped up to hug her friend. "How long are you gone?"

"Five months."

"*Five months!*" the three friends shrieked together.

"*Shhh!* Would you mind not telling the whole train!" Miriam laughed as the other passengers turned their heads to see what the commotion was.

"Where's your bump?" said Clara, shocked, looking at her skinny friend sitting beside her.

"Oh, it's here alright," Miriam said moving aside the big navy-and-white silk scarf that was hiding her stomach.

"You are tiny, Miriam, but how did we not notice?" Helen said.

"Well, we were so excited to see each other, and I have it well hidden," she answered.

"How could you not tell us though? How could you keep this to yourself?" Vivienne asked.

"Well … I wanted to wait for the twelve weeks to be sure and then I needed time to get used to the idea." Miriam felt her stomach muscles relax a little and tried her best to smile.

"So, when are you due?" Clara asked.

"The 3rd of April."

"Oh my God, I still can't believe it," said Helen. "Who else knows?"

"Nobody. You guys are the first," said Miriam sheepishly. "I haven't told my mum or family yet, so can you keep it to yourselves for now, please, girls? And of course, work doesn't know either but I'm starting to show so I'm going to have to tell them after the

Christmas break." Miriam placed a hand on her tummy.

"How do you think your mum will take it?" asked Clara.

"I don't know. Her dementia is pretty bad now, so I don't think she'll understand. Obviously, she would have preferred for me to have walked up the aisle with Mister Right first and, of course, I am thirty-nine so … I don't know what her reaction will be."

"And do we know the father?" Helen asked tentatively.

"No," Miriam answered, feeling sick again. "I went to a donor clinic."

"A donor clinic?" said Vivienne. "I can't believe you went through all this without telling us?" She reached across the table and put her hand on Miriam's.

"I know, I know, I wanted to say something, but this was something I had to do by myself."

Clara leaned in and hugged Miriam. "I am so excited for you, and we will be here to support and help you one hundred percent, won't we, girls?"

The three friends nodded in agreement, delighted for their friend.

"Well, this deserves a toast," said Vivienne as she topped up the girls' glasses and poured Miriam an orange juice.

"*To Miriam!*"

"*To Miriam!*" they all said, raising their glasses.

Miriam forced a big smile on her face as she looked at her three friends' delighted and supportive faces.

Oh crap, she thought as she went along with the celebration. And as her friends chatted excitedly to her about her pregnancy, she felt like such a fraud.

She tried not to imagine their faces if they ever found out that her baby's father was not an anonymous donor but someone they all knew. One of their husbands.

Chapter 3

"Follow me, ladies! And someone help Miriam with her bags," Vivienne said as the train pulled into Galway Station.

"I can manage myself," Miriam protested but Clara and Helen insisted on taking her bags down for her.

"Milk it while you can," said Helen with a wink.

The train station was right in the centre of Galway City and, as the girls left, they could see the main square, Eyre Square, right in front of them. It was the 10th of December 2018, and the square was beautifully decorated for Christmas. Little wooden huts selling handmade crafts lined the pathways, giving the square a Scandinavian feel. A huge Christmas tree stood in the centre of the square with a children's play area around it. There was a giant Ferris wheel at the top of the square, towering over the whole of Galway City. With only two weeks to go until Christmas, the air was buzzing with excitement. Coming out of the station, they walked past the old five-star Great Southern Hotel that ran the whole length of the bottom of the square and the girls got excited, thinking they were staying there.

But Vivienne marched straight ahead across Eyre Square, turning right at the top.

"Where are we going?" Clara asked, dragging her bag over the cobbled street.

"I hope it's bloody close or I'll freeze to death," Helen said, pulling Clara's cardigan around her.

"Almost there," Vivienne said over the shoulder of her full-length camel coat.

"Hey, there's a TK Maxx!" Miriam pointed out to Helen. "You might get a cheap coat there."

"Well, that's handy," Vivienne said, stopping at the TK Maxx entrance, "as we're staying here."

"*What?* In TK Maxx?" said Helen.

"No!" Vivienne laughed. "Up there!" She pointed to what looked like offices over TK Maxx. "Our apartments are up there. They are called the Western City Point Apartments. The entrance is around the corner. You guys stay here while I pick up the keys."

The girls waited with Vivienne's bags as she went off to get the keys from the reception desk in a nearby hotel.

"Well, this is different," Helen said, sounding disappointed.

"Apartments? So much for a pool and spa," said Clara, her heart sinking a little as she said goodbye to her relaxing afternoon beside a pool.

"Well, it's different alright," said Miriam, "but Vivienne has great taste so I'm sure it will be lovely."

Helen's heart also sank as she realized they wouldn't have a bar to hang out in for the afternoon.

When Vivienne returned with the keys, they all tried to look enthusiastic as they took the lift to the second floor.

"Here we are, apartments four and five. Let's unpack and meet downstairs in thirty minutes and we'll go for lunch. I have booked the cutest little restaurant. You're all going to love it."

"Okay, let's move it, I'm freezing out here," said Helen, feeling the frosty December air through her T-shirt and cardigan.

Vivienne and Miriam were sharing apartment Number 5 and Clara and Helen were in Number 4. They usually paired up this way. Vivienne and Miriam both worked full-time and travelled a lot for work, so they had that to talk about. Helen and Clara both had young families and hadn't a minute to themselves, so they had that in common.

Helen turned the key in the apartment door and let out a sigh of relief as the warm air from the central heating melted her cold bones.

"*Oh wow!*" she said as she walked in. "Check this place out!"

Clara followed her in and was amazed at the size of the apartment.

It was huge. There were two double bedrooms, and a modern red-gloss kitchen opening out to an open-plan living room. White marble floor-tiles ran through the whole apartment. Two luxurious white leather couches flanked the living room, drawing the eye to the floor-to-ceiling glass windows and door that led out to a big wooden decking area.

"Look out here, Clara!" Helen said excitedly as she dropped her bag and walked to the window, opening the biggest door and stepping outside. The deck was about the size of the living room. Because the apartments were so high up, they had a wonderful view of the Ferris wheel and the Christmas tree in Eyre Square.

"We'll have to have drinks out here later," said Helen.

"Did someone say drinks?" Vivienne stuck her head around the divider that separated their decked balconies, carrying a bottle of champagne and three glasses.

"Jeez, more drink?" said Clara. I'll be locked at this rate, she thought as her stomach rumbled, missing its Irish Rail fry.

"And a tea for me," laughed Miriam, hugging a hot mug of tea.

"Give it here," said Helen, taking the glasses over the balcony fence.

The four friends stood on their balconies taking in the view.

"You've done it again, Vivienne," said Helen. "This view is fantastic. For a minute there I thought we were staying in the TK Maxx staff quarters!"

Although Clara and Miriam would have liked to be relaxing by the pool of a 5-star hotel, the pals toasted the next part of their weekend.

"Okay, ladies, throw it back!" said Vivienne. "We have to get ready for lunch."

"Guys, I'm going to pop into TK Maxx and buy a jacket for the weekend, so I'll meet you at the restaurant," said Helen. "Vivienne, will you forward me the address?"

"No problem, it's called the Pie Maker. Head straight down towards the Spanish Arch and I'll send you the address."

Chapter 4

Helen grabbed her bag and left a key for Clara.

"*I'll see ye at the restaurant!*" she called as she left.

She looked at her watch. Forty-five minutes until she had to meet the girls for lunch. Not much time. The lift wasn't quick enough for Helen, so she took the stairs instead to save time.

I'd better be quick, she thought, as she entered TK Maxx. The huge shop was packed full of Christmas shoppers. She looked around to see where the women's section was. Damn it, it's upstairs, she cursed when she saw the women's clothing sign. I won't have enough time, she thought, feeling panicked. Turning around, she realized she was standing in the men's department and searched the rails quickly for a small-size jacket. Pulling out a black puffer jacket, she tried it. It didn't fit well and made her look like she had big shoulders but at €29.99 it would do. She headed for the checkout.

The queue was long, and she felt her anxiety rise as she stood in line, impatiently tapping her foot.

"Come on, come on," she said under her breath, checking her watch again.

The staff were wearing Santa hats and trying to be jolly, despite the constant queue of people in front of them.

Oh, hurry up, she thought, willing the queue to move faster. She started sweating and feeling uneasy.

Nearly there, she said to herself, taking deep breaths to calm herself. She picked up a random Christmas card from the display beside her and started fanning herself with it.

"Next, please!"

"Oh, thank god," Helen said under her breath as she rushed forward.

"Would you like a bag?" the smiling staff member said, sweating under her Santa hat.

"No, thank you," Helen said, taking her credit card out.

"We have a special offer on wrapping paper," the teller began.

"Look, I just want to pay for this! I'm in a hurry and I'm going to wear the coat now."

"Cash or card?" said the cashier, dropping her Christmas cheer.

Helen tapped her card.

"Your receipt," the cashier said but Helen was gone.

Rushing out of TK Maxx, she pulled the tags off her new jacket and threw them in a nearby bin. Feeling the sting of the frosty air, she quickly put the jacket on and zipped it up to her chin. She checked her watch. She had thirty minutes now.

Turning up her collar against the wind, she started to walk as fast as she could through the Christmas crowds. Whizzing in and out of Christmas shoppers, she made her way down Shop Street. Having been to Galway on summer holidays with the kids, she knew where the Spanish Arch was, so she kept focused and kept moving. Halfway down Shop Street, she checked the address Vivienne had given her for the Pie Maker restaurant. Standing at the junction of Cross Street and Shop Street to get her bearings, Helen looked around her for somewhere suitable. She needed somewhere nearby so she wouldn't be late for lunch, but not so close that the girls might see her leaving from it.

Walking further down Quay Street, she saw a sign for Jurys Inn Hotel and quickened her step.

Perfect, she thought as she ran ahead.

Walking through the doors of Jurys Inn, she unzipped her jacket and looked around.

"Can I help you, madam?" the receptionist said.

"Yes, I'm supposed to be meeting a friend in the bar."

"The bar is just down the corridor to your right," the young woman replied with a smile.

"Thank you," Helen said, feeling lightheaded as she made her way down the corridor.

Stepping into the bar, the heat from the open fire and the smell of Christmas lunch helped her relax a little. The loud chatter of the busy lunch crowd was just what she was looking for. Groups of people, some on their work break, and others surrounded by shopping bags lunching with friends, filled the busy bar with a lovely Christmas atmosphere.

Helen looked around and headed down to the quieter end of the bar.

"Hi there, what can I get you?" the barman asked.

"Vodka and Diet Coke, please." She took off her new jacket and made herself comfortable at the bar. She checked her watch. "Actually, can you make it a double vodka, please?"

Ten minutes to lunch. She tried to look relaxed, but her heart was racing.

Hurry up, she said to herself, watching the barman chat away to customers as he was pouring her drink.

"Now, there you are," he said smiling.

Helen held out her card to be tapped while pouring the Coke into the vodka with her other hand.

Oh, how I love that sound, she thought as the Coke fizzed on top of the ice cubes.

Around her people were chatting and laughing and Christmas music was playing in the background. Helen blocked them all out as she swallowed the vodka and Coke, allowing the ice-cold liquid to ease down her throat. Relief flooded through her as she felt the alcohol enter her veins.

Oh thank God, she thought, savouring the taste as she looked at her watch, wondering if she had time for another.

Chapter 5

Lunch in the Pie Maker was delicious. The tiny restaurant could only hold eighteen people, so they were lucky that Vivienne had secured a reservation. The four friends sat in a booth of which there were only four. There were also five stools at the counter for customers to eat at while they watched the staff prepare the food. The old traditional Irish décor of the restaurant matched the warm welcome of the staff. Pictures of the Sacred Heart and statues of the Virgin Mary were dotted around the restaurant in a quirky fashion and a whole wall was decorated with school rulers. The menu consisted of different homemade savoury pies with mashed potatoes and peas.

Miriam was delighted to see vegetarian pies on the menu too as she could not tolerate the smell or taste of meat since becoming pregnant. To go from someone who loved steak to someone who couldn't stand the sight of meat was a strange side effect of being pregnant that she had not anticipated. On the other hand, there were so many vegetarian and vegan options in restaurants and cafés these days that she never went hungry. She had bought herself some vegetarian cookbooks and was learning new skills and dishes at home, so it wasn't all bad.

Clara savoured every mouthful as she was still starving, having missed her fry-up. The pastry of her beef-and-stout pie was crumbly and buttery. The beef melted in her mouth, and she closed her eyes as the buttery mashed potatoes filled her with joy.

The ladies finished every bit of food on their plates, each one claiming their pie was the best. It was the perfect food after travelling from Dublin.

"Would you like to see the dessert menu?" the waitress asked.

"Oh no, thank you – we are so full of your delicious pies," answered Vivienne on behalf of everyone.

Clara sighed. She would have loved to try their homemade apple pie with cream but was too self-conscious to say anything now.

"Okay, ladies," Vivienne said as she stood up and put her coat on. "I have a table booked in Cava Bodega for eight tonight. It's a tapas restaurant. The reviews are fabulous, and it was voted Ireland's best tapas restaurant, so it's always busy. Why don't we go for a pre-dinner drink at say seven? That means we will have to be ready to leave the apartment at six thirty. It's half past two now. So what would you girls like to do now? Some shopping?"

"Well, I'm a little tired so I think I'll go back to the apartment for a rest," said Miriam, looking a little pale as she gathered up her coat and handbag.

"You're dead right, Miriam," Vivienne said. "The tiredness of pregnancy really takes it out of out of you."

"I think I'll do the same," said Clara. "I was up last night with Seán so I could do with a nap too."

"Ah, come on, ladies!" Helen said with a wink. "There are so many cool pubs in Galway. It would be bad form not to check a few of them out."

"It's too early for me to go drinking, Helen, or I'll be asleep before dinner," said Clara apologetically.

"Okay. Vivienne, surely you'll join me for a pint?"

"Yes, absolutely! You can count me in. But first I need to do a little Christmas shopping."

"Grand, why don't I come with you? I can carry your bags."

"No! Absolutely not. You hate shopping and the shops will be packed so that will definitely irritate you," Vivienne said with a laugh. "Why don't you go for a wander. I'll do my shopping and I'll meet you in Naughton's pub at say four?"

"Perfect. I could do with some fresh air. That's a plan so," said Helen excitedly, rubbing her hands together.

The girls paid their bill and left the Pie Maker to go their separate ways.

"Are you coming, Clara?" Miriam said, buttoning up her coat.

"You go ahead. I just want to pop into a chemist's. I have a bit of a headache."

"I can wait for you if you like?"

"No, you go ahead and get your rest."

"Okay, I'm exhausted, see you later," Miriam said as she headed up the road.

Turning onto Main Street, Clara walked into the first chemist's she came to and watched Miriam walk up the street from the window. Once Miriam had disappeared into the crowd, Clara walked out of the chemist's and found the nearest Euro shop. She picked up a basket and threw in a pile of jumbo-sized chocolate bars. She also threw in a litre of Coca-Cola and treats for the kids.

She quickly paid, shoved everything into her large shoulder bag and headed back to the apartment.

Although it was early afternoon, Galway's Christmas fairy lights were lit, giving the streets a warm Christmassy feel. Clara passed shoppers laden down with bags. Some looked stressed and some looked excited. It warmed her heart to see little kids in buggies pointing up at the coloured lights with joy and delight on their faces.

She felt lightheaded, so she continued towards the apartment, sweating under her big wool coat. Almost there, she thought as she saw TK Maxx up ahead.

Arriving at the apartment, she let herself in and locked the door. She leaned against the door, letting out a sigh of relief. Throwing her heavy coat on a chair, she pushed the scatter cushions out of the way and fell back on the soft leather couch, allowing it to take her weight. Finally, she thought, closing her eyes, happy to have the place to herself. After a minute or two she pushed herself up to sit, swung her legs off the couch and emptied the contents of her bag on the glass coffee table. Lining the chocolate bars up, starting with her favourite Cadbury's mint crisp, she then poured some Coca-Cola into one of the decorative glasses on the coffee table. Then, starting from the left, she picked up the large bar of mint crisp and gently removed the outer paper wrapper. Folding the paper neatly, she placed it on the coffee table. Next, she peeled a one-inch piece of foil wrapper horizontally, revealing the first line of chocolate squares. She raised the bar to her face and inhaled the wonderful scent of chocolate and mint. Breaking the line of chocolate off and then the individual squares, she slowly placed the chocolate in her mouth. Closing her eyes, she ate each square one by one. The chocolate started to melt in her mouth, revealing the crisp mint chunks which felt like little fireworks of joy. Clara instantly felt euphoric. The rush of sugar was like a drug. Her headache was slowly easing as she continued to eat the jumbo mint-crisp bar before moving on to the next bar. This time she ripped the packaging off and squashed it into a ball. The slow ritual was just reserved for the first bar.

The first bar was savoured, the following bars were devoured. Before she finished one bar, she was opening another, stopping only to wash it down with more Coke. She continued at this pace until every bar was gone.

Then, exhausted from the rush, she tidied up all the wrappers and stuffed them in her bag. Then she kicked off her shoes and slowly put her legs up on the couch. She pulled one of the designer cushions up to use as a pillow and pulled a soft Avoca throw over her. She checked her phone. It was 3.45.

Helen liked her pints, Clara thought, so she won't be back until five at the earliest. She set her phone alarm for 4.30 and dozed off to sleep on a chocolate high.

Chapter 6

Two days before the trip, Clara had looked at the clothes laid out on her bed and sighed heavily. I hate all my clothes, she thought. Packing for this trip only highlighted that she had not lost the weight she had promised herself she would. When the kids went back to school in September, Clara had thought it was the perfect time to go to the Slim4U slimming club. She had planned on walking every morning after the school drop and she thought she would now have loads of time to make fresh salads for lunch and to batch-cook healthy low-fat dinners. *Batch cook.* It was another one of those buzzwords to make women feel inadequate. Organised mums who looked after their families by feeding them healthy meals, were batch-cooking at the weekend, freezing family-sized lasagnas, and casseroles to be whipped out and arranged like a Nigella cookbook at the drop of a hat. Well, at least that was the message Clara was getting.

When Clara tried batch-cooking, she ended up spending five hours of her Saturday peeling, chopping, and frying. Then, before the dishes could be finished, she would have to put Seán in the car and pick up one of the kids from whatever sport they had on. This resulted in coming home to an unholy mess of half-cooked food and scraps everywhere. By then, of course, the kids wanted lunch so that had to magically appear. By the time the batch-cooking was done and put in containers for the freezer, Clara was ready for a lie-down. But, of course, not until she spent thirty minutes cleaning up the mess in the kitchen after using every pot and pan in the house. This resulted in Clara missing her lunch and grabbing a cup of tea and about ten biscuits that were definitely not on her slim4U plan.

Despite the banned biscuits, Clara did lose a few pounds at first. She kept to her walking routine Monday to Friday. James had to be walked to school, so she put Seán in the buggy, took James to school, and then carried on with the walk. It did them both a world of good. Usually, Clara's sleep would have been broken to feed Seán and she was shattered in the mornings, but she pushed through the tiredness as the fresh air cleared her head and she knew the exercise was good for her.

When Seán was born with a cleft palate, Clara had never heard of such a thing. The birth had been by caesarean section and had gone smoothly. Everything seemed fine at first and Clara and Richard were delighted with their new son. But, when Clara had tried to feed her new-born with a bottle, the milk had flowed down the baby's nose causing him to make choking sounds. This was not normal, so Seán was taken to intensive care for observation. The following day an Ear, Nose, and Throat doctor arrived and diagnosed a cleft palate. He explained that Seán's palate had not been formed correctly in the womb, and therefore the liquid from his bottle was being directed to flow out of his nose instead of down his throat. Clara and Richard were shocked and scared and neither knew anything about the condition. Poor little Seán had to stay in intensive care being fed by tubes until a cleft-palate expert could arrive with special bottles and explain everything about his future care. It was a very lonely and sad thing to be the only woman in a maternity ward with no baby and Clara cried herself to sleep over this.

Two days later, an angel in the form of a woman called Anne from Temple Street Hospital arrived with a big smile and wonderful reassurance. Armed with special bottles, she showed Clara how Seán could be fed. It was a slow process and an even slower process winding him, but it could be done. Anne told Clara that everything would be fine and that Seán could have some surgery to fix his cleft. She hugged Clara and told her to enjoy her baby and gave her an appointment for her cleft-palate clinic. She took some of the fear away for Clara and Richard and gave them the confidence that they could look after Seán.

Twelve months later, Seán was thriving. His condition opened Clara up to a world she hadn't been aware of before. Nurses visited the home to keep an eye on his weight. Hospital appointments for clinics were stuck up on the kitchen noticeboard. Richard was researching surgeries that Seán could have down the line.

But Clara was exhausted. Seán had to sleep upright in a baby seat in his cot in their room to avoid reflux. He woke up twice in the night for a feed. The feed took twenty minutes, and the winding took about thirty, and by the time you changed his nappy and settled him the whole thing took at least one hour. Then Clara would have to try to fall back asleep before he woke again four hours later for another feed. Due to his cleft palate, he was on high-calorie powdered milk as he could not eat solids until after his palate surgery. The surgery was coming up soon and, hopefully, it would make life easier.

The lack of a full night's sleep for twelve months meant that Clara needed sugar to keep her fuelled during the day. She took a nap on the couch when she could, but a midday nap was no substitute for a full night's sleep. As a result, Clara didn't lose the baby weight as quickly as she had with her other children which is why she joined slim4U. She joined to lose weight but now she went for the company. For one hour a week, she could go somewhere without the kids and sit and chat with other women. The support and sense of community amongst the women kept Clara going back each week. Even if she put on weight and was disappointed, there would be a sympathetic ear and we're-all-in-this-together atmosphere from the group that fed her soul. Maura, the leader, was a great support to everyone. You were never made to feel bad if you had put on weight but instead were offered sympathetic looks and some tips for the following week. Clara was ashamed to tell them that instead of walking every day and drinking gallons of water, she had lain on the couch when Seán had his nap, watching daytime TV with a mug of tea and a packet of chocolate digestives. She knew she was only fooling herself most weeks, but the people were genuine, and she liked going for the chat. She did believe that if she took their advice she would get there. But she was too tired at the moment to follow the plan properly.

But, looking at the clothes she planned to pack and take to Galway, she wished she had been stricter with herself. Clara loved bright colours but every brightly coloured outfit she tried on seemed to hug her belly too much and some of the sleeves were too tight. The clothes that did fit were loose and black. For just once, Clara thought, I'd like to show up to a girl's weekend away two stone lighter and wearing fabulous, coloured clothes. *Aw*, well, not

31

this year – this year I will be the frumpy friend dressed for a funeral.

But this was not the only thing getting her down. Clara felt lost. Everything had changed since Seán was born.

As a teenager, Clara worked in retail at weekends and during the summer holidays. She loved it. A naturally chatty person, she enjoyed helping people find what they were looking for. Her first summer job was in a local supermarket. She learned a range of skills there from packing shelves, placing items they wanted to sell most of at eye-line level, and creating special shelves for things they needed to shift quickly. She also loved working on the till. She got to know people when they come in every week, and she loved to greet everyone with a smile and ask them how their day was going. Some people just exchanged pleasantries, but others would nearly tell you their life stories as their shopping went whizzing by on the belt. She had particular time for the very elderly ladies and gents who came in every day. Most attended daily Mass and then came over to buy one or two bits for their lunch or dinner. It was a social occasion for them and some of them would not speak to another person for the rest of the day. She took extra time with these customers and remembered their names if they had given them to her.

When she finished school, she went to college to study Retail and Service Management. Upon qualifying, she was immediately offered a job in Marks and Spencer's flagship store in the city centre. Here she used the merchandising skills she had learned in supermarkets and transferred them to clothing and household departments. She was quickly enrolled in their in-house management programme and was a team leader in women's wear within a year. When her first two children, Jessica and James, were born, she went back to full-time hours after her maternity leave.

M&S had very flexible shifts, so she managed to be able to take the kids to school and be there for them when they got home. She organised playdates for her midweek day off and this worked really well. She also loved the work and occasionally was sent on a course in the UK headquarters where she impressed everyone she met with her instinct for what worked well in a retail setting. As a busy mum, she also knew that other busy mums had limited time to run in and buy baby clothes and maybe a little something for themselves. She made a point of emailing her superiors with her ideas. Before Seán was born she had been promoted to assistant to the store manager and she was so happy in her new role.

Clara had been happy with just two children. Jessica and James were great kids and were settled into a routine of school and weekend activities. But Richard wanted another child. He came from a big family of six kids and had loved growing up in a big noisy house. He felt that another child would complete their little family. Clara hoped he would change his mind, but it was something he really wanted, and he offered to come home early to help out and do all the weekend activities so that Clara could go back to work to the job she loved. But the reality was that he never did come home early and so far it had been impossible for Clara to return to work in any form because of Seán's needs. She had discussed this with Richard many times, but he didn't understand why she needed to go back to work, and this irritated her. Although she kept in touch with her managers, unfortunately they couldn't keep her job open for her but told her that she would be welcome back into the company when things settled down for her.

Clara was not happy, staying at home. She needed the interaction of other people. She thrived on it – it gave her energy.

She could not go on like this. She was miserable and she needed this weekend to get her head straight and figure out what she needed to do to get her life back on track whether Richard liked it or not.

Chapter 7

Vivienne left the girls at two-thirty and headed down Quay Street towards the Spanish Arch. Here she turned left along the Quays taking her to the docklands area. Her appointment was at two forty-five and her timing was perfect as usual. It was no coincidence that she had organised the lunch in that location at that time. Lunch had been lovely and relaxing but when the waitress suggested dessert she had to jump in and say no. Whether the girls wanted dessert or not, it was not happening. She could not be late for her meeting. Although the girls didn't know it, the whole weekend was planned around this appointment.

Walking confidentially, Vivienne turned left, entered Dock Street office buildings and took the lift to the 3rd floor. The lift doors opened to the modern plush offices of Jack Brady Solicitors.

"Hi there, I'm Vivienne Jones and I'm here to see Jack Brady," she said to the receptionist.

"Ah, yes, Ms. Jones, he's expecting you – go straight through." she said, pointing towards an open office door.

* * *

Jones was Vivienne's maiden name; McKeon was her married name. She had kept her maiden name for work purposes. Tom, her husband, wasn't happy about it but had to put up with it as Vivienne was adamant about keeping her own name after they married. Their bank accounts were in their married name of Mr. and Mrs. McKeon, but Vivienne had a few accounts that Tom didn't know about.

Of course, when they married and were madly in love, Vivienne had no problem with the joint accounts. But her grandmother had always told her that a woman should always have a secret account of her own. A "running away fund" she called it, just in case. Vivienne had laughed at the idea but, after she became engaged to Tom, she was surprised to find out that her mother also had an account that her dad did not know about.

"Oh, I'm not planning on running away, Viv, but it is nice to have a few bob there all the same. Your dad is very generous, but no woman needs a man questioning how much she has spent on a hairdo or little treats on a girls' weekend away, now does she?"

Although Vivienne could never imagine having to explain any spending to Tom, she took her grandmother's and mother's advice and kept an account in her maiden name, and had a small direct debit go into it every month. Then, as her career progressed, she felt she should keep the odd bonus that came her way as she worked hard to earn it. As Tom considered her job secondary to his, he never asked about her salary and never took much interest in her promotions. It irritated her when he still described her job to people as booking people's holidays. She had staff under her who did that, and he knew it. She ran a corporate team that organised conferences for companies in Ireland and Europe. She used to talk to him about her work projects, but it became obvious that he had little interest, so she just stopped telling him and he never bothered to ask.

Vivienne first came across Tom when she was in college studying Business at UCD in Dublin. He was studying Business and Law but was more known at UCD for his sporting achievements. Tom played rugby for the UCD A team. Born and raised in Blackrock, he had played rugby from the age of five and played all through school, enjoying the success and popularity of being on the Junior Cup and then the Senior Cup teams. He was an average student, but the rugby circle looked after their own and Tom was sure of a job when he finished college whether he was good at it or not. The rugby team was never short of female admirers either. You didn't have to be good-looking to get the girl. If you could score a try for the team it didn't matter what you looked like and you would be treated as a hero in the UCD bar post-match.

Vivienne had no time for the rugby crowd. Although some of them seemed nice enough in the lecture halls, it was a different world from the one Vivienne had been raised in. To her, they looked like entitled idiots full of their own inflated importance. So whenever she saw Tom McKeown around on campus, she turned the other way.

Vivienne had been brought up in a 3-bed terraced house on Dublin's northside. Marino had a wonderful community atmosphere. Everyone knew everyone on her road, and she grew up playing on the street with the neighbours' kids. Young and old said hello to each other and had a chat if they were out in their gardens or heading to the local shops nearby. There was a big green at the top of her road where she and her friends played and where locals would walk their dogs and have a chat each morning. The primary school on Griffith Avenue was walking distance from their house and, when they were old enough, Vivienne and her brothers could walk or cycle there themselves.

Marino had its own set of local shops too. A mini supermarket that was like Aladdin's cave. No matter what you wanted, they had it. Beside it was a newsagent's where Vivienne's brothers used to order comics and magazines. Then there was a chemist's run by two sisters, a bakery, a butcher's, a hardware store, and a hairdresser's. There was everything you needed. Vivienne's dad was a fireman at the local station and her mother was a stay-at-home mum and a volunteer with the local Meals on Wheels, delivering dinners to the elderly in their area. To Vivienne, it was a great place to live, and she got two buses to University College Dublin on Dublin's southside every day. Every summer Vivienne worked in various travel agent's and tour companies and had a few job offers lined up when she left college. As she loved the city centre, she took a job as a travel agent in Dublin's Dame Street. It was a new operation booking holidays, corporate flights, and sports trips but it also ran a domestic company booking weekends away in Ireland. Working for a big travel company like this would give Vivienne experience in many different areas of the business and that was exactly what she wanted. She learned fast and the company was delighted to have her.

It was while she was working one Saturday that Tom McKeown walked into the office. He and his friends wanted to travel to Rome for an Ireland rugby match and Vivienne's company was organising packages for this important game. She recognised him straight away but wouldn't give him the satisfaction of her knowing who he was.

He was very charming and polite and was obviously still playing sport as he was very fit-looking and, although she didn't want to admit it, he came across as a very nice guy. He booked the trip and paid a deposit. His balance was due in a week and Vivienne was angry at herself for looking forward to seeing him again.

When Tom returned a week later, he looked happy to see her too. There was definitely an attraction between them, and Vivienne felt herself blush when he enquired if she would be going on the trip too.

"No, I'm afraid not," Vivienne said.

"Well, that's a pity. I hear Rome is beautiful, very romantic," Tom said, smiling at her and keeping eye contact.

Now, aren't you a smooth one, Vivienne thought to herself.

"So here are your tickets and check-in is two hours beforehand," she said, handing him his documents.

"Can I buy you a drink for all your hard work?"

"Eh, no thanks, it wasn't hard work for me. Just doing my job," Vivienne said, trying to sound professional but feeling annoyed at herself for blushing in front of him.

"Okay, well, how about – if Ireland wins – you let me buy you a celebratory drink when I get back?"

"No, really, there's no need," Vivienne stammered.

"Just one little drink?" Tom said, flirting outrageously now.

"Okay, but only if Ireland wins," Vivienne relented just to get him to leave.

"Great, I'll have to cheer louder now," he said, winking at Vivienne as he left the office.

Oh shit, why did I agree to that, Vivienne thought, putting her head in her hands.

That Saturday, for the first time in her life, Vivienne sat down with her dad to watch a rugby match with her fingers crossed that Ireland would lose. They won 21-20. That 1-point victory sealed the fate of Vivienne Jones.

Two years later Vivienne and Tom were engaged to be married. Tom had swept Vivienne off her feet. She wasn't particularly comfortable around the rugby scene and felt a little intimidated in the company of his privately schooled wealthy friends. But Tom's closest friends were lovely, and she admired their loyalty to each other.

His friends in fairness were also very supportive of her by sending their corporate travel and rugby business her way. She started to like the connections she was making through their business contacts, and it certainly helped her career. The extra business she brought in, and the new accounts she managed, got her promoted to head of her department.

All in all, she and Tom had a very good lifestyle. Meals out at least once a week, weekends away to European cities, and a sun and ski holiday every year. But the one thing that irked and niggled at her about their marriage was their finances. Tom walked into a job in an investment firm in the city centre. He got the job through his rugby contacts and didn't have to do an interview. The pay was good, but Vivienne wasn't exactly sure what he did there. When they first met, she was attracted to his enthusiasm and ambition. She was very ambitious and had long-term work goals and she felt Tom's ambition matched hers. He had often spoken about opening his own investment firm and got excited about their shared ambitions for their future.

But, over the years, he stopped talking about opening his own firm and when Vivienne brought the subject up she was told the time, or the market, wasn't right. As Vivienne rose through the ranks and moved companies to gain more experience or head up new departments, Tom remained at the same firm and seemed to have fewer ambitions.

And there had been other problems, right from the start. Regardless of their financial position, Tom went on rugby trips to support Ireland at least once a year.

In the run-up to their wedding, he had announced that he was off to Paris with the boys for a match. Vivienne was very upset about this.

"You can't go, we're signing for the house on Friday," she had pleaded with him.

"It's fine – the flight is at 2 pm and I've already asked the solicitor to arrange the signing for the morning," Tom answered.

"Wait, you discussed this with the solicitor before you told me?" Vivienne said, shocked.

"I don't see what the big deal is?" Tom said, coming closer and putting his arms around her.

"But this is a special day!" she said. "It's the day we get the keys to our first house, and you're leaving me to sort everything out?"

"You are overreacting – sort what things out?" said Tom, getting cranky.

"The movers! We booked the movers to take all our stuff from the apartment," said Vivienne, annoyed now.

"You are more than capable of dealing with the movers, Viv," Tom said, sounding exasperated.

"It's not that. Do you seriously expect me to spend the first night in our first home on my own?"

"Look, stay with your mum if you like. I am going on the trip, and I'll be back on Sunday night – we can move in then. You know how important rugby is to me, Viv."

"Yes, but we've been saving so hard for the house and these trips are so expensive and we should have spoken about it. Why didn't you tell me?"

"Rugby has always been important to me. I am not going down to the pub every night or betting money on horses. now am I? So I will always find the money for rugby, and I didn't tell you about it because I didn't want to argue about it. It's no big deal whether we move in on Friday or Sunday, Viv."

Vivienne couldn't hide her disappointment.

"Come on," he said, rubbing her neck and kissing her ear. "We'll make up for it on Sunday night. Just you and me, OK? And I'll bring you back something nice."

Vivienne gave in. She didn't want to argue either. Tom got very cranky if he didn't get his way and sulked like a baby anytime they had an argument. But she felt uneasy. She had been putting every penny away to save for the deposit for the house and she thought Tom was too. They each got paid into their own accounts and had direct debits into a joint account. She had stopped having nights out with the girls and had been very careful about buying clothes for the last year as she was transferring everything that she didn't need for basics into the house account. She presumed Tom was doing the same. So where did he get money for the trip, she wondered uneasily. And why wasn't he upfront about it?

When the next trip came around, Tom just announced it after it was all booked and again there was no discussion, and he went off for two nights whether she liked it or not. Everything else in their lives was great so, even though it annoyed her, she decided not to make a big deal out of it, but she did start to put less into the joint account and a little bit more into her own account.

Tom also had credit cards that Vivienne didn't have access to. When she asked about them he told her to relax and enjoy the benefits. These benefits included nights out, weekends away, and expensive presents. Vivienne had to admit that she enjoyed the finer things and was happy not to ask when Tom's gold card came out. She soon got used to going out on a Friday night with his friends to some of Dublin's top restaurants.

When the kids came along, they moved to a bigger house. Tom came up with the deposit after cashing in some investments and, although Vivienne wished he would confide in her more about how much they had and where it came from, she realised that this was one area of their marriage that would never be transparent.

The crunch came six months ago on the June Bank holiday Monday. Vivienne was in the kitchen, chopping vegetables on the marble island, preparing dinner

Tom, who had been in their home office for most of the afternoon, sat down at the island and opened a bottle of wine, pouring Vivienne a glass.

"Wine on a Monday? What's the occasion?" asked Vivienne, taking a sip.

"Well, we are about to make a tidy sum of money," Tom said.

"Oh, and how's that?" Vivienne said, turning back to chop some peppers. She could feel her neck muscles tense. She was in no mood for one of the get-rich-quick schemes that Tom and his buddies got involved in.

As expected, Tom started talking about an investment opportunity that one of his rugby buddies, Gareth, was involved in. It was something to do with an apartment scheme in Bulgaria. Vivienne had no interest but nodded along to please him.

"So this could be a great investment opportunity for us, Viv."

"For us? No, thanks." Vivienne said, keeping things light but not making eye contact with him. She knew he got cranky when he didn't get his way and she was in no humour for an argument.

"Why not? I've checked it out and it's all legit. We invest a lump sum, and the apartments get built and sold immediately, leaving us with a nice little profit," he explained very matter-of-factly.

"It's too risky, Tom. We don't know anything about the housing market in Bulgaria. Honestly, Tom, how has Gareth even got involved in this?"

"Gar has a business client in London who invests in properties in Bulgaria, Hungary, and Poland and he says it's a no-brainer," Tom said, tapping his fingers on the worktop.

She could tell by the atmosphere he was trying not to lose his temper. It was clear that he was annoyed that she was against this.

"A no-brainer? Look, if it sounds too good to be true it usually is," Vivienne said, determined to drop the subject.

"Jesus, do you not want to make a quick risk-free profit?"

"Risk-free?" Vivienne stopped chopping to look him straight in the face. "There is no such thing as risk-free, Tom. Look, if you have a few spare grand to throw away, then you invest. I am not interested." She carried on chopping the peppers as she could feel her anger rising.

"*If I had the full amount, I wouldn't be talking to you about this!*" Tom almost spat out the words.

"Charming." Vivienne said, putting down the chopping knife

and facing him again. "So if you could get away with it, you would just go ahead and risk our money without speaking to me first."

"I'm speaking to you now, aren't I?"

"How much is the investment?" Vivienne thought she would at least hear him out to humour him.

"Fifty thousand."

"*Fifty thousand!*" Vivienne gasped. "Are you kidding me? *No way.* We don't have that kind of money to spare."

"I don't need your approval, Viv. Do you think I'm an idiot? Don't you think I have checked this out?" Tom was standing now, leaning across the island, speaking into her face. "You really have no faith in me, do you?"

"So the only reason you're telling me about this is that you want to take all our savings and put it into this scheme, and you need my signature for the bank?" Vivienne said, holding his stare.

"We'll get double the money back in four months."

Vivienne had to think quickly. She did not want to risk their savings, but she also didn't want to say no straight out and have a row followed by days of Tom sulking. Their marriage was hanging on a thread as it was. She wasn't even sure if she wanted to save their marriage, but she had a very important conference coming up in two days and she needed to be totally focused on that. She had an opportunity to get some big travel business accounts and did not need this distraction.

"Well, if you're serious about this we could get a solicitor to look over the contracts and then see what we could spare but it will be nowhere near fifty thousand." Vivienne felt she was meeting him halfway with this suggestion and this would buy her time to check it out herself.

"We don't have time for that. Contracts have to be signed this week. And I trust Gar. It's a no-brainer." Tom waved his hand, dismissing her idea completely.

"You have to meet me halfway here, Tom. The amount is too big. I can't risk it. It's too dodgy. We can't risk losing all our savings." She was trying to sound calm and reasonable but really she wanted to tell him to go shove it.

"Viv, all the lads are going in on this."

"I don't care, Tom. Use your own money or your dad's but I'm not signing anything."

"*You bitch!*" he suddenly shouted, slamming his empty glass down on the worktop, his words hitting her like a cold slap. "You hardly had your share of the deposit when we moved in here. You came from a bloody council house on the northside! I got you all this!" He waved his hands around in anger. "I introduced you to this area, my friends, a great social life. This was all me. *And you owe me.*"

Vivienne was so shocked by his outburst, she could hardly find her breath. They'd had their rows over the years, but this was different. Whatever was bubbling up inside him was coming out tonight, but she wasn't having it.

"*Who the fuck do you think you are?*" she roared at him, her knuckles clenching the side of the island. "*I worked before I met you. I have paid my way in this house and the house before. I owe you nothing!*" She steadied herself, taken aback by her own rage.

"When did you become such a stuck-up cow? You think your little job booking flights is something special?" Tom hissed, his face red with fury. "I am the one with the connections. My friends are the ones going places. And yours? I don't see your very few friends bringing great investment opportunities to you, now do I? You have this lifestyle because of me and don't forget it!"

Pulling his jacket off the back of the kitchen chair, he stormed out, slamming the door behind him. She heard his car door slam as he drove off at speed.

Vivienne sat down on an island stool. Her legs went weak, and her hands were shaking. She was furious. Deep breaths, deep breaths, she said to herself as she held on to the side of the island. She felt like she had been punched in the stomach. For a long time she had sensed that things would come to a head over money, but the way Tom had just spoken to her and the things he said, well … there was no going back from this. No bunch of flowers or a shiny piece of jewellery would fix this. He had crossed a line tonight and she didn't think there was any way back.

She poured herself a glass of cold water and sat back down. Breathing deeply, she calmed herself. She could see things clearly now. It was as if a veil had been lifted. The façade of keeping a happy marriage going for the kids and her family and friends was exhausting. She hadn't realized how exhausting it had been until tonight. She was now sure of one thing: she didn't want things to go back to the way they were. This revelation saddened her. But she was an independent woman with a very successful career. She could do this. She knew from previous rows that Tom wouldn't be home tonight. He would go drinking with one of his friends and then stay at theirs. She was glad. She didn't want the kids to feel the bad atmosphere in the house if he did return.

Vivienne checked her watch. The kids would be home soon. Taking some plates from the press she took a deep breath to help gather her thoughts. But something didn't feel right. She had a bad gut feeling. If she didn't agree to use fifty thousand of their savings, where would Tom get the money? Why did he need her and not just ask his dad? As she tossed the vegetables around a hot pan, she tried to think of where Tom would get fifty thousand euros. And then it came to her.

Her stomach lurched. She took the pan off the heat and went to the small office they had off the hallway. It was where they kept their legal documents, household bills etc. There was a safe under the desk that held important documents like passports, investment certificates, and saving bonds. She opened the safe, knelt down, and poured the contents out onto the floor. Pushing the passports aside, she laid out the savings bonds. Over the years they had taken a few with various banks financial institutions and the post office. The one she was looking for was the children's college fund, a savings bond of exactly fifty thousand euros. And that was the one that was missing.

Vivienne's heart plummeted. How could he? The selfish bastard! No matter what she would have said today, he was going to do it anyway. He didn't care whether she approved or not. He was going to use their children's college fund. Once again he would do what he wanted and tell her later. But this time he was gambling with the children's money. He did need her signature – it was a joint account – but that bond was with the bank that Gareth happened to be the manager of. They were pulling a stunt.

Vivienne put everything back in the safe and stood up. The shelves in the office were filled with files labelled house, school, medical, etc, that Vivienne had set up to keep everything in order and easy to find. Behind these files was a row of green files where Vivienne kept a copy of everything. She had photocopied every legal document they had and had a file for every document. The files were unmarked, but Vivienne knew exactly what was in them. More importantly, Tom didn't know they existed. She moved her hand along the files until she found the one she wanted. She opened it and there she found a copy of all their saving bonds, jointly signed by the two of them, including the kid's college bond of fifty thousand euros. Vivienne opened up the laptop on the desk. It was Tom's but she needed to print off bank account and saving-bond details now in case he changed his mind and came home tonight. She printed everything she needed and then turned the laptop off. Gathering all the green files, she took them out of the office and up to the spare bedroom. If Tom forged her signature he was breaking the law and, if Gareth overlooked it and approved it, he would lose his job. She had all the evidence she needed. Tom had betrayed her. It hurt and this is not how she wanted things to be, but a line had been crossed and her sadness was replaced by disgust and anger.

That night Vivienne moved all her clothes and belongings out of the main bedroom they shared and into the spare room. She would not be going back to their bedroom. The marriage was over. He had no respect for her. He had gone too far this time.

She guessed that Tom would not be home for a few days. This suited her. She needed time to think and to get one step ahead of him.

Tom stayed away for three days. He sent a text to the kids saying he was away at a conference and that he would see them in a few days. The kids were used to their parents being away for work so this would not be unusual for them.

Sarah was eighteen, studying for her final exams in school. She had already secured a place at the London College of Performing Arts and was moving to London with two friends over the summer to find a flat and look for part-time jobs before college began. Vivienne could hardly believe that her daughter would be moving away soon and starting her own life in another country. She was delighted for her, of course, but she would miss her terribly. Vivienne and Sarah were very alike and had a great relationship. Vivienne had enrolled Sarah in a drama course when she was a painfully shy eight-year-old. It was hard to believe that the skinny frightened little girl who clung to her mother could now perform on stage in front of packed youth theatres and school halls with such confidence. She was so proud of her. As much as she would miss her when she went, Vivienne was proud to have reared a strong independent young woman with ambition and goals.

Alex, who was the image of his father, was sixteen and still had two years in secondary school. He lived for rugby and was out all the time, either playing rugby or going to matches with his friends or with Tom. At almost six feet he was taller than Vivienne and worked out at the gym to build up his rugby physique. Tom had enrolled Alex in the local rugby team as soon as they allowed it. They had a special bond through their love of the game and some of Tom's proudest moments were watching Alex play rugby for his school and his local club. Vivienne had tried to go to his matches but found them too hard to watch and was constantly worried that Alex would be injured. Instead, she bonded with him by teaching him to cook. He wanted to increase his protein to help with his muscle build-up, so he came to Vivienne with suggestions from the rugby coach, and together they worked out meal plans and she was delighted to have Alex cook alongside her. Cooking always relaxed her after a hard day and it was something she and Alex could do together and talk about.

They were both bright independent children. Although Vivienne used to feel guilty sometimes working full time, the kids had grown up well able to look after themselves and were both very sociable. Divorce was not easy for any family, but Vivienne was thankful that they were not younger. They would be leaving the nest soon to lead their own lives and hopefully would not be too scarred by their parents' marriage breakdown. She tried not to think about that part. She only hoped that she and Tom could come to some reasonable arrangement to lessen the disruption to the kids.

The kids adored Tom and, as a family, they all got on great and enjoyed each other's company. When they were younger they'd had some fantastic times, but now the kids were older they preferred the company of their friends and holidayed with them. Tom and Vivienne didn't bother to go on a holiday last year as the kids had their own plans. They each claimed to be busy at work and, although they didn't say it, they both had grave reservations about spending time alone without the kids. Vivienne had suggested couples counselling before, but Tom refused as he did not want anyone to know his business, so they dealt with their lack of connection by using work as an excuse to avoid spending any time alone together.

During his latest absence from the family home, Tom did not contact Vivienne and she didn't contact him either. A quick call to the bank confirmed that the savings bond had been cashed. Vivienne said nothing but kept an account of the phone call. She needed legal advice. Good legal advice. As so many of Tom's friends were solicitors or worked in law firms, she couldn't use anyone local or in Dublin City. Tom had connections everywhere. She needed to find someone outside Dublin who did not know Tom or his cronies.

And then she met Jack Brady. This year Vivienne and her department had organised all travel arrangements for European delegates travelling to a legal conference in Chicago. One of the delegates, a man called Jack Brady, had called her from Dublin airport in a panic as he had left his tickets at home in Galway. Vivienne had quickly reissued his tickets and delivered them to the airport herself. He had been so grateful and charming and had sent Vivienne a huge basket of flowers as a thank-you. She was very impressed by him and took to Google to find out more about him. What she found out impressed her even more. He was a successful hotshot lawyer in the Connaught area. He had worked in Dublin, but his profile said he preferred to base himself in Galway to pursue his water sports at weekends and in his spare time. His Facebook page had some work profile pictures and some sailing and surfing photos too. Vivienne could not find a Mrs. Brady, just pictures of Jack Brady and his Golden Retriever dogs. She liked what she saw.

When she emailed him about a confidential case she wanted his help with, he was happy to help.

"Vivienne, good to see you!" said Jack Brady, coming out of his office.

Vivienne was a little taken aback and flushed a little.

God, was he this good-looking when we met in Dublin? He obviously works out too, she thought as she noticed the outline of his muscles through his shirt.

He shook her hand warmly and his light-blue eyes never left hers.

"Good to see you too. Nice office." She looked around to stop herself from looking into his eyes for too long. His office was modern and spacious with floor-to-ceiling windows that overlooked Galway Bay.

"You have a beautiful view here," she said.

"Yes, I do," Jack said, his eyes still lingering on Vivienne.

Feeling butterflies in her stomach, Vivienne quickly pulled herself together.

"Let's get down to business, shall we?" he said.

Vivienne was here to do business alright, the business of leaving her husband.

Chapter 8

When Miriam left the ladies outside the Pie Maker Restaurant, saying she needed a rest, actually she needed to get some fresh air and clear her head. Although she'd enjoyed the lunch with the girls, she felt a little claustrophobic and needed some time by herself. Having checked TripAdvisor before coming to Galway, she had written a list of some recommended walks to take and cute coffee shops to visit. It was a long time since she had been in Galway and, although most of the businesses on Quay Street were still there, some gorgeous new places added to the creative eclectic mix that made Galway City an exciting place to visit.

Miriam took her list out of her bag. At the top of her list was Cupán Tae, a tea shop that was very close by. Situated at the bottom of Quay Street and opposite Galway's fast-running River Corrib, the beautifully decorated tea shop was the perfect spot for tea and cake.

Before becoming pregnant, Miriam had been so particular about her diet, logging her daily calories in an app on her phone to make sure she was always keeping track of calories in versus calories out.

But, as if to counteract this, since becoming pregnant she had such strong cravings for cake. Not small delicate patisserie-type cakes but big slabs of gateau-type cakes. She tried to give in to her cravings only twice a week but, when she was under stress, a big slice of cake was the only cure.

Miriam reached Cupán Tae in just a few minutes. The outside of the lilac-coloured shop was decorated with real and artificial flowers, giving it a magical garden feel. The window displayed some of the beautiful floral vintage cups and plates that they served the food on. As Miriam entered the shop, a smiling staff member in a vintage floral apron showed her to a table by the window. The waitress's thick red curly hair was loosely tied up with curly strands escaping around her freckled face.

The tea menu was vast, but Miriam's eyes were drawn to the delicious courgette-and-lime cake on the display counter. In the reviews she had read, people had raved about this homemade cake and Miriam was very keen to try it out.

"I'll have a pot of Blue Flower Earl Grey and a slice of that delicious cake over there, please," Miriam ordered. Taking her coat off, she put it on the empty chair opposite her.

"No problem, I'll bring it right over," said the waitress, heading over to the counter which was laden down with home-baked goods.

Miriam gazed out the window. The town was busy today. Shoppers rushed by with Christmas shopping bags. It was a cold but sunny day, and the sky was a perfect crisp blue colour. It had been an early start this morning, so she was happy to sit for a while and take the weight off her feet. Taking her mobile phone out of her bag, she took a deep breath and turned the power on. She had turned her phone off before they boarded the train in Dublin and for good reason. She had three missed calls from her sister Sharon and two texts from her brother Simon.

I am going to enjoy my cake and pot of tea before I deal with these messages, Miriam thought as the lovely waitress placed a slice of the courgette-and-lime gateaux down in front of her. The vintage teapot came with an egg-timer and the waitress explained that the tea needed to brew for three minutes to be enjoyed at its best. The mismatched vintage crockery on the table was so pretty and it was lovely to have old-fashioned doilies on the plates too. Miriam closed her eyes as she tasted the first piece of cake. The smell of lime had her mouth watering, before she even tasted the frosting. It didn't disappoint. The Earl Grey tea was a lovely accompaniment to the citrus cake and Miriam felt so happy sitting in the tea shop by herself, enjoying the delightful atmosphere.

She had left the care of her mother to her brother and sister this weekend. They were perfectly capable of looking after their own mother, so she wanted to enjoy these moments to herself while she could, before she was back at home doing the lion's share again.

Miriam's mother Annie was eighty-five years old and lived alone. Physically she was great for her age, but she suffered from Alzheimer's. Miriam and her siblings only realized how bad her condition was when their father had a massive heart attack and died while playing golf three years ago. Their dad Frank had done everything in the house. He liked to keep busy and loved going out for the weekly shop and chatting with everyone he met.

They had not realised how much housework he did either until he died, and they quickly found out that their mother could not cope with everyday household tasks. They knew their mother was forgetful, but Frank had kept the reality from them. Miriam remembered when they once had a family get-together and Annie seemed confused and forgot one of the grandkids' names. Frank was quick to make a joke about it saying, "Your mother has been on the wine again!" This had happened more than once, but Miriam just put it down to her mother being tired. They had spoken to him about her forgetfulness a few years ago after Christmas dinner in Sharon's house where their mother was very confused and seemed completely disorientated. Frank said it was new tablets Annie was on and promised to contact their GP. When Miriam chased this up a week later, Frank had said the GP changed Annie's prescription and that she was coping much better. Simon had also mentioned an article he had read about the geriatric clinic in the Mater Hospital where their mother could be assessed, and Frank said he would talk to Doctor Ryan about it and get all the information but again assured them that their mother was fine and only got forgetful when she was tired. As Frank was a very capable man, they left him to it. Sure why would they doubt him? So it was only after Frank had died so suddenly that they quickly realized that he had shielded them from the reality of the situation. They understood that Frank loved Annie and probably did not want to face the reality that his wife had dementia and was slipping away from him bit by bit.

Miriam had stayed with her mum in the days following Frank's death. At first, after he died, they thought their mother's reluctance to get out of bed or do basic household duties was grief. It was only when the GP came out for a home visit that they realized he had not seen Annie in over a year, and he too was concerned about her welfare. Doctor Ryan organised referrals to the Mater Hospital and, while they were waiting on the appointment, the three siblings set up a roster of care for their mother. Sharon agreed to bring their mum up some dinners during the week as she was cooking them for her own family of four anyway. Simon and his beautiful Japanese partner Yua had just one child, a little girl, so Simon took over the supermarket shopping and keeping the gardens in order. As Miriam was single, childless, and living closest to the family home, she called in to visit her mum every night Monday to Friday and had dinner and a chat with her. She also did her washing and a little clean-up around the house. Sharon and Simon took over at the weekends.

At the start, Miriam was happy to do as much as she could. She just wanted her mum to be safe and happy. But she felt awful leaving her every evening and the situation was just not sustainable. When Annie's test results came back confirming Alzheimer's, Miriam called a family Zoom meeting to organise home carers to come in to look after Annie. Having spoken to her mother's doctor, she also suggested that they might go and look at some nursing home options for the future, but Sharon and Simon had both been horrified at Miriam's suggestion.

"Look, I have spoken to the Alzheimer's nurse, and I have researched Mum's diagnosis and I just think we have to be prepared for what lies ahead," Miriam had explained. "The symptoms of this disease will only get worse over time, meaning Mum will need more care."

"I can't believe you're suggesting dumping our mother in a nursing home!" Sharon had said furiously.

"I am not saying that. I am saying we have to be prepared and have some sort of care plan in place and maybe a three-to-five-year plan."

"You are not in the boardroom now, Miriam – you can't just shut Mum down like one of the small companies that are of no use to you!"

Here we go again, thought Miriam. Her job involved assessing small and medium-sized businesses for loans or ongoing credit. She had a responsibility to the bank to make good business decisions and, unfortunately, that sometimes meant cutting funding to underperforming companies and businesses. That was her job, and she was bloody good at it. But Sharon always brought it up in any argument, as if Miriam took pleasure from shutting companies down. It was just business and if companies managed their businesses properly then she wouldn't have to do it.

"Give it a rest, Sharon!" Miriam shot back. "Someone needs to be realistic about this."

"Okay, okay, can we not have a conversation without it ending in a row, please?" Simon said as once again he had to come between his two sisters.

"Doctor Ryan is sending an Alzheimer's nurse to the house tomorrow evening at five to meet Mum," Miriam went on. "I can organise someone from Home Instead to be there too and maybe we can all calmly come up with a safe home plan for Mum."

"Well, five o'clock is a really bad time for me," Sharon said. "It's dinner time, and Saoirse has training."

"Can't Paul sort them out? This is important, Sharon, and it's the only time they had."

"Well, I'll see what I can do," Sharon said, in a huff.

"I'm leaving work early so I'll be there to meet them. Simon, can you make it?"

"Well, I'll check with Yua. We take Lin swimming at that time."

"For God's sake, Simon, she's three years old! Surely she can miss it this week?"

"Well, routine is important at this age, Miriam, but I'll sort something out and be there."

"It's not always possible to drop everything when you have kids, Miriam," Sharon cut in.

Rub it in, why don't you? Miriam thought, biting her lip. "Right, that's settled then, see you both at Mum's. This is important, guys."

The meeting had gone well, and Miriam had been so glad that Lucy the lovely woman from the Alzheimer's association had given a clear idea of where their mum was now and how the disease could progress, and what support she would need. It was a shock to hear it and so much had to be done to keep their mum safe and happy in her own home for as long as possible. As Miriam worked in banking, it was agreed that she would take over the finances. Based on the amount of care they were going to need; it was going to cost a fortune.

Meanwhile, Annie was delighted to have a lovely group of people in her kitchen. She made tea and gave everyone cake and asked her daughters who their new friends were. She kept forgetting the two women's names, but she knew they were kind and warm and she was delighted to hear they would be coming back to visit her a lot more.

And so the accounts were taken over by Miriam and a roster of care was organised. One home-help lady came in every morning to get Annie up and dressed. She gave her breakfast and made sure she took her tablets. They then went for a half-hour walk so Annie could get fresh air and exercise. This also meant that Annie should have no reason to go out by herself. Meals on Wheels delivered her dinner at lunchtime and another home-help came at five to take her out on another walk and make her something small for tea.

Initially, the three siblings had a roster for evening visits and weekends. Miriam called up three evenings a week on Monday,

Tuesday, and Wednesday. Sharon did Thursday and Simon did Friday. On Saturdays, Simon did the food shop from a list that Miriam wrote up every week. Every alternate Saturday night Miriam spent the evening and overnight with her mum. Sometimes they went out to dinner or a show or play and other nights they stayed in and watched TV.

Annie loved *Strictly Come Dancing* and danced along to the old-time waltzes. These were the nights Miriam loved. She didn't mind giving up every second Saturday night to dance around her childhood living room with her mum. The joy on Annie's face was worth every minute of it.

The roster worked great for a month or two and then Miriam started to get calls from Sharon.

"Miriam, I can't make it to Mum's on Sunday, Freya has a football match."

"Miriam, I can't make it to Mum's on Friday night, Paul is at a Leinster match, and I can't leave the kids."

"We're going to have to change the roster because, realistically, with the kids' activities, I can only do one day a week and it can't be Sunday because that's family day."

Your mother *is* your family, you selfish wagon, Miriam wanted to shout, but she knew the reply she would get. *You have no children, Miriam, you don't know what it's like. I'm so busy, blah, blah, blah!*

Yeah, like I'm not busy, thought Miriam. Just because I have no partner or kids does not mean I have to do all the care with Mum. She felt guilty even thinking about this. Her wonderful happy mum was a joy to be with but just not seven days a week.

Simon tried his best, but he and Yua were doing this attachment parenting which meant that Lin went everywhere with them 24 hours a day. Having a three-year-old wandering around, climbing on everything in Mum's house, was stressful for her as the house was not child-friendly. Also, Simon and Yau never disciplined Lin for throwing Mum's ornaments around as, according to them, she was expressing her three-year-old self.

Miriam was feeling the pressure and stress of having to organise all her mum's care and hospital appointments and activities. She knew if something didn't change, she could be stuck in this hamster wheel for a long time. She had no chance of meeting someone new or having a child of her own if she were to spend nearly every evening with her mother. Something had to change.

Chapter 9

Helen left the restaurant after lunch and agreed to meet Vivienne in two hours. Thank God she refused my offer to go shopping with her, Helen thought. Vivienne seemed distracted and in a hurry somewhere. Probably a big sale on in Brown Thomas or something. My idea of hell being dragged around BT's. Well, fair play to Vivienne, she works hard enough so she may as well spend her money on nice things.

She headed out into the crowds.

Helen was completely comfortable with her own choice of comfy River Island jeans and her Penny's AC/DC T-shirt and of course her new TK Maxx purchase of the small man's puffer jacket. She had no intention of doing any shopping and, with two hours to kill, she knew exactly where she wanted to go and headed back towards Jurys Inn Hotel.

Quay Street was very busy with Christmas shoppers. Although it was early afternoon, the streets were lit up with Christmas lights strung horizontally down small laneways and stretching across streets from one business to another. Busy mums passed by with bags hanging off their buggies. The mums looked stressed but the kids in the buggies were delighted.

The warmth of the Jurys Inn reception area was very welcome on Helen's cold face. She nodded at the receptionists and headed to the bar. They probably think I'm staying here, she thought. The same barman was still on duty, and he recognised her as she approached the bar. Some of the same lunch crowd were still there enjoying their Christmas drinks.

"Hello again, what can I get you?"

"Hiya, I'm killing time until my friend gets here. Do you sell wine by the bottle?"

"Of course, let me get you a wine list."

Helen looked around for a place to sit. She didn't want to sit at the bar drinking a bottle of wine all by herself. The barman returned with the wine list and left her to look at it while he served another customer.

"Is this seat taken?" Helen turned to see an overweight jolly-looking man point to the seat beside her.

"No, go ahead. I'm not sitting here."

"Cold out there, isn't it?" he said, looking at Helen while pulling his stool closer to her.

"Yes, it's cold alright," Helen replied, keeping her eyes on the wine list and hoping he'd get the hint.

This is all I need, she thought as she nodded at the barman.

"I'll have the bottle of Rioja, please," she said as she handed the wine list back to him.

"Ah, you're not going to drink that all by yourself, are yeh?" said the stranger, smiling creepily at her.

"No, I'm waiting on a friend." She called after the barman, "And two glasses, please!"

"I can keep you company if you like," said the creepy stranger.

For fuck's sake, Helen thought. Can a woman not come into a bar and order a drink in peace without being hit on? Was it too much to ask to be left alone? She would have loved to say this out loud but instead she politely said, "No, thank you," and moved away from him.

"I'll drop that down to you," said the barman, giving the stranger a 'back off' look.

"Thanks," said Helen, taking a complimentary newspaper off the counter to avoid any further unwanted interruptions.

Does he honestly think I should be flattered, she thought, feeling annoyed. She found a big comfortable chair in the corner away from the busy crowd but facing the bar and the door so that she could see all the comings and goings. Putting her coat and bag on the seat next to her, she sat down and relaxed.

Her phone rang in her jacket pocket. It was Jerry. She let it ring out. She didn't want to talk to him.

He would just make her feel bad at the moment and guilty for sitting here in a bar, so she texted him instead.

Hi, I missed your call.

He messaged back immediately: **Yeah, how are things in the west?**

It's freezing but very Christmassy. How's everyone?

Boys are all good. Soccer went well. It was a draw, but Seán is happy. At Cillian's GAA match now. Bloody freezing! Kids keeping warm in the car and then we're off to McDonald's for lunch. You left your jacket on the banister – did you forget it?

Yes, total eejit. I had to buy a cheap man's jacket when I got here.

Maybe it will fit me. How are the women?

All good. Vivienne has us staying in apartments. No hotel for us this time and, oh yeah, big news, Miriam is pregnant.

Pregnant? I thought she was single?

Yeah, she is. She went to a clinic. It was a sperm donor.

A sperm donor? That's very modern.

Yeah, brave girl. I'd better go, Jerry, enjoy McDonald's.

Okay. J

Helen sighed with relief. If she'd called Jerry and he'd heard the background noises, he would have known she was in a bar and she didn't feel like she needed to explain herself. She put the phone on silent and put it back in her jacket pocket, just as the barman arrived with her wine.

He poured the first glass.

"Enjoy," he said, placing the bottle down.

Helen picked up the glass and inhaled the rich fruity aromas as she stretched her legs out under the table into the hotel's deep pile carpet.

Taking a sip of the wine, she closed her eyes and felt her body relax as she swallowed. Jerry would love it here, she thought as she looked around the cosy bar with its warm Christmas atmosphere. Poor Jerry, he really was a good husband and she had been such a moody bitch recently. Recently? More like six months.

Helen tried to think back to the last time she and Jerry had been away together without the kids. When had they even gone out on a date, just the two of them? She knew he wanted them to socialize more as a couple, but these days she preferred to open a bottle of wine and stay in. She blamed her tiredness on being so busy with the boys, but the truth was that she couldn't be bothered to get dressed up, put make-up on, and have to make conversation with people when she could sit at home and drink her wine. *Her* wine. Jerry didn't drink wine, so all the empties were hers. The thought gave her a shiver. She knew she drank too much but her last trip to the bottle bank was an eye-opener when she saw how many wine bottles she went through a week. Jerry volunteered to take the empties bin that they kept outside the back door, but Helen had insisted she take it. She didn't want him to see all the bottles. She knew she was just kidding herself. Many nights he had come down to find her asleep on the couch after polishing off a bottle or two. And they had a huge row just last week because he wouldn't let her drive the kids to school. She shuddered when she remembered his angry face.

"I have to call in late for work today because you can't drive the kids to school."

"Don't be ridiculous, I'm fine."

"No, you are *not* fine. I can smell the drink off you and your lips are still red from the wine you drank last night. You need to do something about this. *You are definitely not fine.*"

Helen had been horrified and embarrassed at first when he left with the kids, but then she was angry. How dare he speak to her like that? But she knew she'd had too much that night because the empties were on the living-room floor when the kids got up for breakfast. Helen felt awful when little Cillian brought them into the kitchen, thinking he was helping her clear up. Had her kids got so used to this? Mammy falling asleep on the couch with bottles beside her?

Helen looked at the bottle in front of her. Something had to change, she knew it. She finished her second glass. But where would she start? An AA meeting seemed over the top and, anyway, she didn't think she was an alcoholic, but she knew she was using alcohol as an escape. Maybe she needed a counsellor or psychiatrist – someone to talk out the issues with? But deep down that's what she was afraid of. She was afraid to explore the reason why she wasn't happy anymore. She adored her kids, and she loved Jerry – but was she still in love with him? These were the thoughts she was afraid of. This is what she was afraid to explore.

Something was missing from their marriage. She knew this. She and Jerry had become more like roommates. At first, she blamed the kids' busy schedules for their lack of intimacy and Jerry was so busy working that he was knackered every night and was happy to kick back and watch a movie or play football with his mates. They had joked about how lazy they both were about their sex life and how they must make more of an effort. But Helen didn't miss the sex. Should she? Did Jerry feel the same? Was he really happy with things as they are? Were they both keeping themselves busy to avoid spending time alone together? Or maybe it was the menopause because her libido had completely disappeared. If Matt Damon walked into this bar to chat her up she wouldn't be interested. She got more enjoyment from her wine.

Could herself and Jerry carry on like this? They got on well and rarely argued and they were so busy with the boys. But was it okay to keep going on like this? Maybe it was. Maybe loads of couples fell into this pattern and were happy because they loved each other. Helen poured another glass of Rioja and felt depressed. She knew she spent too much time indoors at home. She was so busy with the four boys, but was she using them as an excuse? She avoided going out. She felt like her confidence as a person had disappeared over the past few years.

She could never confide in the girls and tell them, could she? Clara and her husband Richard were busy with Seán and his medical issues. They were obviously very committed. Vivienne and Tom had a busy high-class glamorous lifestyle, jetting off here and there. Sure, what could Viv be worried about? No money worries there. And Miriam, well, that was a shocker. A donor too. But Miriam had been carrying all the responsibility of her mother and maybe she felt trapped in the situation because she was the only sibling living on her own, with no children. No, her friends had enough going on in their lives without burdening them with her problems.

When she first met Vivienne, Clara and Miriam five years ago on a Human Resources course, she also was taking an evening aromatherapy course in the same college, mainly to get out of the house two nights a week. Although the aromatherapy was just an afterthought, it was the course she enjoyed the most. She was very interested in the different oils and their uses and, although it felt weird practising massage techniques on strangers through their clothes, she absolutely loved it. The teacher was lovely too and had given her information about becoming a massage therapist. Helen had contacted the college and they had a course that would see her qualified in six months by studying at night. It was a career she felt she would enjoy. Using the oils and giving massages she felt it would help her relax, and working in a quiet spa or therapy centre would be a complete change from her noisy house. She could also work the hours around the school timetable. But, in the end, Helen missed the booking deadline and put it on the long finger.

Now look at me, she thought. I drink too much, my husband has had enough, and I think I might be clinically depressed.

Something needs to change, she thought sadly as she poured herself another glass. But why does everything feel so hard? Why have I no interest in anything? This weekend was her chance to have some head space and come up with a plan but right now all that seemed like so much hard work.

Chapter 10

"Well, what do you think?" Vivienne said, after Jack Brady had looked over her files.

"At first glance, I'd say you definitely have a case here," Jack said, shuffling the paperwork. "Falsifying documents, fraud and collusion from the manager of one of the country's leading banks. If this gets out it could be a national scandal. You could take this further, you know."

"I don't want to take it further. I just want to use this information to get a smooth separation and divorce. I want to end my marriage and move on with my life. I don't think I'm looking for much either. I want him to reinstate the kid's college fund and I want the house to be signed over to me. I know I could stay there until the kids are eighteen, but then we'd have to sell it and split the profits. That's no good to me. I want to sell it as soon as I can and get somewhere smaller, but I need all the proceeds of the house sale to set myself and the kids up for life. Tom's family has rental properties so they can sort him out, he won't be homeless. But he'll fight me on this to save face. We bought the house in the area Tom grew up in. All his friends and family live nearby. I loved the house when we first bought it, but I realise now that I never fitted in in that area and, in the past few years, I have not been completely comfortable living there. It feels more like I am living in his world, not our world. I wouldn't take the kids away from their friends or schools, but I want to move. The proceeds from the sale of the house will set me and the kids up for the next part of our lives. Sarah is doing her Leaving Cert and has secured a place in a drama college in London so she will be moving to London in the summer. A smaller house or apartment in the area will suffice for me and Alex and, it will be easier for Alex to live between me and his dad if I stay in the area. All I want from this is the house."

"Does Tom have any idea that this is coming?"

"Yes and no. We have lived separate lives in separate bedrooms for a while now. He comes and goes without telling me anything. He won't be surprised that the marriage is over, but he will be surprised at how much preparation I have done. He knows he crossed a line using the kid's college money and I told him that it was the last straw for me. I just want to get my facts straight before I talk to him. He is not an unreasonable man, and his family has money but, with Tom, it will all be about keeping face with his buddies. Hopefully he'll be reasonable but if not I need to be prepared. And that's why I need you."

As she said those last three words, Vivienne and Jack's eyes met, and stayed there for a few seconds. Vivienne felt desire flood through her for this handsome man who was her key out of her unhappy marriage.

"I will do everything I can to make this as painless as possible," Jack said, leaning towards her across his desk. "And if Tom and his solicitor friends want a fight, we'll be ready."

Vivienne had to pull her eyes away from his. "Jack, thank you so much for everything," she said, standing up and picking up her bag.

"Leave all these documents with me. I'll go over them in detail and email you on Monday with advice on how to proceed."

Jack rose and came around to stand beside her.

"How long will you be in Galway?"

"Two nights."

"Well, I'd love to take you to dinner if that's not too forward?"

"I'd like that but I'm here with three friends of mine for a pre-Christmas break."

"Oh, I see. Well, here's my card with my mobile number on it. If you get tired of all the festivities, I'm at home all weekend – if you fancy a glass of wine or a walk on the beach." He smiled. "I hope that doesn't sound too unprofessional?"

Viviene took his card. "No, that sounds lovely actually and thank you, but I don't think it will be possible this time."

"Of course, forgive me. Enjoy your weekend. The city looks lovely at Christmastime."

Vivienne knew she had to go but didn't want to leave.

"Are you free right now? For a little Christmas drink?" she blurted out.

"Yes, absolutely." Jack's face lit up. "Let me grab my jacket."

Vivienne looked at her watch. She was supposed to be meeting Helen right about now.

"Great. Let me just send a text. Is there somewhere close by we could go?"

"We could go to the bar in Jurys Inn. It's just around the corner."

"Perfect," said Vivienne, putting on her coat.

Helen can look after herself for an hour, Vivienne thought, as she started to type her a text.

She knew it was risky having a drink with Jack Brady, but she also knew that she didn't want her time with him to end just yet.

Helen checked her watch. She had time for another glass before meeting Vivienne in Naughton's. Just then she looked up and saw Vivienne enter the bar. She was about to wave to her when she saw she was not alone. Helen's high-backed wing chair in the corner meant that she could see everyone coming in, but they might not see her. Vivienne was with a really good-looking man in a business suit, and he led Vivienne to the other end of the bar, gently placing his hand on her back. Maybe she ran into an old friend? Sure I'll pop over and say hello.

Helen was just gathering her things when her phone binged. It was a text from Vivienne.

Sorry, Helen, I'm stuck in BT's. Queues are mental so I won't be able to meet you. See you back at the apartment.

Well, well, well, Helen thought. From where she was sitting she could only see the back of Vivienne's head but, even from this distance, she could see that Vivienne and this mystery man were very relaxed in each other's company. Maybe Vivienne would say it to the girls later. But, if he was only a business acquaintance, why would she lie about being stuck in a queue in Brown Thomas?

Looking around for a convenient exit, she saw a sign for the ladies' toilets on the wall behind where she was sitting, and that corridor led back out to the reception area of the hotel. She gathered her things and went out that way to avoid causing Vivienne any embarrassment.

As she snuck out of the hotel into the evening air, she wondered what the hell was going on with Vivienne.

Chapter 11

They all got back to the apartments in time for some to have a rest and others to have a quick shower and get changed. There was an air of excitement as they all got ready to go out. Complimenting each other, offering advice when asked, and helping each other with their hair was great fun. Clara changed into black tights, black high heels, and a long black-and-gold tunic top which she accessorized with a long gold chain and long gold earrings. Helen stayed in the same black jeans and cowboy boots but wore a red silk shirt on top that looked great with her long wavy black hair and red lipstick. Miriam wore a loose knee-length navy dress with a gold collar over navy tights and knee-high black boots but, although she had reapplied her make-up, she still looked washed out and pale. Vivienne had changed into a red crushed-velvet mini-dress that showed off her toned, strong figure. She wore her hair down, pinned back behind one ear with a hair slide. Her red high heels added to her five-foot-eight height, so that she towered over everyone.

The girls linked each other two by two as they walked from the apartments towards Eyre Square. Squeals of delight could be heard from children as they passed the enormous Ferris wheel at the top of the square. It was lit up and was playing music as it slowly spun around, no doubt giving the occupants a stunning view of Galway from the top.

"*Let's do it!*" Helen shouted, pointing to the Ferris Wheel.

"No way!" Vivienne said, pulling her friend away. "You couldn't pay me to go on that thing – anyway, it must be bloody freezing up there!"

There was a cute free-standing bar in Eyre Square, selling mulled wine, and the sweet fruity smell of Christmas filled the air.

"Come on, let's have some mulled wine," Vivienne said.

They got a mulled wine each and Miriam got a mulled apple juice. They huddled around and raised their paper cups.

"*To friends!*" Vivienne said.

"*To friends!*" they said as they raised their cups in the frosty air.

Miriam felt emotional and started to tear up.

"Ah, Miriam!" Clara said, putting an arm around her.

"Sorry, I don't know what's come over me. Bloody hormones."

"Group hug," Clara said, and they all gave Miriam a group hug.

Miriam laughed it off, but she felt very emotional looking at her three friends' faces. She didn't have many friends outside the workplace. This was going to be a hard year, having a baby all by herself, and she just realized how much she was going to need her friends' help. There was no way they could ever find out who the father of her baby was. She needed them too much.

"Thanks, guys. I'm really going to need you this year," she said, clutching her cup and feeling anxious as the reality of her situation was becoming more real.

"We'll be with you every step of the way, Miriam," Helen said, placing her hand on her friend's arm to reassure her.

"Right, ladies, drink up! Dinner awaits!" Vivienne said and led the way through the crowds.

They headed down William Street, turning left at Abbeygate Street and left again onto Middle Street until they came to Cava Bodega. The tapas restaurant's yellow light spilled out onto the narrow street. The windows were fogged up around the edges, giving it a warm cosy glow. As soon as they entered, a young handsome waiter was right over to take their name and they were led downstairs to their table. The restaurant was full and buzzing with a great atmosphere and the smell of the food made everyone suddenly very hungry.

"I'll just head to the loo," Helen said, turning around and bumping into a waitress.

"Oh, I'm so sorry," she said to the waitress, walking off giggling to herself.

"I think Helen is half-cut already, girls. Has she been drinking all day?" Clara asked. "Was she shopping with you, Viv?"

"No, we didn't meet up after all. I got stuck in BT's so apparently she headed back to the apartment for a rest."

"*Hmm*, well, she was only back an hour before we left," said Clara.

"Maybe she did some shopping herself? Oh, we have to try the patatas bravas and the croquettes," Vivienne said.

"This menu looks delicious," said Clara.

"Why don't we order a selection of starters for the table and then order our own mains?" said Vivienne, taking charge again.

Maybe I'd like to order what I bloody well like, thought Clara but said nothing.

"The toilets are gorgeous here," Helen said, returning to the table. "I met a girl who said we had to try the cider. I forget what name she said but it starts with an L and it's local so I'm definitely having that."

And hopefully some food, Miriam thought, looking at Helen. It's funny when you aren't drinking how you notice when other people are drinking a lot.

The waiter arrived and orders were put in for cider, sangria, and a range of starters. As each plate of food arrived Clara took a photo of it as it was so beautifully presented. The food was delicious, and the meal was a huge success. Vivienne had done it again and picked a perfect spot.

"I remember the first time I saw you, Vivienne," Helen said as the girls reminisced about how they first met. "You were all the business and every man in the place turned to watch you enter the room with your files and snazzy briefcase. Remember, they thought you were the teacher!"

The girls laughed. It was true. Vivienne was so business-like she certainly kept the instructor on her toes with all her questions and work-related scenarios.

"Can you believe that was five years ago?" said Vivienne. "We have certainly had some lovely trips and great nights out since then."

At the time they had met on the Human Resource management course, Vivienne was working in a travel company and had just been promoted to manager of their corporate section. As she would now be heading a team, her company felt it would be useful to attend the six-week evening course as it would help her with people skills and conflict resolution. Miriam worked in the headquarters of a national bank and was looking for a course to help her with her dealings with clients. Every September she picked a different night course to keep her busy and improve her skill set. Clara was working in a big retail store but was tired on her feet all day. One of the staff in the HR department was pregnant and would be going on maternity leave for six months. Clara was hoping to apply to cover her position while she was on leave to see if she might like to work in HR permanently in the future. Helen was doing the course to escape her busy house for one night a week, needing mental stimulation and adult conversation. She booked the HR course for a Thursday and an Aromatherapy course for a Tuesday night, so she was guaranteed two nights out a week.

Apart from the instructor, they were the only women. There were four of them and eight men of different ages. The first night at break time, they gravitated towards each other and had coffee together. Although the men on the course were nice, the girls looked forward to seeing each other every week. They had the same sense of humour and they all just clicked. Helen and Miriam were delighted to be out of the house and to have met such great women. Clara was so glad to meet new women who she felt relaxed with and helped her understand some of the terminologies. She didn't feel confident enough yet to put up her hand and ask a question in class, so the girls were a great help.

Vivienne had had no intention of making friends on this course but chatting with the other three women was so easy. The conversation flowed and she felt relaxed talking to them about anything. It made her look at the women she socialised with, and she realised that she never felt this comfortable with them. At weekends she and Tom went to dinner parties or restaurants with his friends and their wives. The wives had all grown up in the same area and gone to the same school together, so Vivienne sometimes felt like an outsider. They also dressed up every weekend, something that Vivienne enjoyed at first but now, with a busy career and organizing her two kids, she just found it tiring. She realised, when she met these three women, that she could relax and be herself and she liked the feeling. Each of the women got so much out of their friendship that they didn't want it to end.

When it came to the end of the course, they decided that they would go out for drinks afterward. Then Miriam said it was her birthday that week, so Vivienne suggested that the four of them go out for dinner instead to celebrate. They had such a good night and were so comfortable with each other that Helen made a suggestion.

"Okay, I just want to say that I have really enjoyed your company over the past six weeks. It's great to be with women who don't go on and on about their kids or GAA!"

"Yes, the women I see – Tom's friends' wives, in fact – bore me so much these days," Vivienne said.

"Well, I'm so happy not to talk about office politics," said Miriam. "The bitching in the office is unreal sometimes."

"I have loved this too," said Clara. "It's so refreshing to meet you and not talk about work, kids, or husbands."

"I'll drink to that!" said Helen, raising a glass. "So, I have a suggestion. I would like to keep in touch and, as we're meeting tonight for Miriam's birthday, how about we meet up for all our birthdays? We can keep in touch on WhatsApp and meet up four times a year around the time of our birthdays. Whose birthday is next? Mine is September."

"Mine is in June," said Clara.

"And mine is in March," said Vivienne, "but that's ages away."

"I know, why don't we meet up for a Christmas night out too?" said Miriam.

"That's a brilliant idea," said Helen and they all agreed.

So for the last five years, the girls had been meeting in March, June, September, and November for each other's birthdays and in December for Christmas. The first year they went for a meal in Dublin for their Christmas night out. The following year their favourite restaurants were busy most weekends, so Vivienne suggested they go away for an overnight stay in a hotel instead. Everyone loved that idea.

"Oh my God, that's a fantastic idea!" Helen had said. "I so need a night away for my sanity's sake and, with the prices of restaurants and taxis in Dublin, the cost won't be much more."

And that's when the tradition started. It went from one night away to two and sometimes three. The first one was in Ireland, then London, Paris, and Rome. Those weekends were treasured by the girls. A time for them to relax and be themselves.

As they lived in different parts of Dublin, neither their husbands nor children knew each other. And, as they did not have friends in common, they felt they could be completely open and honest with each other, knowing that everything they divulged about their lives would be confidential. That was the part of their relationship that they treasured the most.

Helen's tip about the cider was bang on. It matched the food they were having so well that they ordered another round.

"Can we have another jug of sangria, please?" Helen added to the order as she seemed to be drinking faster than everyone else.

Clara felt relaxed and happy. Having been initially worried about the bitesize tapas coming to the table, the plates just kept coming. The food was so rich and delicious, she savoured every bite. Vivienne was drinking very little, and Miriam noticed her checking her watch a few times, but she seemed to be enjoying herself and told a few hilarious stories from work. She looked stunning tonight, and her make-up was perfect. She so often wore her hair pulled back tight from her face which gave her a very severe and sometimes cold look, but when her hair was down like tonight, she looked so much more relaxed and warm.

Miriam was very happy to be out and having fun, even if it was without a drink. She didn't socialise with her work colleagues if at all possible and what other few friends she did have she had no time to see because she was caring for her mother. She gently rubbed her little bump under the table. I hope everything works out okay, she thought nervously. I hope I am up to this.

"Hey, missus, wake up! You were miles away," Helen said to her.

"Oh sorry, a wave of tiredness just came over me. It must be all this food."

"I can walk back to the apartment with you after dessert if you like?" Vivienne said.

"Ah no, I can make my way back, thanks. You girls have to go out drinking. I thought you were going for some cocktails?"

"Honestly, it's no problem – let's get the dessert menu," Vivienne said, catching the waitress's eye.

"You will come back out, Vivienne? We have to go for a cocktail," Helen insisted in a slightly slurred voice.

"To be honest, I'm exhausted too. I meant to have a nap today but got carried away with my shopping, so I never got a chance.

Sure we have tomorrow night too. I'll be happy to get to my bed tonight."

Helen was visibly disappointed. "Clara, you're not going to leave me drinking on my own, now are yeh?" she said, putting her arm around her friend.

"No, I'll come for a cocktail with you. A nightcap now, I don't want to be out all night, thank you."

"Just the one, I promise," Helen said, smiling now.

Clara didn't fancy a cocktail at all but there was no way she could let Helen go to a bar on her own as she was half-locked already. Why was she drinking so fast? She was already tipsy when they were leaving the apartment and has been throwing back the drink ever since. Clara was worried about her friend. Something else is going on there, she thought. Maybe if it's just the two of us she might say something. Or maybe she just needs to let her hair down a bit. Clara understood this too.

Deserts were ordered and there was a delicious selection of Basque cheesecakes, delicate deep-fried churros, and Catalan crème. Coffee was ordered too, and Helen and Vivienne had an Irish coffee as a nightcap. When the bill came, they divided it into four and got ready to go. It had been a long day and the Irish coffee on top of a delicious meal made everyone feel relaxed and satisfied.

The waiter arrived with the credit-card machine, and each paid her share.

"I'm afraid that didn't go through, madam," the waiter said to Vivienne as the others were counting out change for a tip. "Would you like to try again?"

"Oh sorry, I must have put in the wrong pin," Vivienne said as she typed in her credit card pin again.

"*Em*, I'm afraid that didn't work, madam," he said. "Do you have another card?"

"Yes, of course," Vivienne said, confused. That's our joint card so I know there is money on it, she thought, as she produced another card from her wallet.

She started to feel anxious as she waited for the payment to go through.

"I'm afraid that card is not working either, madam."

"That's ridiculous, I know checked that account today. Let me try again, please."

"You can put it on my card," Helen offered, "and give it back to me tomorrow."

"That won't be necessary. This card is fine," Vivienne said, feeling hot and bothered now.

"I'm sorry, madam, the payment won't go through," the waiter said, putting it as politely as he could.

"Here, take this," Helen said, thrusting her card at the waiter.

She entered her pin, and the payment went through straight away.

"Thanks, Helen. I don't know what's going on there," Vivienne said, feeling very uneasy.

"It happens, Vivienne," said Miriam. "Sometimes the bank system goes down or is being updated and the last people to know are the customers."

Suddenly Vivienne felt very sober. Miriam was being nice, but Vivienne's bank cards were from two different banks. But they were both from their joint accounts.

Just then her phone buzzed with a text.

Vivienne glanced at it and saw it was from Tom.

She felt suddenly anxious as she opened his message.

Enjoying your night out?

Vivienne froze and looked around her.

"Are you okay, Vivienne? You look very pale?" Clara asked.

"I–I–" Vivienne stammered. "I just feel very hot all of a sudden. I think I'll head back."

"Well, I'm ready, so let's get some fresh air," said Miriam.

Vivienne did not want company, but she couldn't let Miriam walk back on her own.

"Sure, let's go," she said, feeling a tightening in her chest. What the fuck was going on? Tom's text unnerved her. *Enjoying your night out?* He was barely talking to her. And why text now at this time of night? What was going on? Did Tom know why she was here? How could he? Her head was spinning. She needed to act calmly, but she needed to get to an ATM fast.

Vivienne and Miriam hugged the girls and headed back up the main street toward the apartment.

"I just need to stop at an ATM and check my cards, if that's okay," Vivienne said.

"Sure, there's one beside the shop there." Miriam pointed as they made their way through the busy street. "I'm going into the shop for some water. Do you want anything?"

"No, nothing thanks," Vivienne said as she queued up for the bank machine. When it was her turn, her hand shook as she put their joint credit card into the machine.

CARD CANCELLED came up in big writing across the screen.

She quickly withdrew that card and put in the debit card from their joint account.

This card worked. She knew there was over €3000 in it today

when she went shopping. She checked the balance: **0.00**.

Oh my God, Vivienne said to herself, holding her breath as she pressed transaction history.

€3250.70 had been transferred out of that account at 6.30 pm that day.

Balance **0.00**

Vivienne placed the cards back into her wallet, her hands shaking with rage. She wanted to ring Tom and roar down the phone. That was her money too. But no, she needed to gather her thoughts and figure out her next move.

"*Fuck him*," she said between clenched teeth.

"Everything okay?" Miriam asked, appearing at her side.

"No, it's not okay, but I will wait and check again tomorrow," she said.

But she knew that checking tomorrow would make absolutely no difference. She needed to get back to the apartment and get some time on her own to think straight and figure out her next move very carefully.

Chapter 12

Helen and Clara left the restaurant and headed for the main street in the town.

"Let's go to the Quays," Helen said. "It'll be hopping."

"Yeah, sure, but listen, I'm not staying out all night, my feet are killing me," Clara said, cursing herself for wearing heels in a city full of cobbled streets.

The Quays bar was hopping alright. It was a huge pub, and it was packed with groups meeting up for a Christmas drink and office Christmas parties. The atmosphere was festive as people danced and mingled and shouted over the music. They squeezed through the crowd and walked towards the back of the bar, looking for a seat.

Clara spotted two women leaving a table and shouted to Helen over the noise. "*You grab those seats and I'll go to the bar. What do you want?*"

"Rum and Coke," Helen replied. "Actually, get me a double so we don't have to go back up to the bar again. It looks very busy."

"Okay," Clara said. She was very unsure about buying Helen a double drink as she watched her bump off people making her way to the free table. She had definitely been drinking all day and was looking the worst for it now.

The bar was very busy, and people were two lines deep. The barmen were quick though and kept the line moving as best they could. Clara looked around to see Helen talking to two women at the table behind theirs. Maybe that will sober her up a bit, she hoped. She really couldn't be left on her own now. Maybe she was just letting off steam. It couldn't be easy in a house full of active boys. Either way, Clara could not have let her go to the pub on her own, the state she was in. She could understand Miriam wanting to go back to bed – those early months of pregnancy could be exhausting. But she was surprised at Vivienne. Usually, Vivienne knew exactly where to go after dinner. She would have researched all the cool bars and the girls would have just followed her. But she seemed distracted tonight, stressed even. Maybe it was her work or maybe it was that husband of hers, Tom. He didn't sound very supportive of her at all.

"A double rum and Coke and one gin and tonic," Clara ordered when it was her turn.

I'll enjoy my drink here and then get Helen home; she thought as she carried the drinks back to the table. But Helen wasn't there.

"*Clara! Clara!*"

Clara turned around to see Helen in the middle of a group of men. They were wearing shirts and ties and Santa hats, obviously an office party.

Clara reluctantly made her way over.

"Here you go!" she said, passing Helen her drink.

"*This is Clara!*" Helen shouted over the music to the men.

Clara had no interest in making conversation with drunken party-goers.

"*What happened to our table?*" Clara shouted back to Helen.

"*Too quiet. We need to mingle and get into the Christmas spirit!*" Helen said, dancing to the music and bumping off an equally drunk man in the group.

"*My feet are killing me! I'm not standing all night,*" Clara said, looking around for a stool or a free seat anywhere.

"*Jesus, you're no craic! It's Christmas, for god's sake!*" With that, another Christmas song came on and Helen started singing it at the top of her voice, throwing her arm around one of the men. "*Oh, I wish it could be Christmas every daaaay!*"

Clara swayed along, not to be a killjoy, as she watched Helen knock back her drink. Her feet were burning. But Helen didn't care as long as she was having a good time. Clara could feel herself getting pissed off. Did no one give a shit about her feelings? It was always good ole Clara helping everyone else and being considerate of other people, not the other way around. One of the men attempted to chat Clara up and put his arm around her shoulders while leaning in and breathing alcohol fumes into her face. She pushed his arm away and moved away from him. Pulling Helen's sleeve, she motioned to her that they should move on, but Helen was having none of it as she had her arm around another man's neck, singing and swaying to the music.

"*I'm going to the bathroom!*" Clara shouted over the music. "*Are you coming?*"

Helen just ignored her. For fuck's sake, Clara thought, heading off to find the ladies'. She took her drink with her as she squeezed through crowds singing and swaying, her frustration rising. As was usual in pubs, the queue for the ladies' toilets was very long. Sipping her drink, she leaned against the cool wall as she waited in line. She slipped one shoe off and balanced one foot on top of another to get some relief for her aching feet. She'd had a lovely day up to now. Okay, it was disappointing not to be staying in a hotel with a pool and a spa, but Galway was such a beautiful place at Christmastime. She finished off her gin as the queue moved along. Once inside the toilet cubicle, she slipped off her two shoes, cooled her feet on the bathroom tiles, and was grateful to be able to sit down. She was really tired now and just wanted her bed.

Right, she thought, I'm going to get Helen and go. She's had more drink and she's locked. I don't care if she thinks I am a spoilsport. I've had a drink with her and now I'm done. It's obvious she doesn't even want my company, she seems very happy hanging out with those bloody men. She put her shoes back on and headed back out to the bar. She pushed her way through the crowd back to where they had been, but she couldn't see Helen. One of the men pointed to Clara and then pointed further up the bar. Helen had moved on to another group of men, a much younger group. As Clara approached she could see Helen with her arm around one fella who was young enough to be her son.

Clara felt embarrassed for her friend as she made her way through the crowd to her.

"Clara! Clara! These lads just won their hurling match today and we're celebrating!"

"No, thanks, let's go. Come on."

"No way, sure the night's only getting started."

"No, Helen, it's time to go. We agreed on one drink!"

"You go then, I'm fine here with these lads, but have a shot first before you go." Helen cheered as the barman arrived with a tray full of shots.

A cheer went up from the young lads as Helen handed out the shots.

"Come on, Clara, have one!"

"No, I don't want one."

"Come on, don't be so boring!"

Clara's blood started to boil. "I'm going back to the apartment."

"Go then," Helen said, turning her back on Clara as she started a countdown with the lads 5-4-3-2-1 and they knocked back the shots.

"Right, come on, Helen," Clara said, noticing the lads moving away from Helen once they finished their shots.

"Clara, you are such a downer. Look, the lads have moved away," Helen said, annoyed.

"They have moved away to talk to girls their own age," Clara said. "And I'm knackered, and I want to go home."

"Go then! I'll be fine," Helen said, slurring her words.

"No, I can't leave you, Helen."

"Jesus Christ, Clara, I'm not a child!"

"No, but you are pissed so I think you should come with me. We have all day tomorrow and tomorrow night."

"*For fuck's sake, it's Crisssmas!*" Helen said, looking in her bag and swaying.

"Come on, Helen, you've had enough."

"Okay, I'll go, but only because I have no cash left," Helen said grumpily, still rooting around in her bag.

"Right, follow me," said Clara, linking her arm through hers. It took ages to push through the crowd and get outside.

"*I ssspose I am tiiiired too*," she slurred as Clara tried to negotiate the busy street crowded with partygoers.

It was one o'clock in the morning but as busy as one in the afternoon with people of all ages out celebrating the run-up to Christmas. Clara kept her eyes on the lit-up Ferris wheel as a guide to where they were headed.

Helen kept stopping. She wanted to stop at every busker and sing along with them. Clara was losing her patience, dragging her friend up the road like a bold child.

"*Supermacs!*" Helen cried out when they reached Eyre Square. "*We haaave to get ships*," she slurred.

"No way, just keep walking, we're almost there."

"Nooo – I'm getting shipsss, and you can do what you like," Helen said, releasing herself from Clara's grip and staggering towards the door.

Just then two lads in the queue in front of Helen started a row. They started to push and shove in the queue, nearly knocking Helen over.

Clara hurried over and pulled her friend from the queue.

"I'm not leaving you here. You can come back tomorrow," Clara said, totally fed up now.

Helen glared at Clara but looked back at the two lads fighting and reluctantly went with her.

Helen was shouting and swaying and complaining that Clara was a killjoy when they finally reached the apartments.

Once inside the lobby door, Clara had had enough.

"*I am never going out with you again, you selfish bitch! You drink all day and throw a strop when you can't have another. What the hell is wrong with you?*" she roared.

But Helen was so drunk it was a waste of time arguing with her now.

Helen slumped at the bottom of the stairs.

"I'm so *tiiired*. I'm staying here."

"Come on, Helen, get up. I'm fed up with this!"

Helen curled up and told her to fuck off. That's it, Clara thought, I have no choice but to ring Viv and Miriam. I can't deal with this on my own. She phoned up to their apartment to get help.

"Hi, Viv. Listen, I'm downstairs with Helen. She's pissed sitting on the stairs and refusing to get up and I can't move her by myself. Can you give me a hand?"

A few minutes later Vivienne and Miriam appeared and came down the stairs. Miriam was in her pyjamas, and Vivienne had changed into cream lounge bottoms and a matching top.

"I'm sorry, girls, but I'm going to need your help getting her up to the apartment. Miriam, you can't lift anything so just take her handbag there, okay?"

"Jesus Christ, what happened? She wasn't this drunk in the restaurant," Vivienne asked.

"What happened?" Clara answered. "She has been drinking all day and just didn't want to stop. It's been a bloody nightmare just getting her here."

"Okay, let's get her up."

Vivienne took one arm and Clara took another. Helen stood up and woke up again. They got her up three steps before she started shouting at them.

"*Leeeave me alone, I'm fiiine!*" she slurred.

"Just keep moving, Helen, we're just trying to help," Vivienne said.

"*I don't need your bloody help!*" Helen shouted as she pulled her arm away from Vivienne. Her arm swung back and hit Miriam who was following behind, carrying Helen's handbag. Miriam took the full brunt of Helen's flailing arm and fell backward down three steps, landing on her back.

Everyone froze. Miriam turned white and looked horrified as she looked down and placed her hands on her bump.

Chapter 13

"Oh my God!" Helen's voice was the first to break the silence.

"Don't move, Miriam," Vivienne said, kneeling beside her.

"*I'm sso ssorry, I–I–*" Helen stuttered.

"Shut up, Helen! Clara, can you …?" Vivienne nodded toward Helen.

"Yes, of course. Helen, come on."

"But I musht help … Oh God, Miriam … I …"

"*Just go, Helen!*" Vivienne shouted.

Helen burst into tears and made her way up the stairs towards the apartment.

"Miriam, are you okay? What can I do?" Clara asked.

"I don't know how I am … I …"

"Okay, I'm calling a taxi and we're going to the hospital," Vivienne said, taking charge.

"The hospital?" Miriam said, starting to sit up. "Do you really think I need to go to the hospital?"

"Yes, I do. I'm sure everything is fine but after a fall you need to get a scan."

Miriam started to cry.

"Oh, babe, I'm sure it is fine, but we just need you checked out, okay?" Vivienne said, stroking Miriam's hair.

Miriam nodded. "But I'm in my pyjamas."

"You can have my coat," Clara said.

"Clara, can you stay with Helen in case she does anything else stupid?"

"Are you sure? I can come with you?"

"No, you stay here, and I'll call you from the hospital once we've been seen. But do you have any cash on you? My cards wouldn't work in the ATM either ..."

"Of course," said Clara, taking two fifties out from her purse. "Take this and let me flag a taxi – there was a queue of them outside when we were coming in."

"Thanks, Clara. Can you stand, Miriam?"

Miriam got to her feet slowly. She felt a little lightheaded but not faint.

"The taxi is here," said Clara, arriving back. She took off her coat and wrapped it around Miriam's shoulders, then held the door open as Vivienne helped Miriam through.

Miriam's pale face looked terrified as she eased herself into the taxi.

"Ring me, Viv," said Clara as they exchanged concerned glances.

Clara climbed the stairs to the apartment. The door was open, and Helen was sitting at the kitchen table with her head in her hands.

Clara stood in front of her.

"Oh God, I'm sso ssorry. Ish all my fault," Helen sobbed as she looked up at Clara.

"*Yes, it is all your fault,*" said Clara angrily.

"But I didn't mean to … I wass …"

"*Drunk?* Is that the word you were looking for? I asked you to stop drinking and leave the bar with me because you were so drunk. *So, yes, it is entirely your fault!*"

Clara stormed off to her room and slammed the door behind her, leaving Helen shaking in shock at the kitchen table.

Exhausted and angry, Clara took off her clothes and dumped them on the floor before changing into her pyjamas and removing her make-up. Opening her bedside locker, she took out the chocolate treats she had bought for her kids and laid them out on the duvet before climbing into bed and eating the lot.

The taxi man, seeing Miriam clutching her stomach, took the quickest route to the maternity section of Galway University Hospital and they arrived in less than ten minutes. The nurses dealt with them immediately and brought them to a cubicle to check Miriam's blood pressure and to get the details of her fall. They had no choice but to tell them everything and the nurse left them while she went to get a foetal monitor and the doctor on duty.

"I can't believe this has happened," Miriam said, starting to cry again.

"Now, now, don't upset yourself. We're in the best place to get you checked out," Vivienne said, squeezing her friend's hand.

"Doctor Molloy is in surgery and will be another twenty minutes," the nurse said as she popped her head around the cubicle curtain. "Can I get you a cup of tea, Miriam?"

"No, thank you."

"Okay, you relax there, and the doctor will be here as soon as she can."

"Is there a bathroom I could use?" Vivienne asked.

"Yes, the visitor's toilet is just outside the door you came in."

"Thank you, nurse. Miriam, do you mind if I go to the loo before the doctor gets here?"

"Of course, go. I'm fine here. They're all so nice," Miriam said, looking better now with some colour returning to her face.

"Okay, I won't be long," Vivienne said as she headed out.

Miriam sighed. She was grateful for Vivienne coming with her, but she needed a minute to herself. She felt so guilty. All this time she had kept her pregnancy a secret. A secret from her family, a secret from her work colleagues. She had been worried about what people might say about being almost forty and deliberately bringing a child into the world to raise alone. But now that something could be wrong, or there being a chance that she might lose the baby … Miriam started to cry again. She cradled her stomach. "Please be okay," she whispered to her baby, "please."

Vivienne sat on the toilet and leaned against the cool wall of the bathroom cubicle. Her head was pounding. This weekend was a disaster. She was already in shock at her accounts being emptied when this happened. *Bloody Helen.* What the fuck was going on with her? Obviously, she didn't mean to hurt Miriam but, Jesus Christ, she was so drunk. Had she been drinking all day and if so, why?

She looked at her watch. It was a quarter past two. Too late to text Jack. She needed to see him tomorrow. She wanted his advice before she rang Tom to see what was going on. She quickly typed out a text.

Jack, Vivienne here. I need to see you tomorrow. Something serious has come up and I need your advice.

Her finger hovered over the send button. Fuck it, she thought, and pressed send. She washed her hands and splashed her face.

Then her phone buzzed.

Anytime. Ring me tomorrow. I'm here for you. Jack

I'm here for you? Vivienne smiled to herself, feeling warm inside.

X, she replied as she went back to support her friend.

Saturday

Chapter 14

Helen turned over in her bed and squinted to look at the time on her phone which was propped up on her bedside locker. She tried to sit up but felt strangled by the bedclothes.

"*Oh God ...*" she sighed when she looked down and realized that she still had last night's clothes on. "*For fuck's sake!*" she shouted as she untangled herself from the duvet.

Sitting up too soon, the room started to spin.

"Oh God," she whispered, holding the base of the bed, eyes closed as she tried to steady herself. Glancing down, she kicked off the boots that were still on her feet, taking deep breaths in and out to slow her racing heart. Her heartbeat pounded in her head. It stings, it hurts, everywhere hurts. My mouth is dry, so dry. I need water. She looked around at the bedside locker for a glass of water but there was none there.

"The bathroom, I need to get to the bathroom," she whispered, eyeing the bathroom door and grateful that her bedroom had an ensuite. An image of Clara shouting at her last night came to mind. "Not now, I can't deal with that now."

Slowly getting to her feet and feeling very unsteady, her stomach lurching, she knew what was coming next. Weaving her way to the bathroom, she switched on the light, managing to reach the toilet bowl before she threw up. Her stomach continued to lurch even when there was nothing left to come up. Her hands shook as she gripped the sides of the toilet bowl, tears mixing with the snot and sweat on her face. Slumping down on the cold tiled bathroom floor, she closed the lid and flushed the toilet, laying her head on the lid, waiting for her body to calm down after all the stomach spasms.

"*When will I ever learn?*" she moaned.

When the nausea passed, Helen pulled herself to her feet and moved to the sink to splash her face. The sight that greeted her in the mirror shocked her. Her pale, almost grey face with smudged make-up and black slug-like trails of mascara was an awful sight. Her face was swollen from either vomiting or crying, and her hair tangled and sticky. Shivering in the cold bathroom, she gently washed her face. She contemplated a hot shower but was afraid she might fall as she still felt so unsteady.

Fall. Fall. Fall. Oh my God! Helen's hand instinctively covered her mouth in shock. *Miriam!*

Her stomach lurched again but this time she did not get sick – she just felt sick with shame and disgust. She looked at her reflection. "What have I done, what is wrong with me?"

Looking away from the mirror, she dried her face and went back to the bedroom. Shivering now, she climbed into the bed and pulled the duvet and sheets up to her chin. Images of the night before shot across her mind like scenes in a horror movie – the final scene Miriam's pale face as she lay at the bottom of the stairs, the stairs that she had pushed her down. The horror of what happened terrified her.

What kind of person have I become? She heard her husband Jerry's words now: "If you don't stop, someone will get hurt." She had laughed it off, thought he was overreacting. Yes, someone had reported her to Cillian's teacher for arriving to collect him smelling of drink. But she was completely sober and, if there was a slight smell of wine, that would have been from the night before, and the bitch who had reported her had caused a whole lot of trouble over nothing. The poor headmaster was mortified talking to her. She could see how ridiculous he thought the whole thing was. What an overreaction! Or at least that is what she thought at the time. She would never endanger her children. But now look at what she did to Miriam. It was an accident, of course, and she was entitled to have a few drinks when she was away but ... this was different. Miriam was pregnant and, accident or not, she had fallen down those stairs because *she* hit her.

Helen checked her phone. She scrolled through her messages. There was a message from Vivienne to the WhatsApp group at 3 o'clock in the morning.

All fine, rest needed but they are both okay.

"*Oh, thank God!*" Helen whispered with relief. Miriam and the baby were okay. But what if they hadn't been?

She went on to the Irish Rail app and googled train times. She needed to leave. She couldn't face the women. Again she remembered Clara shouting at her last night – quiet Clara. She had to leave and go back to Dublin. How could she look at them after last night? She had fucked up. They all probably hated her now, especially Miriam. Nothing she could say to her could make up for what she had done.

It was six now. There was a train at nine-thirty. That's what I'll do – I'll pack and leave a note and slip out, she decided.

She sat up but the room began to spin again. I'd better rest first, she thought, feeling overwhelmed by tiredness. She set an alarm on her phone for seven thirty. She'd get up then and sneak out. She would send them a message from the train as well. It would be easier to apologise when miles away on a train rather than endure the shame of having to look everyone in the eye.

I just need some more sleep, she thought as she lay back down and fell asleep.

Chapter 15

Clara woke up to go to the toilet. She looked at her watch which she had forgotten to take off and was now tight around her swollen wrist. 4 o'clock. God, I hate getting up to go to the loo, she thought, as she climbed out of bed.

She tried to remember the layout of the unfamiliar room. The bathroom light screamed too bright for this hour. She did a quick wee, keeping her eyes half-shut, not wanting to wake up fully. After rinsing her hands, she wiped them on her pyjama top, eager to get back to bed and back to sleep.

Hurrying back into bed, she pulled the duvet up to her chin and closed her eyes.

Nothing.

"*For fuck's sake*," she whistled between her teeth and turned over, squeezing her eyes shut. It was no use.

She sighed loudly and, feeling frustrated, turned on her back and looked at the ceiling. There was a trickle of light peeking through the curtain from the streetlight outside that stretched thinly across the ceiling. Feeling hot, she threw back the top part of the duvet to allow the air at her. She heard a crinkling sound. Without turning she put her arm out over the duvet to the other side of the bed. Her hand picked up a bunch of wrappers. *Oh, dear.* Her heart sank. She could have turned on the light, but she didn't need to. She remembered these were the wrappers of the chocolate bars that she demolished after shouting at Helen. She had been so mad at her. The memory of it didn't make her remorseful, it still made her angry. Her jaw stiffened as she realised she was still furious.

She made me so angry, she thought, trying to pinpoint what made her so furious. There was a lot to choose from. Helen annoyed her by not leaving the bar, and by ordering drinks for strangers to delay going home. For ignoring her. For being a pain getting home. For causing such a fuss. For knocking Miriam down the stairs. For ignoring her.

For ignoring me. Clara kept coming back to this thought. Helen did a lot to annoy everyone, but it was the fact that she had ignored her, ignored the fact that she wanted to go home. Helen had no appreciation of the fact that she had stayed out with her, something Helen wanted to do, not what she wanted to do. She never even thanked her. She just presumed she would hang around.

She even went off to talk to other people, Clara remembered. It didn't matter that I was there at all. What about what *I* wanted to do? *What about what I want to do? What about my wants? What about me? What about me?*

Her outburst of anger wasn't completely about Helen at all. She was just the tipping point and, seeing as how the night ended, she was an easy target for her anger and frustrations. But she wasn't only angry at Helen's drunken behaviour. Helen had used her. She didn't consider her at all because that's what other people did too. Nice obliging Clara had been a wingman for most of her friends all her life. She was usually the nice friend who looked on while prettier girls got the popular guy. She sat on the side-lines while sporty girls got picked for the school teams. Nice Clara had friends but seemed to play the supporting role in everyone else's life rather than the starring role in her own. Who put her first? Of course, when she met Richard he put her first, but this wasn't about him. He was usually supportive of her. He valued her and made her feel special. She knew she was loved and appreciated at home. But outside the home?

Clara lay still staring at the ceiling. She knew her anger came from a deep place. She knew she could not say it out loud because of what people might think. But she knew she wasn't the only mum of a special needs child who felt the same as she did. She loved Seán, she adored him. The fact that he was so reliant on her made her even more protective of him, more so than her other kids. She loved them too of course but they would grow up and go out into the world and make their own choices and decisions. Seán's future was not so clear yet. He would need their help for years to come. His would be a harder journey. Thinking back, the start of his journey was also the start of a new journey for her, one that she did not see coming and was still coming to terms with.

There was no way she could return to work and function as she had before. She had no choice but to hand in her notice. And then there was the guilt. She knew Seán took up a lot of her time, so she tried to spend time with Jessica and James and take them out for treats without Seán or spend individual time with them at home. But this was not always possible.

She had agonised over the decision to leave work because

although she didn't earn much, it still meant one less salary coming into the house. They had to look at their household budget very carefully. They changed electric and gas suppliers and she shopped in Aldi and Lidl to save money. She even cancelled her much-loved magazine subscription to cut down on expenses. Every penny mattered now. She felt she was doing the right thing and her decision was proved right when, on a routine hospital check-up for Seán, it was discovered that he was not responding to the routine hearing test. An audiologist was called in to do a thorough test and she confirmed that Seán had a hearing loss in both ears.

The news was like a knife through Clara's heart. Her poor beautiful boy smiling up at her from her lap would have to have surgery before his first birthday for his cleft palate and after that his hearing problems would have to be dealt with. He needed her more than ever now and for a long time into the future.

It was in the waiting room of one of the hospital appointments that Clara looked around to see a room full of women just like her. Tired worried mums, hoping that maybe this next appointment might bring some good news for their beautiful smiling babies. Clara had a word for these mums and herself: 'battle-weary'. They looked battle-weary because everything was a battle. Feeding your baby, stimulating your baby, trying to see the right doctors and therapists for your child, and accessing services for your baby. All the women who had careers or full-time jobs had to try to juggle with these new demands and many gave up work or went part-time if they were lucky enough to get it. Financially there was a carers' allowance but there were two things wrong with it. Firstly, no mother calls herself a carer for her own child – they are just being a mum putting the child's needs first. Secondly, the allowance was means-tested on the whole family income so usually the main earner's salary tipped them over the allowed amount. After spending ages filling out the complicated form and getting the doctor to fill in the medical sections, Clara was refused because of Richard's salary.

But what about her? Nowhere was she a consideration.

It made her very angry. She had worked, and she had a salary, but she had no choice but to give up work and lose that salary to look after her child with additional needs. Why not just means-test her? Her salary was gone. Her income was now zero, but this didn't seem to matter. When you get rejected for a small allowance it feels like the authorities are saying "We don't consider your caring job worthy. We don't see you." It's exhausting and frustrating and the anger builds.

She loved Seán so much it hurt but she was angry that they had to fight for him all the time. She was angry about how their prospects had changed due to the lack of support. Due to the lost salary, they would not be going on an annual holiday anymore. She and Richard could not go on many date nights because money was tight, and her mum was the only one who could babysit as only she knew how to feed Seán. The nice things had to go, and this made Clara sad and angry.

She was angry too that she couldn't talk about it to her friends. They had been very kind when Seán was born but hospital appointments don't make interesting conversations. They always asked about him, but they couldn't understand what her life was like now and it was nobody's fault, but it did make her feel detached from them and feel like she had less in common with them. It felt a bit isolating and lonely. If Seán had been born with no problems, she and Richard would be planning another great summer holiday.

she and Richard would be putting money away for the children's college fund.

Although she adored Seán and wouldn't be without him she was perfectly within her rights to sometimes say "This is shit." But Clara didn't say these things out loud. How could she? She had tried talking to Richard about her feelings, but he just didn't get it. Was she angry at him too? She had been so happy with two children and a career that she loved. He had pushed and pushed for another baby, and she had given in. But had he considered her views at all? These thoughts kept coming up more and more. Even now, did he have any idea how much her life had changed while his had changed little?

Richard was a great dad and he loved Seán, but he went out every day to work and had an after-work pint every Friday. He was not exhausted all the time as he didn't do the night feeds. She had tried telling him how she felt but she didn't want to sound like she was moaning all the time. But a mix of anger and sadness was how she felt most of the time now.

Was this depression? She didn't know. She was so busy all the time at home that she didn't spend much time figuring out her feelings. But this break away from home was a great opportunity to have some headspace to think about everything. Normally she kept these feelings inside and, when those feelings bubbled up, she shoved them down with chocolate. She hid chocolate around the house and then threw the wrappers out before Richard or the kids saw them. Chocolate filled a void and gave instant pleasure. But then that also brought guilt and disgust. Clara realised now that her chocolate overeating was a way to keep her anger at bay. But it was not helping, and it wasn't working anymore. She sighed, wiped a tear away, and turned over in the bed, willing sleep to come.

Chapter 16

Miriam got discharged from the hospital at 2:30 am and the women felt both exhausted and relieved as they took a taxi back to the apartments. Miriam had been very well looked after. The staff had been wonderful and caring. They had put a baby heart-monitor belt on her tummy to keep track of the baby's heartbeat and they also kept an eye on her blood pressure. Both were fine. The heart-monitor belt was attached to a printer and the nurses came in every twenty minutes to check it. Seeing the printout reassured Miriam that everything was okay. Lying there in the hospital, she felt so close to her unborn baby.

Before this, she had kept the pregnancy a secret. She wore loose clothes at work so nobody had noticed her changing shape. She was arguing with her siblings over her mum's care, so she certainly did not want to confide in them. Also, she didn't want to answer their questions. Who was the father? Was she bringing up a child on her own? How would she manage? What would she tell the child? Miriam hadn't told anyone about the baby because she didn't want to answer these questions. She thought she could just push it to the back of her mind and deal with it when she could no longer hide her pregnancy anymore.

But now she didn't care who knew. The girls had taken the news very matter-of-factly and had offered to help, no questions asked. Miriam had been so nervous about telling them, but she needn't have been. Seeing the baby's heartbeat on the monitor and the relief when the doctor said that everything was fine brought with it a huge surge of protectiveness. Miriam was overcome with love and want for this baby, and now she didn't care who knew about it.

Vivienne messaged the girls from the taxi as they sped home.

"You've been fantastic," Miriam said, leaning over and squeezing Vivienne's hand.

"Don't be silly, I'm just so happy everything is okay. You will still have to take it easy, though. Stay in bed tomorrow. You've had a shock and we've been up most of the night."

"Yes, I think I'll have a pyjama day tomorrow alright," Miriam said, yawning.

"*Hmm ...*" Vivienne was looking out the taxi window, wondering what tomorrow would bring for her.

"You okay?"

"Yes, just tired. The girls will be so relieved to know that everything is fine. I'd say the atmosphere has been very frosty in that apartment. Clara looked furious and Helen was a mess."

"Yes, I'm glad I'm sharing with you. I just couldn't face anyone else now, especially Helen."

"Well, I'm sure she'll want to apologise to you tomorrow."

"We'll see," Miriam said as the taxi pulled up at the apartment block.

They made their way to their apartment and said their goodnights as they went to their separate rooms.

Miriam lay on the bed, but her mind was full of plans. The sooner she let her brother and sister know about them the better. She turned on her side to try to sleep but her mind was busy figuring out how she was going to get her points across clearly. She didn't want to face the two of them together. No, an email would be better. That way she wouldn't get flustered, and she could say everything she needed to without interruption. She tried to find a comfortable position to sleep, but she was wide awake.

There is no point in lying here awake, she said to herself. She was exhausted but knew she wouldn't sleep until she resolved this. Her laptop was at the side of her bed, so she opened it up and wrote the email to her brother and sister.

Hi Sharon and Simon,

I am writing this email to you both, as it is easier than making two phone calls. My big news is that I am pregnant, five months pregnant and my baby is due on the 3rd of April. I am delighted and cannot wait to become a mother and all the changes that entails. As I am not in a relationship, I used the services of a sperm donor agency, so you won't be meeting the father. I am very happy with my decision, and I hope that you will both be happy for me.

At the moment, I go around to Mum three nights a week and you two call in on Saturday and Sunday. We have home help coming in at breakfast and meals-on-wheels delivering lunch and dinner, but it's not enough. As you also know, Lucy from the Alzheimer's Association recommended we visit St Patricia's nursing home and possibly put Mum's name down. Both of you refused to go but I went and took the tour and met the manager and I agree with Lucy that it is the best place for Mum. She can have her own room and be cared for 24 hours a day by people who understand her condition.

Two weeks ago when Mum's doctor and Lucy called a meeting, again you both were too busy to attend – but I went, and Mum's condition has deteriorated so much that very soon it will be deemed a health risk to leave her in the house on her own.

I am now five months pregnant I will not be able to continue staying with Mum three times a week and some weekend days when you guys can't do it. So the time has come to make some hard decisions. Things cannot remain the same. I know it is difficult for all of us to see Mum move into a nursing home, but we have to be realistic about this and do what is best for her and her safety.

The alternative is to have home help come in 24 hours a day. I have attached the figures for both options. You will see that although both options cost a lot, the nursing home option is 500 euros cheaper a week and less disruptive for Mum. The other option is that you two take over most of the care, as due to my age I need to take extra care during my pregnancy. After the baby is born I will not be able to commit to anything until I assess my situation.

Please do not reply to this email immediately. I have been dealing with this for months. I suggest that both of you organise a visit to St Patricia's and speak to whoever you need to and when you have done that, and looked at the figures, maybe we can sit down and make a plan for Mum. At the end of the day, it is Mum's happiness and health that is all of our concern.

Miriam

Miriam took a deep breath and saved the email in drafts. She would send it in the morning when she woke up and then she would turn her phone off for the day. She'd had enough drama for one weekend and knew Sharon would be on the phone looking for a row. She put the laptop away and fell asleep immediately.

Chapter 17

Vivienne woke at nine. She was so exhausted when they got back that she fell into a deep sleep – but not before setting the alarm on her phone. She didn't want to waste a morning by sleeping in. As she lay in bed recalling the previous night's events she believed that the drama delaying her confrontation with Tom was a good thing. She had been so angry. But now with a bit of space, she knew she had to plan her next move carefully. How much did he know? How much would she tell him? She needed to figure all this out.

There was obviously a reason why he cancelled their credit card and cleared out their joint account without telling her. If there had been an emergency, he would have called her. So the obvious conclusion was that he either found out what she was doing in Galway, or he was getting advice himself from a solicitor friend. She had been so careful to keep her motive for this trip under wraps. How could he know? Anyway, she needed to get advice from Jack. She didn't want to involve the women – they didn't need their weekend ruined by her personal affairs. Well, one thing was sure now, things had escalated. The separation was definitely on and by the looks of it was going to be a messy one.

Vivienne went into the bathroom and turned on the shower. Standing naked, she looked at herself in the mirror. Her weekly trips to the gym combined with yoga and watching her weight had paid off. She brushed her hand across her breasts and then down across her flat stomach. It had been a long time since Tom had excited her with his touch.

They used to have such fun in the early days of their marriage. Romantic weekends away and socialising every weekend. Tom's friends went out in a group every Saturday night. Every weekend they attended a different dinner party, a charity gala dinner or a group outing to the newest restaurant around town. It was all very exciting then and Vivienne enjoyed it. But she never fully felt she fitted in.

There were coffee mornings the women in the group held, that she was never invited to and would only hear about in passing.

When she asked about it, Cathy the main organiser in the group replied, "Oh we just presumed you would be too busy, Viv".

"Well, keep me informed – I might be free for the next one," Vivienne had said, smiling through gritted teeth, not convinced that was the reason at all.

The other women in Tom's friends' group all grew up and went to school together. Many times over dinner Viv had to sit and listen to a story being retold from their past while everyone laughed or added their version. She wasn't part of any of that. At first, she found it funny but after a while it irked her when the same stories were brought up, the same shared memories that she was not part of. She said it to Tom.

"Do you guys have nothing else to talk about, nothing else in common?

119

"What do you mean? Of course we do. They just forget that you weren't there, that's all."

"Well, it's getting a bit boring for me having to listen to it every time we go out."

"Hey," Tom had said, putting his arms around her, "forget about the other women. They probably don't have that much else to talk about, but they are nice people and they go way back."

"Yes, but when I bring up anything about the state of the world or politics or general stuff they just don't want to know."

"Politics!" Tom had laughed. "Jesus, Viv, you should know by now that the only politics the women are interested in is who will get on the parent-teacher board! Their world is different from yours, okay, but that doesn't make them less kind or fun. And, anyway, I love my brainy career wife." He caressed her neck. "I'm hoping I can retire and be a kept man. Then I can spend my days going to coffee mornings and Pilates classes." He laughed as he pulled her close.

Vivienne had laughed it off but, the fact was, although she was married to Tom, had kids in the same schools, and saw so much of these women, she would always be an outsider. When she thought about it, they never asked questions about her job or her travels. Oh, they occasionally asked about her work but zoned out when she told them about it. Or they would say things like, "Viv, I don't know how you manage to do a full-time busy job. I don't know where you find the time," which didn't quite feel like a compliment. Vivienne couldn't understand it because all of these women went to college and got degrees but gave up their jobs or careers once they got married and had children. Was it because they never had to work for their college fees that they didn't appreciate it? It was a mystery to her, but she carried on with the weekend dinner parties and the group ski holiday every year or so. She went along with everything to keep Tom happy.

That is until the guys returned from their annual rugby trip five years ago.

Tom had arrived home from the rugby trip absolutely wrecked and reeking of alcohol. He had gone straight to bed when he got home, and Vivienne set about emptying his bag. She took out his dirty clothes and was separating them for the wash basket when she smelt the perfume. She recognised it immediately as Chanel No. 5, a perfume she never wore. She picked up three different tops Tom had brought and sniffed the collars. They all smelt of Chanel No. 5.

"What's this?" she had said, storming into the bedroom, holding the tops.

"What?" Tom had said, half asleep with his eyes closed.

"Tom, open your eyes. There's a woman's perfume all over your clothes."

"Don't be ridiculous," he said without opening his eyes.

"Tom, I'm not joking."

He sat up suddenly. *"Oh Jesus, I'm so hungover! Will you just leave me alone with the nagging!* One of the lads sprayed me with perfume in the duty-free, okay? Now leave me alone, I need to sleep."

"But these clothes were in your bag and –"

"Leave it!" he shouted, then added more quietly but firmly, "Just leave it, Viv. That's the end of it now."

Vivienne felt sick in the pit of her stomach. She left the bedroom and shut the door quietly behind her. He was lying. She knew it. She felt it in her gut.

In a panic, she rang Caroline whose husband also went on these annual trips. She was one of the quieter women in the group and she felt she could trust her. But Caroline's response shocked her.

"Look, Viv, just ignore it."

"What do you mean ignore it? His clothes smell of Chanel No. 5! I would recognise that perfume a mile away."

"Look, what happens on these trips just happens, okay? Don't give it another thought."

"*What?* Are you serious?"

"Viv, it's just the way things are. The lads go away on the annual rugby trip, the girls go away for their weekend, and nobody asks any questions. At the end of the day, Tom comes home to you and David comes home to me and life goes on. Seriously, put it out of your mind. If you want my advice, leave it be. Buy yourself something nice and expensive on his credit card and forget all about it. Now I have to go. Thanks for ringing but I don't think we need to talk about this again, okay?" And, with that, she hung up.

Vivienne stood there, looking at the phone. She could not believe it. So it was quite acceptable to this group of so-called happy couples to go off for one weekend a year and – what, snog? Have sex? And for nobody to talk about it or be bothered at all by it? Was this why the women were starving themselves half the time and dressing up every weekend? Vivienne had always thought they did that because they enjoyed it, but now she wasn't sure who it was for.

She had tried so hard over the years to fit in and be accepted but she was not like them. She wasn't going to try anymore. She felt more herself with the lovely women she had met on the Human Resources course who she had nights out with a few times a year. They were so down to earth and interested in her and life in general and they, those strangers, made her feel more comfortable than these people she had been trying to please for years.

Something shifted in Vivienne that day. She would deal with Tom. She was not going to ignore this. But one thing was clear: her life changed right there at that moment by just emptying Tom's weekend bag.

Tom refused to talk about that weekend and Vivienne refused to go out with their friends. She just felt the whole thing was a fraud. The atmosphere in the house was awful. When she suggested couples counselling, he laughed in her face.

"Nothing happened, now get over yourself," he had said.

After a few days of them avoiding speaking to one another, he came home with flowers and chocolates and tried to charm her.

"Nothing happened, you have to believe me. We can't go on like this."

"I just want details and an explanation. I'm not like those other women. I can't sweep this under the carpet as if nothing happened."

"Oh for Christ's sake, look at you!" he said, frustrated. "You are so high and mighty. Who do you think you are? Look around you. Who pays for your nice house and your nice car? I do. I never heard you complaining when you enjoyed your nights out in top restaurants. I never saw you picking up the bill. You have me to thank for the life you have. I'm not coming home every night to this atmosphere and your sanctimonious attitude. If you are not happy with the way things are, then you know where the door is. We're finished speaking about this. Now I am going out to meet my friends for pints and dinner. Are you coming?"

"No," Vivienne had said in a whisper, shocked at what he had said. And when he left she cried and cried and cried.

Things changed for Vivienne after that night. She tried to figure out a way forward, but if Tom didn't want to try counselling to save their marriage, she didn't want to keep up the charade. She did see the women when she went to Alex's rugby games, but everyone looked different to her now.

This game they played might work well for them, but it would never work for her. Had he been unfaithful on every trip? She would never know. When she thought of all those trips and all the time she and the kids would run to welcome him home, peeking in his bag for some duty-free goodies! It made her feel sick now, but she couldn't keep going over this. Was she overreacting? It was the not knowing that was worse. If she knew, they could try to fix it. She didn't want to break up the family but there was a gap between them, and Vivienne didn't know if they could get back to the way they were. They still shared the same bed, but something had shifted for Vivienne. Tom stayed out late with his pals more and more and occasionally he didn't come home at all on rugby match days. They argued about that too.

"Why don't you trust me, Viv? The problem is you not me," was Tom's usual answer.

After a while Vivienne got tired of asking him so she gave up and they both led their own lives living under the same roof and were civil to each other for the sake of the kids. Vivienne threw herself into her work and once she got over the heartbreak of it she didn't care anymore. It was just sad.

Vivienne pulled back the shower curtain and turned the shower on to hot. Taking another look at her naked body, she found herself wondering if Jack Brady would appreciate all her hard work. She was sure she could feel sexual chemistry when she sat beside him in

Jury's Inn. And she had flushed when he held her gaze as she spoke. She closed her eyes as she remembered the feel of his hands on her shoulders as he helped her with her coat. He kept them there for longer than he needed to, and she hadn't minded at all.

"Oh God, what am I like?" She laughed as she stepped into the steaming hot shower.

Chapter 18

Helen woke suddenly and sat up abruptly. She could hear something – the sound of teacups and saucers and people mumbling.

Oh no, she thought, *shit!* She had hoped to sneak out and get the train home but now the girls were up and having tea in her apartment. She must have slept through her alarm. She tried to grab her phone but it fell to the ground with a thud. *Shit!*

She had no choice but to face them. She couldn't pretend to be asleep because of her phone falling, which they would have heard through the bedroom door.

Getting out of bed slowly, she pulled on a fresh T-shirt and leggings. Her head was still pounding, and her stomach muscles felt sore from vomiting.

I'd better face the music, she thought, taking a deep breath and opening the door to find Clara sipping tea at the table and Vivienne in the kitchen.

"Good morning," Vivienne said, looking over her shoulder.

"Eh, morning," Helen said sheepishly, avoiding Clara's eye and feeling utterly awkward just standing at the bedroom door. "How is Miriam?"

"Miriam is fine," Vivienne said. "It was a long night, but she was given the all-clear. Do you want some tea?"

"No, I'm just going to speak to Miriam and then I'm going."

"Going where?" Clara asked, looking at Helen for the first time.

Helen couldn't judge her mood by her tone. "I'm going home. I've caused enough trouble this weekend."

"Helen, sit down," Vivienne said, wiping her hands on a tea towel and walking over to the kitchen table.

"No … I feel awful … I …"

"*Sit down*," Vivienne repeated, sitting down and pulling out a chair beside her.

Helen sat down, feeling mortified. "Look. I'm so sorry for last night. I was out of control, and I can't believe I …"

"Yes, you were drunk and a bloody pain," said Vivienne, "but what happened was an accident. Please stay."

"I'm so embarrassed and something awful could have happened."

"Well, thank God things turned out okay. Look, I don't want to preach, but it could have been very different. I don't know what's going on with you, but you were completely out of line."

"I'm sorry," Helen said, just wanting to run out the door.

"Listen, running back to Dublin won't solve anything. We're your friends. If there is anything going on you can talk to us."

"No, there's nothing wrong," Helen said, feeling very uncomfortable to be under this scrutiny. "I just had too much to drink."

"Okay, well, stay then," Vivienne said, looking from Helen to Clara for a reaction. "If you go home, you'll be straight into a house with four boys and a load of washing waiting for you."

"Well, that's true." Helen hadn't thought this through. If she went home now, she would have to explain why to Jerry, and lie about having a plan in place about her drinking and lie about the new person she was going to be. She was not ready for that conversation.

She looked over at Clara, trying to gauge if she was still talking to her.

Just then Vivienne's phone vibrated. "I just need to reply to this text," she said, standing up and moving into the kitchen.

"Is everything okay?" Clara asked her when she came back and sat down.

"Yes, it's just a client I have to meet this morning," Vivienne said.

Helen was about to ask if it was the same client she saw her with in Jurys' bar yesterday but decided to keep her mouth shut, afraid to put her foot in it again.

"Can I go and see Miriam?" Helen asked.

"Not now, Helen, she's sleeping. But, honestly, she's fine and knows it was an accident. She was awake earlier. I brought her a cup of tea, some pastries and the papers. She looked good actually. She said she's going to lie around in her jammies and then meet us at the spa later."

"The spa!" said Clara, her eyes nearly popping out of her head.

"Yes!" Vivienne said, taking two brochures out from her bag. "Now come on, you didn't think I'd let this weekend go by without a spa treatment, did you? The Skylight Hotel has a great spa and I have booked the four of us for four o'clock for a one-hour treatment of your choice."

"Oh, great!" said Clara. "Just what I need!"

"The three of us can go out to breakfast now and then we can split up and do our own thing and meet at the Skylight later. We can decide then if we want to eat out tonight or get takeout and have it here. Maybe have a quiet night here in our pyjamas?"

"That sounds heavenly," Clara said.

"Girls, I just don't know, I'm so embarrassed," Helen said, feeling awful. She also felt too hungover to even think about food but didn't want to admit that.

Vivienne glanced at her phone messages then, leaning across the table, she put a hand on Helen's arm.

"None of us are perfect," she said.

As they headed out for breakfast, Clara couldn't help noticing how casually Vivienne was dressed this morning. She was wearing a big white parka jacket, black leggings, and black Nike runners which was such a contrast to her office-type clothes of yesterday. She was glad Vivienne was relaxing, as she seemed a little distracted in the restaurant last night and didn't get a good night's sleep after the dash to the hospital with Miriam.

"We'd better get a move on. The restaurant we are going to is very popular," Vivienne said as they weaved through the Saturday morning shoppers. "It's called Ard Bia at Nimmo's and it's right down at the Spanish Arch. The food is delicious, and the building is gorgeous."

"Lead the way," said Helen.

The cold air had helped wake her up a bit more, but she was dreading having to sit through breakfast. She had sent Miriam a text message and Miriam had replied with a heart. She still felt awful but hoped to buy Miriam a little something today to make up for it and she was going to try to stay off the drink. She had promised Jerry she would come back with a plan so she might as well see what a booze-free day felt like. It starts right here, right now, she said to herself, feeling nervous and unsure.

The girls arrived just before a group of Americans formed a queue behind them. It certainly was a popular spot. They didn't have to wait long before a smiling waitress showed them to a lovely table by a window that looked out onto the River Corrib. The menu was a mix of traditional Irish breakfast items as well as some new popular ones like smashed avocado on sourdough bread with poached eggs, and buttermilk pancakes with fresh berries and local organic honey.

Clara and Vivienne placed their order.

"I'll just have coffee and toast for now," Helen ordered. She was very unsure how long she could even sit in the restaurant surrounded by food.

When the food arrived it was served on mismatched vintage Irish plates that matched the Irish cottage feel of the place. The staff were lovely and friendly and the décor inside of whitewashed walls and small red window-frames gave a warm comforting feel. The girls enjoyed their breakfast but Helen left her toast untouched – she was just happy to keep the coffee down.

Vivienne checked her watch and stood up.

"I'll see you later at four, yeah? Here's some money to cover my food. You relax and enjoy your cuppa." She put some cash on the table. She had gone to an ATM earlier on, before anyone was up, to take cash out from her personal account. She put the joint account cards away and would only use her own debit card from now.

"See you later, enjoy your day." And with that, she was gone.

"She seems very keen to get going," Clara said, hoping to break the ice with Helen. It was just the two of them now and she didn't want an awkward atmosphere between them.

"Yeah, and she looks different today, more relaxed," Helen replied. "Listen, Clara, about last night. I'm sorry. I was over the top. I feel awful about what happened to Miriam, but I know I ruined your night too. I'm just in a shit place right now and I need to sort myself out."

"I don't hold a grudge, Helen, but I was worried about you – anything could have happened."

"I know, I know," Helen said, dropping her head and staring into her cup.

"You know you can talk to any of us if you want to? Nobody's life is perfect."

"Thanks, I appreciate that. I just need to get things straight in my own head first," Helen said, grateful for Clara's offer.

"This is a strange weekend though, isn't it? Miriam is pregnant by a donor and Vivienne isn't herself either. She seemed so stressed yesterday and today she is a different person. She even has her hair down!"

"I know!" nodded Helen, "I like the new-look Vivienne I must say. Okay, let's get out of here. I'm going for a wander. I want to buy Miriam something for last night. I saw some lovely pottery on one of the market stalls outside at Spanish Arch so I might head there now. What do you plan on doing?"

"I think I'll take a walk out to Salthill to clear my head and then go back to the apartment for a rest. I'm so glad we're going to the spa. It'll be great to have some real girlie time."

"Yeah, I know what you mean. With an all-male household, I rarely think of pampering myself. Look at the state of my nails, for god's sake!" Helen laughed as she showed Clara her bitten nails. "I don't think a manicurist could save these now."

"I'm not sure whether to have a facial or a massage. I'll see how my face looks after a walk in this cold Atlantic air."

"Right, I'll see you at the spa," Helen said, getting up and putting her coat on.

"Yeah, see you at four."

Clara stood up and hugged her friend. She was still angry at her but felt she really needed a hug.

Chapter 19

Helen wandered around, looking at the stalls of the Christmas crafts market. There were painting stalls, food stalls, baked goods stalls, and beautiful ceramics by local artists. She picked up a lovely vase with a seascape design on it. This could hopefully be a peace offering for Miriam, she thought as she paid the lady for it.

"Is it a gift?" the artist asked.

"Yes, yes, it is actually."

"I can gift-wrap it for you, no extra cost?"

"Oh, thank you, that would be lovely!"

The artist wrapped it and put it in a lovely box.

While she was waiting on her change, she removed her scarf and opened her jacket. Bloody hot flushes. They were always worse after alcohol, especially wine. Something to do with the sugar, Helen remembered hearing somewhere. Maybe it was one of the Menopause Hub's videos. Helen's sister was seeing a menopause expert in a clinic in Dublin called the Menopause Hub and kept telling Helen to make an appointment with them. They had changed her sister's life. God knows I could do with a change for the better, Helen thought. Picking up the wrapped gift, she made her way to a small wall beside the river where she sat down to cool off. The menopausal hot flushes and night sweats were not helping her problems at all. Waking up in the middle of the night with night sweats was horrible and then it took ages to get comfortable again to get back to sleep. The broken night's sleep meant that she was tired and cranky the next day which made her irritable with the boys. Jerry was probably delighted to leave the house for work to get away from her mood swings. And as for her libido? Helen almost laughed. That had disappeared altogether.

Maybe if I get my menopause symptoms under control, I might feel better about myself and be nicer to be around, she thought as the wind blew her hair back. It would be a start anyway.

She felt anxious thinking about Jerry. Vivienne was right about not going home. She wasn't ready to face him, with him expecting her to come home with a plan to deal with her drinking. Well, at least she had a plan to see the menopause doctor and, if the doctor was nice, maybe she could build up the courage to ask her for tips on how to cut down on her drinking. Maybe.

God, this is so refreshing, she thought, sitting with her coat wide open while people rushed past bracing themselves against the cold wind.

She looked across at Jury's Inn. There was no reason to give up the drink completely, she thought, if she could control it better and maybe not drink mid-week. But she knew Jerry wouldn't go for that.

Then another thought crossed her mind. Maybe if I were happier I wouldn't need to drink? Why am I not happy? When did I stop being happy?

Helen felt miserable. Sitting on the wall, she looked to her right again at Jury's Inn. I could go over for just one, she thought, standing up and zipping up her jacket.

She walked towards the hotel.

And then she stopped herself. Oh for God's sake! What am I doing? What is wrong with me?

She quickly ran across the road into the crowds of shoppers and headed back to the apartment before she changed her mind.

Helen's palms began to sweat as she tapped on Miriam's door. This would have been the perfect occasion for a drink to steady my nerves, she thought. She heard a shuffle behind the door and then Miriam opened it. She was wearing a navy hoodie over light-blue pyjamas with tiny daisies on them. She looked sleepy with no make-up on but had colour in her face at least.

"I'm so sorry, Miriam. I feel terrible about last night, and I –"

"Come in, for God's sake – it's freezing out there."

Miriam led the way into the identical apartment. "Do you want a cup of tea? I think Viv got milk," she said, having a look in the fridge.

"No, I just wanted to pop in and give you this," Helen said as she handed her the big box.

"What is it?"

"It's just a small gift to say I'm sorry."

"Helen, there was no need," Miriam said, putting the box on the kitchen table. "It was an accident and I'm fine now, no harm done."

"Yeah, well, if I wasn't so drunk it would never have happened and that's a fact. I am so ashamed of myself. If anything had happened to your baby,..." Helen sat down as she was feeling lightheaded. Menopause and a hangover from hell did not go well together. Her palms were sweating but she felt cold.

Miriam was taking the vase out of the box. "Oh, Helen, it's beautiful! Honestly, I love it."

"You're welcome. I wanted to speak to you myself and clear the air before we meet the others at the spa. I'd hate for there to be an atmosphere between us."

"Come here, give me a hug. We're all good, okay?"

"Thanks, Miriam," Helen said but she still felt like shit. "I'll leave you to rest up."

"No need, I'm grand. I'm thinking of getting some air actually."

"Well, it's freezing out there so wrap up. I'll walk to the spa with you later, if you like?"

"Yeah, that'd be great. We can leave here at a quarter to four – it's only up the road."

"Grand, I'm going for a rest now. Can I get you anything?"

"No, I'm fine, thanks."

"Okay, I'll knock for you at a quarter to, then," Helen said as she went to the door. "And Miriam? Thanks for being so nice about it."

"Go on, everything is fine now. I'll see you later."

Miriam was so generous about it, Helen thought as she went next door to her own apartment, but it felt so awkward. She hated feeling shame, but that's all she seemed to feel these days. Ashamed of herself. She took a glass from the kitchen and went into her room. Opening her shopping bag, she took out the magazines she had bought at the Tesco Express on the way back to the apartment. Then she took out the litre of Diet Coke and filled her glass. She was so thirsty that she drank it back in one go and then poured herself another glass.

She then opened her weekend suitcase that she still hadn't unpacked and took out the small naggin of vodka that she had brought with her on the trip and poured it into the Coke. She knew she couldn't drink tonight or, if she did, the women would be watching her. More shame. But she needed something to settle her. Taking off her leggings and her boots, she threw them on top of last night's bundle of clothes on the floor and got into bed.

She finished off her drink and poured another one. The vodka was working its magic. She could feel herself relax. Just one more and a little sleep and nobody would know any different. She was exhausted from the drama of last night and the shame and judgment today. She just needed a little break from everything.

Vivienne pulled the hood of her snow-white parka up over her head and tucked her hair into it as she walked over the Corrib and headed out to Salthill. The wind was cold, but the sky was blue, and the sun was out. So as long as you were wrapped up and moving you were fine. Taking out her phone, she checked Jack's directions for where to meet him and his dogs.

Meet me at the junction of Father Burke Road and Grattan Road.

She typed this into Google Maps. It was a twenty-minute walk from the restaurant, maybe less as she was walking fast in these temperatures. She was glad she had packed her walking trainers and this walk would do her good before meeting Jack.

She wondered if Helen and Clara had believed that it was a client texted her earlier. Helen had looked at her a little oddly and seemed about to ask her something, but then subsided.

But no matter – she was so excited about seeing Jack again. She was definitely attracted to him, but she needed him as her solicitor and needed his impartial advice. It would be foolish to cross the line between business and personal. So what was she doing rushing to meet him like a sixteen-year-old on a first date?

Once she crossed the bridge from the city, she continued left to keep on Father Burke Road. It wasn't long before she saw the sea in the distance. How wonderful to have the beach so close to the city, she thought as she got to the junction with Grattan Road. She stopped for a moment to take a deep breath and take in the view of the Atlantic Ocean. Walkers and joggers passed her as they made their way down the promenade.

Just then, she saw Jack and waved in his direction. He hesitated for a second and then waved back. He was leaning against a Land Rover wearing jeans, hiking boots, a green wax jacket, and a matching green scarf tied loosely at his neck. Beside him, his two Golden Retrievers wagged their tails in anticipation of their walk.

"I hardly recognised you," he said, smiling as she approached. "Forgive me but I have only ever seen you in work clothes."

"Well, I'm off duty today," Vivienne said, smiling as she knelt to greet his dogs. They wagged their tails as she hugged them and scratched their backs.

"I can see you are well used to dogs," Jack said. "Meet the ladies in my life, Molly and Milly."

"I love dogs," Vivienne said, wondering if these were the only ladies in Jack Brady's life. "We always had dogs growing up, but Tom never wanted one. I tried for years to convince him, but he never allowed it. One of our many differences. I go home to my mum and dad to see the dogs." She laughed. "They think their daughter misses them but it's really the dogs!"

Jack laughed too. He was liking this relaxed dog-loving version of Vivienne, a huge contrast to the perfectly groomed businesswoman who arrived in his office yesterday.

"Thank you so much for seeing me today," Vivienne said, standing up. "I need your advice and I'll pay you, of course, for your time."

"Hey, don't worry about it ... but you do need to earn my attention," he said, looking into her eyes and holding her stare.

"Oh, okay. What have you got in mind?" Vivienne replied, holding his gaze and feeling butterflies in her stomach.

"Let's start with this," he said as he handed her a lead and a ball. "Let's go walk these ladies and talk business later, if that's okay with you?"

"Yes, that sounds perfect." The credit-card disaster could wait. Time to relax.

They headed off down a few steps onto the beach. It felt like the most natural thing in the world to do, walking dogs with Jack Brady. Vivienne couldn't remember the last time she felt so relaxed and comfortable and, yes, happy.

Chapter 20

Clara left the restaurant, pulling up the collar of her wool coat, and turned left over the bridge. The River Corrib was flowing fast and furious. She stopped for a minute to look over the side. If you fell in there you wouldn't have a chance, she thought, before moving on. This side of Galway City had been developed into a creative quarter since Clara had last been here. There were artisan bread shops, lots of restaurants, and lovely tea shops.

I might pop into one of those tea shops on my way back, she thought. Right now I just want to walk and clear my head.

Reaching the beach, she took out her phone to send Richard a quick text but decided to call him instead.

"Hiya, love," she said.

"Ah, there ya are – how's Galway?"

"Cold, freezing cold, but dry and sunny. How are the kids?"

"Grand, everything is good here. We're at James' match and we're going to McDonald's after. Are you having a good time?"

The wind was making it a bit difficult to hear him.

"Yeah, well, it's been eventful."

"*Get in there! Get the ball!*" Richard shouted. "Sorry, love, did you say eventful?"

"Yeah, well, Miriam announced she was pregnant. Can you believe that? Then she had a little fall last night, so Vivienne took her to the hospital to get her checked out. Thank God she was okay, but it was very dramatic, I can tell you, and we –"

"Sorry, love, did you say Miriam is pregnant?"

"Yes, she used a donor. Very modern. But fair play to her. She got fed up waiting for Mister Right to arrive. It won't be easy. We're all delighted for her though."

"Well, that's some news alright!"

"Listen, I'm going to go. It's very windy here. I'm off on a walk to Salthill and I can barely hear you. Say hi to the kids for me."

"Sure. Enjoy yourself."

"Yeah, see ya."

"Bye, love."

That was it, short and sweet. Putting the phone back in her pocket, she walked on.

The wind was blowing against her now. Clara felt pressure in her head. The wind was bitterly cold, but she kept her hood down. She liked the feel of the sea air through her hair. She had a lot to think about. Her outburst with Helen last night and subsequent restless sleep exposed the anger that had been building inside for some time. She couldn't ignore it any longer or it was going to make her ill. She kept walking. Salthill Beach was further than she thought, so when she saw a sign for Grattan Beach, she took that turn instead. She had the idea that she would walk for miles on the beach when she got there, but by the time she reached it she was winded. I'm so unfit, she thought. That's another thing to add to my to-do list.

She stood, looking out to the sea. The wind was bitter now. She turned around to see people coming out of a small café across the road from the beach. Feck the walk, she thought, it's a warm drink and a sit-down I need.

She headed back across the road to the café. Her timing was perfect as the people leaving the café had vacated a table at the window. She was delighted. She had a wonderful view down the strand from the heat and comfort of this cosy café. Paintings by local artists hung on the walls and there was an old cottage-type dresser with beautiful pottery pieces on it in sea colours of blues and greens. Clara took off her coat and her gloves and felt very comfortable here indeed. She had planned on just ordering a pot of tea, but the display case of cakes and tarts was making her mouth water.

"Good morning, what can I get for you?" a young smiling waitress asked. She was so funky-looking. Her long hair was braided with different-coloured threads and her nose and eyebrow were pierced. Her name badge read *Fern*. How perfect, Clara thought, her name totally suits her. I wish I could have been brave enough to look like her when I was younger. She felt disappointed once again in herself and her compliant ways.

"I love your hair!" The words were out before Clara realised it.

"Oh, thanks so much. I just love a bit of colour. It just gives you a lift, doesn't it?"

"Yes," Clara said, "it really does."

"Just to let you know we have two apple tarts made fresh this morning and a blackberry crumble. We also have plain or fruit scones."

"So much choice!"

"The apple tarts are very popular because my gran makes them."

"Well, that has to be the one then. I'll have apple tart and a pot of tea, please."

"Great. The apple tart comes heated with either cream or custard."

"Oh my! Custard, please. I haven't had custard on apple tart since I was a child. That's what my grandmother used to give me."

"Gran insists on custard being an option, so custard it is." Fern headed off behind the counter.

What a breath of fresh air, Clara thought as she watched her. I wish I had taken more risks as a teen or even into my twenties.

She sighed, gazing out the window. Nobody told her not to dye her hair or get piercings. Her younger sister had every hairstyle going and their mother didn't mind at all. Clara didn't know what held her back. Thinking about it, she didn't like being the centre of attention and if she had a wild hairstyle then she would have got attention. She had felt more comfortable blending in rather than standing out. But now she felt so blended in that she didn't know who she was anymore. What did she like, what did she want, who did she want to be? She didn't need to become a different person, just a different version of herself. She was tired and bored with this version.

Fern arrived with her pot of tea and her apple tart. There was a small jug on the side with the homemade custard. All the delph was the same blue-green colours as the delph on the shelf. The colours swirled into each other like the waves of the sea.

"Thanks, Fern. That looks delicious."

"Just give me a shout if you need anything else," she said, putting down some napkins.

"Actually, would you have a pen and a sheet of paper?"

"Sure," Fern said, tearing out a few pages from her order book and giving Clara a pen from her apron.

"Thanks so much, you're very good," Clara said.

She poured out the tea and put a drop of milk in. She then poured the silky custard over the apple tart. The smell of the custard brought her right back to her grandmother's kitchen. She used to visit her grandmother every Sunday for tea when she was a child and continued to call in every Sunday evening after she was married for some of her apple tart and custard. She felt a pain in her heart as she remembered. She missed her grandmother so much. She always seemed to sense when she was sad. She never asked for details, she just hugged her and sat close to her telling her she was beautiful and clever and kind. And Clara would close her eyes and inhale the scent of her grandmother and it felt like inhaling love, pure love.

Brushing the memory aside, Clara tucked into the apple tart and sipped her tea. She laid out the sheets of paper and started a list. She had always liked lists. They put an order on things, and she needed some order, some direction right now.

She headed one piece of paper: *Things I don't like.*

The next one: *What I want.*

And the third one: *How can I make it happen?*

Then she opened her bag and took out her birth control pills and swallowed one with her cup of tea.

Picking up the pen, she wrote on the "*Things I don't like*" page.

1) Lying to my husband.

Chapter 21

Clara had been lying to her husband for nearly a year now. She remembered the moment she started lying to Richard. It was Christmas Eve, and the kids were fast asleep in bed. Clara and Richard had just made love downstairs in front of the fire. This was a rare enough occurrence in itself as they were kept so busy with the kids and Clara was so self-conscious about her extra weight that she hated to see herself naked, never mind being naked in front of Richard. She knew he would never remark on her weight gain, he probably didn't even notice it, but it affected her self-esteem, and she didn't have the energy to do anything about it. This made her feel down which, in turn, made her eat sugar to cheer herself up, which kept everything going around in a circle of disappointment in herself.

"We should do this more often," Richard had said. "We're so good at it."

Clara had laughed. Richard was so happy. The flickering light from the open fire had made her feel sexy and unashamed of her shape. She was blissfully relaxed.

"No, I mean it, love. I think we should do it more because I think we should try for another baby."

Now Clara did laugh. "Are you serious?"

"Yes. Think about it, a little brother for Seán."

"No way, Richard, I ... I just couldn't manage."

"But we'd all be here to help. The kids would love a little brother or sister. I just feel that one more would complete the family, love."

"I don't think so. I feel so stretched as it is, and we don't know what the future holds for Seán."

"Exactly, the new baby would be a welcome distraction and our focus wouldn't be so much on Seán. We would all have something positive to look forward to."

"But what about me? I'm hoping to go back to work at some stage, even part-time."

"You don't need to, love. We're doing okay and the kids love having you at home."

"But I have enough on my plate as it is. I'm exhausted all the time and I need to get some piece of my old life back. I've told you before how I feel."

"But Seán needs you here, love, and things are so much easier when you're here at home."

Easier for you, you mean, Clara thought, feeling anger and resentment rising in her. Had he not listened to her at all? Or had he heard her and just decided that he wanted things his way?

"I have told you so many times that I need to get some of my old life back. I was happy before with just Jessica and James and you pushed for one more baby. And then we had Seán and our lives turned upside down, but mine has been affected the most."

"Jesus, Clara, he needs you!"

"I know and I adore him, but at some stage I would like to work outside the home even part-time or do some volunteering for the sake of my sanity."

"Okay, well, will you think about it at least?" Richard said, kissing her shoulder.

Clara could tell he was not listening to her, not really listening. Did he not understand how much extra pressure a new baby would put on her? She could feel herself getting annoyed, but it was Christmas Eve and they'd had a lovely night, so she just let it go.

"I'll think about it," she said, knowing her mind was already made up.

"Oh that's great," Richard said, looking excited. "I do love you, Clara!" And he lay back on the rug, looking so happy.

As Clara looked at him, a sadness came over her and, not for the first time since Seán was born, she felt distant from her husband. Did they want different things now?

After Christmas, as soon as her GP's office was open, she renewed her prescription for the Pill and had been taking it ever since.

There never seemed to be a good time to tell Richard about her contraception, and she thought he had forgotten about having another baby, but then he started asking about her cycle and this just made her feel stressed and pressured. She felt he was only having sex to get her pregnant and this was really annoying her. She needed to speak to him, but she couldn't find the right time to bring it up. Or was she avoiding it? Why couldn't she tell him? She didn't know. But now she was away from the situation, she knew that she had to tell him. Her mind was made up. She was not having another baby, ever. She needed to get her life back and do things for *her*. Another baby would tie her down for God knows how long.

So having written 1) *Lying to my husband* on the *Things I don't like* page, she took the

What I want page and wrote 1) *To tell Richard we won't be having another baby.*

Then on the *How can I make it happen?* page she wrote 1) *Tell him when I get home but no need to tell him about the birth control as he will feel lied to and betrayed (damage limitation). BE BRAVE!*

Clara sighed. It felt good to write the words down and read them.

She continued.

Things I don't like

2) How I look.

What I want

2) To not care what other people expect and try to show my real self.

How can I make it happen?

2) Buy funky clothes, and change my hair. BECOME YOURSELF!

The next one:

Things I don't like

3) Not speaking up for myself.

What I want

3) Confidence to speak up.

How can I make it happen?

3) Start today, and value my own opinion. YOU MATTER!

Next:

On *Things I don't like* page:

4) Feeling guilty for taking time for me.

What I want

4) To not feel selfish for self-care.

How can I make it happen?

4) Schedule it every week to do yoga, walk, and apply a beauty treatment. TAKE CARE OF YOURSELF!

Clara sat back and looked at her notes. She felt a weight lift. With these three pieces of paper, she had a pathway, a roadmap. If she could start with these four items on the lists, and work on them, she could move on to four more. Slowly but surely she could step into the person she wanted to be. If she worked on the outside first, it might give her the courage to work on the inside. Feeling excited and ready for these new plans, she wondered if there was anything she could start today.

Fern arrived back at the table.

"Will I get you a fresh pot? You were so engrossed in your writing I didn't want to bother you."

"No, I'm full of tea now," Clara smiled "but you might be able to help me with something else. I want to get my hair done today, something different, something funky. Would you know anyone by any chance?"

"Yes! My mate Frank has a place down the road. It's on Henry Grattan Road on the way back into the town. It's over a tattoo parlour so you mightn't see it at first. He's very nice and you have gorgeous hair. He could definitely do you something funky. I can give him a call if you like?"

"Yes, please. Does he ... eh, do women my age?" Clara asked nervously.

"Of course! Will yeh go way! Sure you're only a young one. Hang on."

Fern took out her mobile

"Hey, Frank, how's it going? Fern here. Yeah, I'm at work. Listen,

I have a lovely woman here looking for a funky new hairdo – can you fit her in today?"

She put her hand over the phone.

"Can you go right now? He's just had a cancellation."

"Yes, absolutely."

"Yeah, Frank, she can be there in ten minutes. Cool, thanks, mate." Fern finished the call.

"Thank you so much, Fern."

"No problem. You'll love Frank – he's a dote".

"You're an absolute star," Clara said, delighted with herself.

"Not at all!"

Clara carefully folded her lists and put them away in a zipped pocket in her handbag for safekeeping. Putting her scarf and gloves on, she stood up to put her coat on.

The sound of dogs barking made her look outside to see two Golden Retrievers hop into the back of a jeep belonging to a tall handsome man across the road … *and was that Vivienne?* Clara squinted her eyes and craned her neck to get a better view. That is definitely Vivienne, she said to herself but who was the man she is laughing with? They seemed very friendly. She did say she was meeting a work client. Just then she saw Vivienne put a hand on his arm and smile at something he said. He then opened the jeep door and Vivienne got in. Well now, that was very interesting. Even from here Clara could see there was chemistry between the two of them and Vivienne had looked so relaxed in his company. Was he the reason we came to Galway, she wondered. Ah well, we all have our secrets, I guess.

She gathered up her things and went up to the counter to pay for her tea and cake.

"That will be six fifty, please," Fern said.

Clara tapped her card and then gave Fern a ten-euro note.

"What's this for?" Fern said.

"It's for you. To thank you for all your help."

"But I only made a call for you," Fern said, baffled.

"No, you did way more for me today, Fern, more than you know."

"Ah, thank you so much – you are so kind," said Fern as she popped out from behind the counter and hugged her.

The hug was a shock and a surprise, but it made Clara feel like she was not invisible anymore. Something had shifted in her attitude to herself today. And it had shifted for the better.

Chapter 22

"Thanks so much for this, I really needed it," Vivienne said as climbed into Jack's jeep. She pulled down the visor of the passenger seat, fixing her windswept hair in the mirror and then laid her head back on the headrest.

"These girls will take your mind off your worries alright," Jack replied, looking into his rear mirror at his two panting retrievers.

They drove along the promenade and then turned up a tree-lined road. Jack pulled up outside a closed driveway and pressed the sensor on his keys to open the gates. The curved driveway meant that the house was unseen from the road, so they were halfway up the drive when the house came into view. Jack parked outside the front of what looked like the regular whitewashed detached one-storey bungalow common in this area. Heather plants and grasses in various shades of purples and blues were growing in a border across the base of the house and contrasted beautifully against the bright white stone walls.

Jack let the dogs out of the boot, and they waited at the front door for Jack to open it.

"Come on in and let's get the kettle on," Jack said, holding the front door open.

Vivienne stepped in, unzipping her coat.

"*Oh wow!*" she said, looking around with her mouth open. "This is incredible." The outside of the house gave nothing away as to what was inside. Most of the interior walls had been taken away. On the white walls hung various colourful paintings and pieces of art, and the polished wooden floors gave the open-plan layout a modern art-gallery look.

"Come on into the kitchen," Jack said, leading the way.

The kitchen was around the end of a curved wall to the right, even though it was part of the open-plan first floor. But as Vivienne walked towards it her eyes widened. The whole back wall of the house was a floor-to-ceiling wall of glass that opened onto a raised deck. Beyond that was a magnificent view of Galway Bay.

"I'm speechless," she said.

"Yes, it's some view alright," said Jack, filling the kettle and taking down some mugs from beautiful light wood cabinets.

"You would never think that this was the inside of this house from the road."

"It took a lot of work, but I love architecture and design, so I worked with a local firm and drew up most of the plans myself. When I first viewed this house, the back garden was completely overgrown so, unless you were a local, you would have no idea that a view of Galway Bay was behind the jungle of a garden. A simple look at the plans would have told anyone that, but the house hadn't been lived in for years and the garden was a big job, so my offer was the only offer put in for the house. I got lucky."

"You must have a great eye, Jack. Not everyone could do this."

153

"Well, as I said, I have always had an interest in architecture and the design of buildings and their functionality. When I left school I was completely torn as to what college course to do. It was a toss-up between law and architecture. I often wonder if I chose the right path. So buying this house gave me a design project I could really work on. Tea or coffee?"

"Tea, please."

The dogs had found their way to the wood-burning stove in the corner of the living-room section. There was a large green-and-blue rug in front of it and the dogs immediately stretched out and fell asleep.

"Are you hungry?" he asked. "Can I get you something to eat?"

"No, I'm fine, thanks. I had breakfast with my friends at Nimmo's and the portions are huge there. I'll have something small later before I head to the Skylight."

"Oh yeah? Are you going to the spa?"

"Yes, we are, and I can't wait to have some of my stress massaged out," she said, blushing a little.

"Let's join the girls," Jack said, carrying the tea to the couch.

Viviennen sat down on a huge burnt-orange L-shaped couch in front of the fire and he handed her a mug.

"So, tell me what's up?" he said, joining her on the couch. "Something has happened since yesterday, right?"

Vivienne settled in her seat and told Jack about Tom moving the money out of their joint account and their joint credit card being declined. And she also told him about Tom's sly text saying, "Are you enjoying your night?"

"*Hmm.* Did you ring him last night to ask him about it?" Jack asked.

"Well, I was going to, I was furious. At least half of that money in the joint account is mine so he has no right to touch it, but we had some drama last night. I won't go into the details but Miriam, one of my friends, had a fall last night and she is pregnant, so I had to take her to the hospital and get her checked out."

"Jeez," Jack said, looking concerned.

"That's why I texted you so late. I was in the hospital until two this morning. My head was so taken up with looking after Miriam that it got too late to ring Tom and there was no point in having a row at two in the morning. So I thought I'd talk to you first. The women I'm with don't know I'm separating. We're very close but we don't see each other that often and they have never met him, so I didn't want to burden them with my problems."

"Whose name is the credit card account in?"

"It's actually in Tom's name but we have two cards from it. He thinks that he's hurting me by cancelling that credit card, but actually that leaves him with the bill. It's emptying the joint account that annoys me more." Vivienne felt her jaw stiffen. "At least half that money was mine."

"Okay, well, you could call him today and confront him or confront him tomorrow in person. We know he forged your signature to access the children's college money. Are there any other accounts he could get to?"

"We have stocks and shares or bonds, but I have all the documentation on those. We have a savings account in the EBS with no cards and I have the savings book, so he won't be able to access that."

"Why do you think he has done this? Do you think he found out that you're seeing me – professionally?"

"I have been racking my brain. I don't know if he knows I am here in Galway speaking with you or if he has just done this off his own bat."

"I think you need to call him and see which it is. You'll know where you stand and what you are walking into when you go home."

"Yes, you're right. I don't want to be ambushed. I didn't expect things to get nasty so quickly." Vivienne looked down into her mug.

"Now, now," Jack said, turning to face her. "I don't want you worrying about this. Facts are power and when you have the facts you will be able to see where this thing is at. Have you spoken to your kids this weekend?"

"Yes, I rang the kids on the way here and they said nothing unusual. They said they had take-out with Tom last night and that they were all going to a rugby match later, so I don't think he's changed the locks or anything. But you're right, I do need to speak to him."

"Print out a list of the lodgements you made to that joint account in the last year. I wouldn't worry about the credit card. Are you okay for money?"

"Yes, yes, I am. I have my own personal account and a secret one," Vivienne smiled.

"A secret one?"

"Let me explain. Before I got married my grandmother told me to open an account that my husband knew nothing about. She called it 'your running away money'. I thought it was very funny at the time and totally unnecessary but, oh, how right she was!"

"She sounds like a wise woman. More tea?"

"No, thanks. I have to get back actually. I will ring Tom from the apartment before I meet the women. Can you go ahead and draw up whatever documents we need for the legal separation case? I feel we need to move as quickly as possible now."

"Yes, of course, and don't worry. You hold all the cards, and I will do everything I can to get you what you want."

"Thank you, Jack," Vivienne said, putting her hand on top of his arm. "I really appreciate you seeing me today. I'm sure you put all your clients at ease in this beautiful house."

"Actually, I don't bring clients here," he said, holding her gaze. "You are the only one."

"Seriously? Oh, I'm sorry, I hope I haven't imposed myself on you?"

"No, I have enjoyed every minute of your company, Vivienne."

There was a silence and Vivienne had to pull her eyes away from his before she might do something unprofessional.

"I'd better go," she said, almost in a whisper.

"Let me drop you back. After walking my dogs with me, that's the least I can do." He stood and took their mugs into the kitchen.

They drove back into Galway City in comfortable silence.

When they got close to Spanish Arch, Vivienne asked to be dropped off outside Jury's Inn.

"Are you sure? I can drive straight to the apartments?"

"No, thanks, I could do with the walk to figure out what I'm going to say to Tom."

As they pulled up to Jurys, Jack leaned across to release her seatbelt and the smell of his aftershave almost made her lean forward and kiss him. The sexual tension in the jeep was so strong that Vivienne didn't know if she wanted to hop out of the car and get fresh air, or drive straight back to Jack's house and go straight to his bed. She felt he knew what she was thinking so she laughed nervously, thanked him, and jumped out of the jeep before she changed her mind.

Chapter 23

Vivienne walked briskly back to the apartment, going over in her head the conversation she planned on having with Tom. I must try not to get angry and try to keep calm so I can get an idea of why he cleared out the account and how much he knows, she thought.

She let herself into the apartment and immediately saw a note from Miriam on the kitchen table.

Gone for some fresh air. See you at the spa. M x

Vivienne was relieved. She did not want Miriam to overhear her conversation.

Taking a deep breath, she dialled Tom's mobile.

"Hello, Vivienne, having a good time?"

Vivienne detected a sneer in his voice. "Well, I was until you moved our money out from our joint account and cancelled the credit card. What's going on, Tom?"

"Well, you tell me, Vivienne. It seems you've been very busy."

"What are you talking about?"

"Busy downloading account information from my laptop, Viv. Does that jog your memory? Alex needed help printing off a project for school so we used my laptop in the office. And when I went to clear the history, it was all there."

Shit, she thought, breathing deeply. The night she had downloaded and printed off the documents she had used his laptop. She didn't have a choice as she wanted to work quickly, and her laptop was in her office. But she was sure she had deleted the history and covered her tracks. Obviously she hadn't.

"I have nothing to hide. I am entitled to any information about our finances. The question here, Tom, is why did you clear out our joint account? At least half the money in that account is mine. Why did you do that?"

"I'm protecting my assets. My question is why would my wife print off every financial account we have? Can you answer that?"

"We're not getting anywhere here," Vivienne said, exasperated.

"Well, if you're trying to build a case for a separation, remember I know all the top solicitors in this city who will be happy to represent me. So do your worst and be ready for a fight."

And then he hung up.

That bastard, Vivienne thought, almost shaking with rage. But then she'd known he would become defensive – she just didn't expect him to clear out their account like that.

She took a deep breath to calm herself. Everything was going to be okay. She would get a printout of the statements, like Jack said – it would prove that at least half that money was hers.

She grinned when he said he knew all the top solicitors in Dublin. That might be true, but she had the top solicitor in Galway and all the information to implicate his solicitor and banking friend in fraud for the deal they pulled with her forged signature. She was going to let him think he had the upper hand

– that way he would be less prepared.

Oh, I really need that massage now, she thought, rubbing the knots in her shoulders after that conversation.

She would call Sarah later to get an idea about Tom's mood and also if he had said anything to her and Alex. They would have to sit them down soon and tell them they were separating as it looked like things were going to get very messy.

Chapter 24

Vivienne arrived at the reception desk of the Skylight Hotel. She looked around but she was the first to arrive. This gave her time to get directions to the hotel spa from the receptionist. She was about to sit down when Helen and Miriam walked through the door. Vivienne was delighted to see them linking each other, obviously having got over the drama of the night before.

"Hey, you guys!"

"Hi, Viv," Helen said. "Thank you so much for organising this."

"Oh, it's purely selfish on my behalf, I desperately need a massage. My shoulders are so stiff," answered Vivienne, rubbing her shoulder.

"I think I will have a facial and a manicure," Miriam said. "I can't remember the last time my nails saw some love."

Just then the door opened.

"Oh *wow*, Clara!" Vivienne said as the others turned around and followed her gaze.

Clara had arrived with a fabulous new hairdo. Her long black bob was cut very short on one side, shaved at her temple, and over her ear. Her new side parting fell softly around her face on the other side and was shorter but kept the same bob shape. There were blue and green steaks of colour all around the front strands of her hair, lighting up her whole face. Also, she was no longer wearing the heavy wool coat she had on this morning. Instead, she was wearing a short black denim jacket and a huge green scarf to match the green in her hair.

"Oh wow, your hair!" Helen said.

"It's gorgeous. You look so different, so young. It takes years off you," said Miriam.

"Thanks, girls, I know it is different, but I so needed a change," Clara said.

"It's so funky, Clara, and the colours are fab," Helen said.

"Apparently they are called mermaid colours and I love them."

"Did you book it before we came down?" asked Vivienne.

"No, I met a lovely girl in a café with fabulous funky hair and I just thought I want something like that. So she rang her hairdresser and here I am."

Clara was delighted with her new hairdo. It was outrageously different for her but exactly what she was looking for.

She'd had no problem finding Frank's place and he was waiting for her when she arrived. Despite being young and trendy and covered in tattoos, he didn't bat an eye when Clara explained what she wanted.

"I'm sure you probably think I'm mad?" she had said to him, a little embarrassed.

"Mad? No, why?"

"Well, because of my age?"

"No, not at all. Age is just a number, darling. I only wish more women came in and got the hairstyles they really want and not copy someone else's. You are going to look amazing, and it'll knock years off you too. It will give you such a lift."

And he was right, she did feel amazing, and it did knock years off her. If a young cool guy like Frank thought she looked cool, then why should she be worried about what anyone else thought? She loved her new hairdo and she felt great, and that was what mattered right now.

Vivienne was taken aback at Clara's new image. Not only was her hair way 'out there', there was something different about her. Her jacket and scarf had to be new too. She was glowing. Her energy had definitely changed since yesterday.

"Ladies, we need to go. We don't want to be late for our treatments," Vivienne said, and they headed off behind her.

Clara was delighted with her friends' reaction. She felt amazing. She wasn't sure if Richard would like it, but she realized today that she didn't care whether he did or not.

The spa was in the basement of the Skylight Hotel. When the lift opened, a long corridor lined with stone sculptures and beautiful paintings of seascapes led the way to the spa reception.

The receptionist was waiting for them, wearing a big smile.

"Hello, ladies, you are all very welcome to the spa. If you can just sign in here first, we will get you sorted."

She was a young therapist in her early twenties, wearing a spotlessly white uniform top over black trousers. Her hair was tied back very tightly, and her make-up was flawless. She handed each of the ladies a plush fluffy towelling robe and a pair of white spa slippers.

"If you ladies would like to go to the changing rooms, you can leave your clothes in the lockers and then take the key with you. You can then meet back at the waiting-room area where you can fill out forms and decide on your treatments. I will leave a list of the treatments there for you."

The waiting area had low lighting, plush chairs with footrests, and aromatherapy oils burning in the diffuser. The colour scheme was soft blues with white furnishings.

After they had changed into their robes, they relaxed in the plush seats of the waiting area. When they sat down, a different therapist came in and offered them a glass of herbal tea.

"I will be back in five minutes for your forms, so you relax here," she said in a soft voice.

"I'm relaxed already," said Clara, closing her eyes and lying back, listening to the gentle music that was piped through the spa.

When the therapist returned she took all their forms. "You will all be taken to our relaxation room following your treatment, for refreshments," she said.

Shortly after, one by one, different therapists came by and called one of their names.

"See you on the other side!" Vivienne said as she headed off for her treatment with her therapist.

Chapter 25

"Helen?"

"That's me," Helen said, standing up as her therapist called her.

"Follow me and I'll take you to the therapy room. My name is Grace, and I will be looking after you this afternoon."

Grace looked around the same age as Helen and had a very kind smile. Helen was glad to have a therapist her own age because it made her feel less self-conscious about her stretch marks and her Pennys underwear.

Grace's brown hair was cut very short in a pixie style, showing off her flawless skin.

"What treatment are you having today, Helen?" she asked as she led Helen into the therapy room.

"I was thinking of an aromatherapy massage."

"A good choice," Grace replied.

"Oh, this room is lovely," Helen said, looking around the small room.

There were no windows or outside light. The lighting was dimmed and there was relaxation music playing in the background.

There were fluffy towels in a soft coffee colour that matched the walls and the carpet. It felt so relaxing.

"Yes, it is a lovely environment to work in alright. I have four boys at home, so I certainly appreciate coming in to work here."

"I have four boys too!" Helen said.

"Oh, they can be a handful, can't they? Are they here with you?"

"God no! No, I'm away on a girls' weekend and God knows I need it."

"Yes, it's a lot keeping up with all their activities and their mess and their noise!" laughed the therapist.

"Oh, I'm so glad I got you today, Grace. At least you understand. I feel like I'm giving out when I say those things to my friends."

"I hear ya, Helen. We love them to bits but sometimes it's hard being the only woman in the house. You can hang your robe on the back of the door and make yourself comfortable on the plinth and pull a blanket over you. I'll be back in a minute. I'm just going to get a jug of water and then we'll have you relaxed in no time."

Helen felt so relieved. Grace was lovely and now she could totally relax and enjoy her massage.

When Grace returned, Helen lay back and let her work her magic. She warmed the oil in her hands and gently applied them to Helen's shoulders. Her hands expertly eased out the tension in her neck too. Helen didn't realise how tense she had been until she felt the muscles relax. The aromatherapy oils filled the room.

"*Mmm* ... that smells good – is it ylang-ylang?" Helen asked.

"No, it's Clary sage mixed with lavender," answered Grace.

"Oh, I haven't heard of Clary sage. I did an aromatherapy course myself a few years ago. I really enjoyed it. It was so relaxing and interesting too."

"Did you go into the business?"

"No, not at all. I wouldn't know how to go about it and my life was so hectic with the kids then. To be honest, I only signed up for the course to get out of the house. But I was surprised at how much I loved it. I meant to go on and do the certificate course but didn't get around to it."

"Well, if you like it, why not? I started out taking a course on aromatherapy oils too and I loved it, so I did an aromatherapy massage therapist diploma course at night. That took one year but it covered everything from learning about the oils to learning massage techniques. Sorry, am I talking too much?"

"No, not at all. Were you qualified to practise then?" Helen asked.

"Yes, I joined the Association of Aromatherapists, and I got insurance. I started by volunteering in hospitals and nursing homes to gain confidence and get some experience under my belt. And then I just applied for jobs. This hotel suits me best because I just work a few hours a day. Do you work yourself?"

"Well, I was doing some voluntary work in our local charity shop at the start of the year, just a few mornings a week because the hours suit me, and you don't have to commit to anything long-term. But there hasn't been much work there lately, only one morning a week because all the Transition Year students are doing it – don't get me wrong, it's great to see teenagers doing a bit of charity work – but being at home so much doesn't suit me."

Helen left out the part about her awful timekeeping and the fact that the charity shop stopped calling her to offer her any shifts.

"Yes, it is handy having flexible hours around the school runs alright and I know what you mean about being at home too much."

Grace laughed. "God, I'd be hitting the bottle if I didn't leave the house every day!"

Helen blushed and felt mortified. She also felt very hot. "Sorry," she said, sitting up, "Can I have a glass of water, please? I feel very hot all of a sudden."

"Of course, here you are," said Grace, passing Helen the glass, looking concerned. "Are you okay? Is it too hot in here?"

"No, no, it's just a hot flush. It will pass in a minute."

"You take as much time as you like. I know all about hot flushes – they are bloody awful," said Grace.

"It must be uncomfortable to get hot flushes when you are working on a client alright."

"Oh, I didn't hang around when I got them. My sister had very bad menopause symptoms and she waited, thinking she could manage without medication, but she just got worse."

"With the flushes?" Helen asked.

"Not just them. She had insomnia and mood swings and she got so down that her doctor wanted to put her on anti-depressants. Can you believe that? So I did a bit of research and found a menopause clinic for her. So many GPs haven't a clue, you know – they get so little training on menopause. So anyway off she went and was put on HRT immediately and it changed her life."

"*Wow.*"

"So when it came to my turn I went straight to the experts and got the right prescription for me. Now it doesn't suit everyone but there is so much misinformation out there. It is so important to find a menopause expert because there are more than twenty different symptoms of menopause and women are getting misdiagnosed all the time. So if you have any symptoms, Helen, get it checked out. Don't suffer, love."

Helen started to cry.

"Oh, I'm sorry, have I said something wrong?" said Grace. "I'm always talking too much."

"No, you have hit the nail on the head, Grace. I have been so miserable, and I have all these symptoms and I just never thought they could all be linked to menopause."

"*Aw*, pet," Grace said, giving Helen some tissues. "I'm telling you, go and see an expert. It might not solve all your problems, but it might just fix some of them."

"Thank you so much, Grace. I'm so glad I got you today."

"It was meant to be, Helen. No such thing as a coincidence. Now lie down on your front and let me massage out all that stress and you cry if you want to. I will stay quiet now for the next twenty minutes. This is your time."

And Helen did what she was told and let Grace take over. She shed some more tears, feeling it safe to do so and then she went into a deep sleep.

When the session was over Grace gently woke her with a gentle hand on her shoulder.

"Take your time getting up. I have left some fresh water for you and when I come back I will take you to the relaxation room where you can spend as long as you like."

Helen lay there thinking about their conversation. She needed to see a menopause expert and get her symptoms sorted. Apart from the hot flushes and night sweats, she had felt low for a long time and had no enthusiasm for anything. And the insomnia was crippling. It was one of the reasons she had started drinking – to fall into a deep sleep. Maybe, if she could sort those things out, things might turn around for the better. And, if she got her old self back, maybe she could get a qualification in aromatherapy and become a therapist. Maybe she could be a good person and learn to like herself again.

As she stood up and put her robe on, she felt so much lighter.

Chapter 26

Miriam followed her therapist into the therapy room.

"So, Miriam, have you chosen which facial would you like today?"

"I don't mind really. The only thing is that I'm pregnant, so some strong smells can make me nauseous."

"No problem. I have a lovely facial mask based on seaweed products, so it is very natural, and the scent is very fresh and mild."

"That sounds lovely," Miriam said, looking forward to being pampered and drifting off.

Buzz, buzz.

"Oh sorry, I forgot to turn my phone off vibrate," Miriam said, fishing her phone out of her robe.

She had put her phone on silent once she arrived in Galway to avoid getting calls from her brother and sister. Having sent the email to both of them last night, she knew they would be calling and texting her to try to speak to her. She was not ready to speak to them though. Glancing at her phone as she was just about to press the power-off button, Miriam saw a text on her screen.

"*Oh no!*"

"Are you okay?" the therapist asked.

"*Em*, yes, sorry, I *em* ..."

"Do you want to sit down?" the therapist said, looking concerned.

"Yes, thank you. I'll be okay in a minute. I'm fine, really." But she was not fine at all.

Miriam looked at the message again.

Miriam, call me. We need to talk. I just need to be sure. J

J for Jerry. Bloody hell! What does he want? He needs to be sure! I thought I was very clear.

Miriam had known that the women would be in touch with their husbands over the weekend and that there was a big chance they would mention her pregnancy to them. So she had no choice but to ring Jerry before the weekend.

"Can you give me a few minutes?" she asked the therapist. "Of course, I'll come back in five," she said and left with a smile.

Miriam took a deep breath and tried to calm herself.

She texted Jerry quickly: **Can't talk now. But, yes, you can be 100% sure.**

She had phoned him on Thursday evening and it had been difficult. Very difficult.

"Hi, Jerry, it's Miriam here." Her voice had been steady enough.

"Oh hi, is everything okay?"

Did he sound a bit apprehensive?

"Yes, everything's great!" She tried to sound as upbeat and carefree as possible. "Actually, that's why I'm ringing you. You're the only person who knows my donor story and, well ... I just wanted you to know that I tried again immediately and ... this time it's been successful!"

172

"Oh! You mean you're …?"

"Yes, pregnant."

"That's great news! Congratulations!"

"Thanks. Eh, nobody knows yet."

"Oh … okay …"

"Yes, and the reason I'm telling you is that, as you know, I'm going away with Helen and the others this weekend and I'll be telling them then and …"

"And …? Oh, I see."

"Yes, I didn't want you to get a heart attack and think that maybe it was because of what *we* …"

"I get it. And you're sure …?"

"Yes! One hundred per cent – I can hardly believe it but I have a letter to prove it!"

"No, I meant … and you're sure it wasn't me?"

"I'm sure, Jerry. Positive. You can relax about that."

"Good. Okay, well, I appreciate you calling me … and I'm so happy for you."

"Thanks, Jerry. And … can you keep this to yourself, please? I don't want Helen to ever know what happened between us – and, now that the donor clinic has worked, well … everything is great now and I just want to look to the future."

"Of course."

"Okay, well, that's it."

"Best of luck with it all and thanks again for letting me know."

"Okay … bye then."

Phew! Job done.

Miriam took a deep breath. I just have to keep to my donor clinic story, and everything will be fine, she told herself as the therapist returned

"Would you like a glass of water?" the therapist asked, concerned.

"No, I'm fine now," Miriam said, turning her phone off. "It was just a wave of nausea."

"I'll tell you what, sit up there a bit. I won't put the table back too much so that you're not lying flat – that will help with nausea."

"Yes, great idea," Miriam murmured.

I don't care what you do, she thought, just don't talk to me. I need to get my story right and clear in my head. Jerry can never know that he's the father of my child. It was a great passionate once-off, a stress-relief more than anything, and that was the end of it. She needed to come up with a plan to keep Jerry off the scent and she needed to do it fast.

Miriam considered herself to be a very independent woman. She owned her own house and was very efficient and hard-working. When she first got the keys to her house, she took some courses in her local Woodies store on basic DIY, so she never had to ask for help putting up shelves or putting flat packs together. She was very proud of this. But when it came to plumbing or electrics she did not dare to try. Instead, Helen's husband Jerry would come over and sort the difficult jobs out. He was in the construction business and knew a bit about everything. Helen had given her his number on a night out and said he'd be delighted to help her out.

This time Miriam was getting a new Ikea bed delivered. Although she could probably put it together herself, she was so busy with work and minding her mum that it was easier to ask Helen if Jerry could do it. He was always so obliging and easy company to be around. Jerry rang her to sort out the details. The arrangements were made and, as usual, he was bang on time.

"Thanks a mil for coming, Jerry," Miriam said as she opened the door.

"No bother at all, glad to help out," Jerry said as he stepped into the house, wearing jeans and a white T-shirt and carrying his toolbox.

Not for the first time, Miriam reflected that Jerry was very attractive. He was in great shape and tanned from the work he did outdoors. Lucky Helen, she thought as she glanced at his strong arms. He ran a hand through his floppy shoulder-length hair as he smiled at her.

"You look the part anyway," said Miriam, smiling back.

"*Ha, ha*, very funny," he said, passing Miriam in the narrow hallway of her small townhouse.

She inhaled his cologne as he passed. God, he smells good, she thought.

"Do you want a cuppa?" she asked, pulling herself together.

"No, thanks. I might have one afterward. Let's see how long it takes. How're things with you?"

"Grand, yeah, nothing much happening," Miriam said with a shrug.

"Okay, show me the way and I'll get started."

Miriam walked up the stairs ahead of Jerry suddenly feeling self-conscious about how her backside looked as she walked ahead of him but then shook the idea out of her head as she showed him into her bedroom.

"Well, at least they carried it up the stairs for you," Jerry said, looking at the huge package.

"I pulled the poor helpless woman's face," Miriam laughed, tilting her head and fluttering her eyelashes jokingly.

"You women get away with murder," he said, laughing.

They both stood, looking at the giant box in the bedroom. Miriam felt a little flushed. Was she imagining it or was there some chemistry in the air? Maybe it's because we're in my bedroom, she thought, feeling silly for thinking that and mortified for thinking that way about her friend's husband.

"Okay, if I remove the cardboard, will you take it downstairs, so it will give me more room?" he said.

"Sure, I've made space in the green bin for it," Miriam replied, glad of the diversion.

Together they worked side by side, taking all the packaging apart. When all the bed bits were laid out, Jerry took out his toolkit.

"Right, leave me to it."

"Are you sure?"

"Of course I am. I'll give you a shout when I'm done and I'll have that cuppa then."

"Deal!" said Miriam as she moved the cardboard out onto the landing and headed off with as much as she could carry to the green recycle bin in her front garden.

Back in the house, she did some jobs around the kitchen before making a second trip to the landing and out to the bin again.

Then, on the way back into the house, she noticed that the post had arrived. Her heart skipped a beat when she saw the envelope.

Sitting down at the kitchen table, she slowly opened the envelope from the fertility clinic. She quickly scanned down the page until she saw the word 'unsuccessful'. The sperm donor insemination had failed. She was not pregnant.

Miriam sighed. I suppose deep down I knew, she thought, as she hadn't felt any different. Every little cramp or twitch normally had her wondering if she was pregnant but for the last two weeks she had felt nothing. She wiped her falling tears away with her sleeve as they started to roll down her face. She tried to hold it in, as she could hear Jerry working upstairs, but she couldn't. Her shoulders began to shake, and she put her head down on the table and sobbed.

"*Any chance of that cuppa now, Miriam?*" Jerry shouted from upstairs.

Miriam jumped, stood up, and walked to the kitchen door, wiping her eyes.

"*Coming!*" she shouted up the stairs and then blew her nose and walked over to put on the kettle. She tried to look at her reflection in the kettle as she was sure her eyes were puffy and red from crying.

Shit, she thought, all my make-up is upstairs. Ah well, I'll just tell him I have allergies. She made two mugs of tea and headed upstairs.

"Here we are," she said, trying to sound cheerful.

"Ah, thanks a million," Jerry said, turning around to take the mug. Then he stared. "Jesus, Miriam, what's wrong?" He took the mugs from her and put them down on her dressing table.

"Nothing ... I'm fine," she stuttered, trying to pull herself together. But she failed miserably, and the tears came flowing again.

"Hey, hey, come here," Jerry said, putting his arm around her shoulders and leading her over to sit on the bed with its new mattress.

"What's happened? Are you okay?"

"I'm fine, there's nothing wrong, it's just ... I'm so sorry, Jerry, and I'm so embarrassed," she sobbed.

"You have nothing to be embarrassed about – just let it out."

Miriam laid her head on his shoulder. It felt so good to be held.

"If you need to talk, I'm a great listener."

"I don't want to bother you with my problems."

"Hey! Come on now, it's no bother. I hate to see you this upset," he said, giving her a side hug.

"It's just that I got some bad news, well, more like sad news really. Please don't tell Helen. I haven't said anything to the girls."

"Scout's honour, I won't say a word," Jerry said, making a silly Scouts sign to try to cheer her up.

"Well ... I've been to a donor clinic to try to get pregnant and I just got a letter to say it was unsuccessful. I don't know why I'm so upset because I haven't felt any different since they planted the eggs, so deep down I expected it but ... it's just hard seeing it in black and white."

"*Aw*, Miriam, I am so sorry. I had no idea you were trying."

"Nobody does. I haven't told anyone. You're the only one who knows." She looked into his eyes. "It was hard enough to decide to have a child on my own, but now it is the only thing I want. I've given up looking for someone to have a relationship with and I'm not getting any younger, so even if I did meet someone they would run a mile if I said I want a baby like right now." Miriam shrugged. "I tried online dating and then Tinder."

"Tinder?"

"Yes, well, without being crude I had planned to hook up with someone on Tinder when I was ovulating and hopefully get pregnant and never see them again."

"Jesus. It just sounds so ..."

"I know how it sounds, Jerry, and although I'm not proud of it I tried it twice. But it wasn't successful, and I couldn't do that again. It's not who I am. At the end of the day, it was the sperm I needed.

So I contacted a fertility clinic and to be honest it was easier than I thought. Expensive yes, but I have the money. Everything was going so well. I chose a sperm donor, and my eggs were taken and replanted. I had no side effects, and I was hopeful. But it seems I failed," she sighed. "I can try again in a month, and I will, but I just thought ..."

"Oh Miriam, I'm so sorry."

"Thanks, I'll be grand. I just feel a bit stupid. How did I think it was fine anyway? What do I know about being pregnant or ... anything?" She started crying again. "Oh sorry, Jerry," she said as she sobbed into his nice white T-shirt.

"Now listen here," Jerry said, turning to face her, taking her face in his hands. "You are a beautiful, clever, amazing woman. Any man would be lucky and so proud to have you in his life. You are stunning."

For a moment they just looked into each other's eyes and then it happened.

Afterwards Miriam couldn't remember who kissed who, but all of a sudden they were kissing, tender and slow at first, and then deeper and more passionate. Without saying a word, they started to remove each other's clothes. The tempo increased and suddenly they were having passionate sex on the new Ikea bed. The plastic wrapping was still on the mattress, making it a noisy affair but neither of them could stop. Miriam felt wild and free. She felt all the stress crashing like waves from her body. They both roared as they came together and fell back sweaty and exhausted.

"Oh God, I'm sorry. I have never done this before," Jerry said breathlessly.

"Well, you have four kids, so I think you have," Miriam said, smiling, trying to make light of the situation. "Honestly, Jerry, it's fine."

"But, oh God … Helen …" he said, sitting up with his head in his hands.

"Look, Jerry. We're friends, okay, nothing more. You love Helen. She will never know about this. This was just one of those things. If that letter hadn't arrived today while you were here, this would never have happened. I don't feel guilty. It felt great to be wanted and not treated like a medical procedure. This will never happen again. Please don't feel bad. Can we agree to pretend this never happened?"

"Yes, we can. Thank you. I love Helen and she's going through a hard time at the moment, but I don't want anything to change between us."

"Is she okay?"

"It's menopause-related, I think – maybe a little depression. I don't know – she won't open up about it but she's working through it."

"Okay, well, let's just leave it at that, yeah?" said Miriam, feeling uncomfortable talking about Helen.

"Oh yeah, sure, of course … *em*, so what should we do?"

"Nothing. You probably need to get going," Miriam said, not wanting things to get awkward.

"Okay," said Jerry, "if that's not too rude?"

"No, you go, please. And thanks for today … the bed … I mean," Miriam shook her head, getting flustered.

"You are very welcome!" Jerry laughed as he picked up his clothes and trainers and left the room.

"Thanks!"

"I'll just put the rest of the cardboard out and head off," he said from the landing.

"I'll deal with that, just leave it!" Miriam called from behind the door.

"Really? Well, if you're sure?"

"Yes, I can handle it from here."

"Okay … well, I'll be off so, and I meant what I said, you are amazing and good luck with everything."

"Thanks, Jerry … and mum's the word, yeah?"

"Mum's the word."

A few weeks later Miriam was back at the donor clinic for an appointment with her consultant to consider another round of donor plantation.

She felt unwell in the doctor's waiting room. It was early in the morning and a wave of nausea came over her. She rushed to the bathroom and threw up. She didn't throw up much because she hadn't eaten anything that day – she couldn't even face her much-loved morning coffee. Sitting in the toilet cubicle, she realised that she hadn't been able to drink her coffee for a few days now. She thought it was the brand of coffee or the milk, but she just couldn't stomach it. Even the smell of coffee in the office made her feel sick. And that's when it dawned on her.

Oh my god, she thought as the penny dropped and she emptied her handbag on the bathroom floor searching for her diary. With shaking hands, she counted the days and realised she was five days late. Normally she would know her cycle off the top of her head and would be watching for any changes but, for the past two weeks, she had been staying with her mother and had disturbed sleep every night. Her mother's tablets had changed, and it always took her about a week to get used to them and settle down. Miriam was exhausted, so she had not been so vigilant about her cycle. Also, the disappointment of the last failed donor plantation had hit her hard and she just didn't want to think about it for a while. She gathered up her things and left the toilets, walking through the consultant's office.

"The doctor can see you now," the secretary said.

But Miriam couldn't speak with the shock and walked right past her and straight out the door to the nearest chemist's and then raced home with five home pregnancy tests.

Lining the five positive test results up in a row, Miriam cried for joy. She was finally pregnant. She was so elated. But, between the laughing and the crying, she knew she couldn't tell anyone. Not yet anyway. She had to come to terms with the news herself. Then she had to figure out what to tell people in her family and her workplace.

And then she had to figure out how she felt about carrying a child fathered by one of her closest friends. And she had to figure out what to tell him.

And I thought the hardest part was getting pregnant, Miriam thought as she tried to relax on the beauty therapist's chair. She sighed deeply, lay back, and tried to enjoy her seaweed facial.

Chapter 27

As they each finished their treatments at different times, they arranged to meet in the hotel bar after the relaxation room. Helen was invigorated after her talk with the lovely Grace who had planted the idea of enrolling in an aromatherapy and massage therapist course. She could now see a tiny light at the end of the tunnel or, at least, the start of a plan that she could work on.

Vivienne looked positively glowing after her massage. She had kept her hair down and loose today which softened her look. This weekend she looked like a different person.

Clara felt amazing. She had a lovely young therapist who admired her hair and said it looked cool. This made her feel relevant and seen. If a young therapist thought she looked cool, she should give herself a break and be kinder to herself. She told the therapist she was looking to update her wardrobe with cool bohemian clothes and the girl gave her the names of some boutiques and good-quality charity shops in Galway. Clara was planning to check them out after her treatment. She felt years younger and was delighted with herself. If she could look how she wanted, maybe she could feel how she wanted.

Miriam was the only one who looked very pale after her treatment. The text from Jerry had made it impossible for her to relax and, in the end, she asked the therapist to finish up early. She used the pregnancy nausea as an excuse and asked the therapist to leave her for the last fifteen minutes so that she could have space to think.

"Let's grab a table in the conservatory," Vivienne said, leading the way. "I'll head to the bar. I'd love a gin and tonic, anyone else?"

"Well, if it's okay with you guys, I want to get to a couple of shops before they close," Clara said. "The therapist gave me a list of places to try, and they all probably close in an hour."

"Sure, see you back at the apartment. We still have to make dinner plans – do you have any preference?" Vivienne asked.

"None at all, you guys decide," Clara replied and headed off.

"You're a bit pale, Miriam, are you feeling okay?" asked Helen.

"Oh yes, I'm okay – it was just very warm in the therapy room. I think I'll have a cup of tea, Viv, and a glass of water, please."

Helen craved a vodka and Coke but there was no way she could order one in front of this lot after last night's fiasco.

"I'll have a tea and a water too, Viv," she said instead.

"Grand, I'll get them in. I'd better give Sarah a call too and make sure they're being fed properly." Viv laughed as she headed to the bar.

"What can I do for you?" asked the barman.

"A gin and tonic, two teas, and two glasses of water, please," Vivienne said as she dialled her daughter's number.

"Hi, Sarah!"

"Hi, Mum, how's your weekend?"

"Oh, it's great, love. Galway is gorgeous at Christmas. It's freezing though."

"Yeah, it's cold here too but sunny so it's not too bad."

"Did you go to the rugby with the boys?"

"Yeah, me and Alex met Dad and Clodagh there. It was good fun."

Dad and Clodagh? Vivienne was taken aback but tried not to show it.

"Why were you meeting them there – did you not go with Dad?"

"No, Dad was at a dinner party in Clodagh's last night and stayed over. He said they all drank too much to get taxis, so we just met them there."

"Really?" Vivienne could feel her jaw stiffen.

Clodagh Walsh was an old friend of Tom's. They grew up in the same area, hung around as teenagers, and had definitely hooked up once or twice in their teens. Tom had always said it was nothing, a few drunken encounters, and that they had never officially gone out with each other. But Clodagh had always been a bit too tactile with Tom for Vivienne's liking and it had always bugged her. She always seemed to sit herself beside Tom on nights out. She also loved bringing up old times or trips the gang took when they were teens, knowing that Vivienne was not around then so couldn't relate or join in the conversation. It was bloody rude.

Tom had dismissed Vivienne's concerns when she brought it up, insisting that Clodagh was an old friend and great craic and to leave her alone. Clodagh had married quickly after Tom and Vivienne got married but her marriage didn't last long. She was separated and divorced after two years. She also had no children and always encouraged Tom to stay late drinking when Vivienne wanted them to go home as they had to get up early at weekends for the children's activities. Vivienne always felt she did it to try to show that she had a hold over Tom. And, of course, if she needed something put together in her house it was Tom she called. It always irritated Vivienne, but she took Tom's word that nothing would ever happen between them.

It now sounded like Clodagh had been more than an understanding ear for Tom. I bet she was only delighted for him to stay over at hers, Vivienne thought.

"So, is Dad home now?" she asked, keeping her voice light.

"No, he and Clodagh were going to the pub after the match to meet the gang. He's staying out tonight, I think, because he gave us money for a takeaway."

"I'll ring him. He should at least stay home one of the nights I'm away." Vivienne could feel the anger rising.

"No need, Mum, we won't be here anyway. I'm going to Cassy's for the night and Dad arranged for Alex to stay at a friend's house."

"Whose house?"

"I don't know, one of the lads on Alex's rugby team."

"For god's sake!"

"Mum, it's fine! Alex was delighted. Just enjoy your weekend, everything's fine here. Look, I have to go."

"Okay, love, have a good night."

"Bye, Mum."

And with that, Sarah was gone.

Everything is fine? I bet it bloody is, thought Vivienne. Part of her was fuming and part of her was sad that life was going on without her. They were just doing their thing and the kids did not bat an eye about their dad staying overnight at Clodagh's house.

Jesus, how quickly you can be replaced, she thought. How quickly I have been replaced.

"Hello there? That will be sixteen fifty, please."

"Oh sorry, I was miles away." Vivienne hadn't noticed the barman standing in front of her with the drinks.

"I'll carry them down for you," he said, taking her cash.

"Thanks, we're over there." She pointed to the women. "I'll follow you down. Can you tell them I'm just on a call?" She held up her phone.

She left the bar, headed out to the reception area, sat down on one of their big reception chairs, and dialled Alex's number. It went straight to voicemail. He probably forgot to charge it again, she thought, putting her phone back into her pocket. Her son was staying in someone's house, and she didn't know who they were or where they lived and there was absolutely nothing she could do about it. She suddenly felt very lonely. Is this the way her life was going to be now? It looked like Tom was fooling around with Clodagh and the kids were doing their own thing. Vivienne had a glimpse of how things were going to be. When the divorce was done and the house was sold, Sarah would have moved to London. And Alex? He might decide to spend more time with Tom or with his rugby mates than stay at home with his mum at the weekends. Vivienne hadn't thought that far ahead. She had thought that she had everything figured out, but the reality might be very different. She knew her marriage was over. She did not want to live with Tom anymore – she could barely stand to look at him. But, in her vision, she had been looking forward to living in a new place with Alex. But the reality was that he was not her baby anymore. He was a six-foot-two, rugby-loving teenager who had a few girlfriends on the go and a party to go to most weekends. Would it be enough for her to stay at home on her own at weekends? Vivienne took a deep breath. This is what I want, and this is the time for it. I just have to deal with things as they arise. She straightened herself up and held her head high as she made her way back to the girls and her much-needed gin and tonic.

Chapter 28

Clara left the Skylight Hotel and headed back towards the town centre. Galway was such a great city because you could walk everywhere. No need for buses or taxis. It was early evening and Clara quickened her step as she wanted to get to the shop her therapist recommended before it shut. The directions were straightforward and even though she had only been here two days, Clara felt she knew the town well enough to find her way around. She loved the atmosphere of Galway. It was so artistic and bohemian that she felt like her old self here, a feeling she hadn't had in a long time. She didn't know what it was about it, but the culture and the influence of the arts could be seen everywhere. Here she didn't feel like a frumpy blob.

Imagine a girl like Fern not batting an eye when she wanted to get her hair dyed with blue and green mermaid stripes! And the clothes shops the therapist recommended sounded right up her street too. Clara realised that today she had felt seen. She had confidence here that she could look cool and colourful and not ridiculous. She caught her reflection in a shop window and was delighted with her new hair. It had given her such a boost. She felt such new energy. It was like she had woken up again. She wanted to look different, and she wanted to feel different. She needed this boost of confidence to look at her life and see what she wanted for herself.

She had been in a rut, feeling pressured by Richard to have another baby and not knowing how to tell him that this would never happen. When she got home she was going to sit him down and tell him that she wanted to go back to work, even a few days a week. She had more to offer. Her job had energized her and gave her an identity outside the home. She planned to contact HR and see if she could go back maybe two days a week at first or even casually just to get back into it. And, if they couldn't accommodate her, she would try somewhere else. With her years of retail and management experience, she was sure she would be an asset to any shop.

Clara checked the address again and arrived at the shop. The building was a lovely lilac colour, down a side street, with a string of fairy lights blinking around the window frame. An old-fashioned bell rang as Clara entered and the warmth from a small electric heater was a welcome relief from the frosty air outside. The shop itself was an Aladdin's cave of colour that lifted her heart.

"Hello, let me know if you need help with anything," a voice said from behind a counter in the corner.

Clara was delighted to see that the shop assistant was a woman near her own age. The lady had black hair with silver streaks around the front, loosely tied up in a bun with two chopsticks, crisscrossed, sticking out of it. She was wearing a long cotton dress with big pockets and a long red silk kimono over it. Clara smiled in awe at her unique and stunning style.

"I'm sorry to arrive so late, I'm sure you're closing soon but I was recommended to come here, and this was the first chance I got. I will try to be quick."

"Take your time, my dear. My son is collecting me, and he won't be here for another twenty minutes. I like your hair, by the way."

"Oh, thank you very much," Clara said, bringing her hand up to her new blue streaks. "I just got it done today so it's new to me. I'm still getting used to it."

"Well, it suits you. Are you looking for anything in particular?"

"Well, I don't really know what I'm looking for," Clara said, looking around, feeling overwhelmed. "I know this sounds silly but, since getting my hair done, I feel like my clothes don't match my new look. My clothes feel like the frumpy old me, so I want something colourful and funky without making me look stupid or ridiculous for my age."

"Well, I don't think you look frumpy or old and I'm not just flattering you for a sale," the lady said, smiling. "But I know what you mean. It is possible to look colourful and funky and be comfortable in yourself too."

"Yes! That's it. I want to be comfortable with myself. I've lost my way a bit. I have no idea what I like or what would look good on me. But I really like your dress!"

"Well, this is a tunic, and it is so comfortable. You can wear it casually or dress it up with jewellery or a colourful coat as I have."

"I love your look. Do you have something like it here?" Clara said, looking around.

"Come with me and we'll have a look. I'll just put the closed sign on because it's nearly that time anyway and we're the only ones here. That way we won't be disturbed. I'm Sylvia, by the way."

She locked the door and put the closed sign on.

"You're so kind, Sylvia, I'm Clara."

Clara followed Sylvia down the shop and Sylvia took items off the rails, matching them up as she went. With an experienced eye, Sylvia needed to only glance at Clara to know her size and save the embarrassment of asking her. As most of the clothing was loose-fitting Scandinavian-style smocks and tunics, there were lots of options on the rails.

"Here you go, try these combinations on and tell me what you think," Sylvia said, hanging all the clothes up in a little changing room at the back of the shop. "I think the purple tunic with the blue buttons would go very well with the light-blue long jacket and the colour would match the blue in your hair, but go by how you feel, how the clothes make you feel, and what colours make you feel good."

Clara's eyes lit up. The two items on their own were beautiful but together were stunning. The tunic skimmed over her hips and the block colour made her wobbly bits disappear somehow. The half-sleeves covered the parts of her arms she hated too. She loved the colour purple and standing there, looking at herself, she wondered why she had no purple at all in her wardrobe at home. The blue coat on top of the purple dress was just perfect. Sylvia definitely had an eye for colour. Clara would never have put these two colours together. She could hardly believe the image staring back at her from the mirror and her eyes started to fill up.

"Is everything okay in there?" Sylvia asked.

Clara pulled back the curtain.

"Those colours are so lovely on you. You are glowing!" Sylvia said.

Clara wiped a tear away.

"Are you okay?" Sylvia asked.

"Yes, I just haven't seen myself look like this in a long time."

"Oh darling, you look lovely," Sylvia said, handing her a tissue. "Now don't ruin it by having big red eyes!"

"Oh thank you so much, Sylvia. I'll take this outfit. You have been so kind."

"Not at all. You look great. Take your time and I'll meet you at the till."

Clara could not believe how nice everyone had been today. Everyone she had met had given her a confidence boost. To think I was so nervous about coming and not looking right, she thought. I didn't feel right in myself because I wasn't myself.

New hair and new clothes wouldn't change everything, but they were helping her figure out who she wanted to be from now on.

Just then her phone buzzed. It was a text from Vivienne.

Hi Clara, no rush but we want to go ahead and order Chinese takeaway. Do you know what you want, or should we wait for you?

I'm just finished here but order me a Chicken Chow Mein and I will see you in about twenty minutes. C x

Great, we are eating in our apartment and the dress code is pyjamas!

Clara smiled to herself. Today had really turned this trip around. Looking in the dressing-room mirror at her new hair and new clothes, she realised that she hadn't felt this good about herself in a long time. Why hadn't she been happy? Why was it so long since she had felt this content? She needed to use her remaining time here in Galway to have a long think about all these questions and try to come up with answers that worked for her firstly, and then Richard and the whole family. One thing she was certain of – a different Clara was going to step off that train in Dublin to the one who had left two days ago.

Chapter 29

When Clara arrived back at the apartment, she hung up her new purchases. She would keep them for going home tomorrow. She quickly changed into her pyjamas, threw a hoodie on, and joined the girls in Vivienne and Miriam's apartment. The smell of Chinese food made her mouth water. The girls were already there in their pyjamas, looking relaxed. All the dishes were on the table for everyone to tuck in.

"This was a great idea," Miriam said.

"It is so relaxing not having to get dressed up and go out in the cold, isn't it?" Vivienne said. "Especially after being so warm and relaxed after our treatments."

"This food is so good," said Helen, tucking into the barbequed ribs.

Clara was delighted to see that the girls had ordered loads of sides too. The table was full of main dishes and sides of ribs and spring rolls and other small cartons that she was eager to try. There was no shortage of food tonight.

"How did the shopping go?" Miriam asked, passing the prawn toasts around.

"Oh, brilliant. The shop manager was so nice and took her time with me. It helped that she was the same age as me," Clara said, adding some spring rolls to her plate. "So she picked some lovely pieces that are funky but not too young if you know what I mean."

"And when will we get to see them?" asked Helen, passing around the fried rice.

"Don't worry, I will model them tomorrow when we head home," Clara said with a laugh. "What do you fancy doing tomorrow? Christmas shopping maybe?"

Before they could answer, Clara's phone rang. "Oh sorry, ladies, it's Richard. I'd better answer it. Can I take it in your bedroom, Viv?"

"Of course."

"Okay, I won't be long. Keep me one of those ribs – they are delicious."

Clara shut Vivienne's bedroom door and sat on her bed to answer the phone.

"Hey there, how are things?" Clara asked cheerily as she answered the call.

"Well, you sound in good form."

Clara could tell from Richard's snide tone that something was up.

"Is everything okay? You sound funny."

"Funny! You think I sound funny. Well, I suppose you are having a great laugh at my expense with your friends, aren't you?"

Clara was taken aback. "*What?* What are you talking about?"

"What am I talking about? Well, how about Richard the idiot who thought we were trying for a baby but found out today that you have been on the Pill all along?"

Clara suddenly felt cold. She felt sick. She didn't know what to say.

"Have you nothing to say? Okay, I'll speak for you. I went to collect Seán's prescription from the chemist's and the girl behind the counter said, 'Oh, do you want to collect your wife's prescription while you are here?' She put the two prescriptions in the one bag so when I got home and took Sean's out, I found out that my wife is on the Pill."

Clara was sweating now. She felt awful.

"I'm sorry, Richard, I'm sorry you found out that way. I should have told you. I was going to talk to you when I got home."

"Oh really, well, how am I supposed to believe that? How long were you going to string me along?"

"Richard, don't."

"Don't what? Don't get annoyed because my wife has been lying to me for God knows how long? Don't get annoyed because while I thought we were on the same page about having a baby you were doing everything you could to make sure that didn't happen. As if I would force you to have a child. Why didn't you say anything? I feel like such an idiot."

"I'm sorry," Clara whispered.

"I am so hurt that you couldn't talk to me."

There was silence on the line.

"I have to go," he said.

"I am sorry, Richard. Can we talk properly when I get home?"

"Whatever. God forbid I put a downer on your weekend."

"Richard, come on. We can talk now if you like."

"Clara, just leave it. I am too angry to talk to you now anyway. Just leave it. Bye." And he hung up.

Clara stayed sitting on the side of Vivienne's bed, staring at the phone.

"*Damn it.*"

She felt awful, hearing the hurt in his voice. She would have to think about how she was going to approach this when she got home. Taking a deep breath, she joined the girls again.

The girls stopped talking and eating when Clara returned, looking like she'd had a shock.

"Clara, are you alright? You look a bit shaken. Is everything okay at home?" Vivienne asked.

"Well no, everything is not alright. Oh God, I feel terrible."

"Hey, sit down, what happened?"

"It's okay, I don't want to ruin your night," Clara said.

"Don't be silly. We are here for you, Clara. Maybe we can help?" Vivienne said.

"Well, thanks, but I don't think you can help with this problem," Clara said, sitting down.

"A problem shared is a problem halved. You were in such great form tonight – I hate to see you like this," Vivienne said, sitting beside her and putting an arm around her.

Clara looked around at her friends' worried faces.

"Well, maybe you're right. It couldn't hurt to get an outside point of view, I suppose. Basically, for the past year nearly, Richard has been talking about having another baby. He thinks it would complete our family. I don't. I have enough on my plate with Seán. I have tried to tell him more than once how I feel, and I also want to return to work part-time, which he is not overly happy about. When I met you girls on the Human Resources course I realised that HR was really where I wanted to be. While I was an assistant store manager at the time, I also did another night course in HR to boost my qualifications. I forwarded my qualifications to my head office, and I planned to move into the HR department when a vacancy came up. With all my retail experience I know I could get a part-time job in some big company. I need something for myself. Richard knows this but he thinks the kids will benefit more from me being at home. I am ready to go back to work and, as soon as I can find a position with hours I can work around, that is exactly what I will do."

"Surely he can't object to that?" said Helen.

Clara sighed. "Last Christmas he was going on about having another baby so much that I agreed to just think about it. Really, I was avoiding talking about it or having any arguments. But, honestly, I felt really let down. It was like he didn't take my return-to-work plans seriously. I was so annoyed, but I didn't want to ruin Christmas, so I bit my tongue. I said I'd think about it and he seemed happy with this. Anytime I have brought up going back to work, he says, 'Let's wait and see' or 'Haven't you got a lot on your plate already?' But that is exactly why I want to go back, to get some space for me and use my brain again. But, after Christmas, I went to the doctor and renewed my prescription for the Pill. I just don't want another child and I kept meaning to talk to Richard about it, but time just flies by, doesn't it? Anyway, today he went to the chemist's to pick up medicine for Seán and the young one behind the counter gave him my prescription too."

"What? Did he open your prescription?" asked Helen, shocked.

"No, the girl put the two things in one bag so he couldn't not see it. So understandably he is angry and feels betrayed. He thought we were trying for a baby, and I was making sure we weren't."

Her friends were quiet for a moment, letting it all sink in.

"But you told him you didn't want another baby," Vivienne said.

"Yes, but I should have made it crystal clear. I chickened out because then where would it leave us? He wants one, I don't. Would he always resent me for not having another baby? I was worried things might change between us. I should have had a proper discussion but, to be honest, I was just too tired. We seem to want different things, and I didn't want to deal with what that meant for us as a couple. Going on the Pill was giving me more time, I suppose. Will this drive a wedge between us now, wanting two different things?" Clara sighed, putting her head in her hands.

"Oh, Clara," Helen put her arm around her, "you have a right to a way of life that makes you happy."

"You have to do what makes you happy or nobody will be happy," said Vivienne.

"I know. And thanks for listening. I was looking forward to coming on this weekend for a break and a rest. But I have had the time to think and see clearly what I want. I have been invigorated. I feel like me again. I just don't know if Richard will like the new me."

"Of course he will," Helen said. "Richard loves you. You guys are as thick as thieves. I'm sure once you've explained everything, he'll see your side. And maybe knowing about your prescription might make him sit up, take note and look at things from your side."

"Well, I hope you're right because right now he is just feeling angry and lied to. Maybe by the time I get home tomorrow, we'll be able to sit down calmly and discuss it. If not, maybe we'll need therapy. One thing is for sure though – I want a change and I don't want things to go on as they are."

Vivienne felt for Clara. She could see how conflicted she was, but she could also see a determination in her to change her life. She decided to take a deep breath and share as well. It might be a help to Clara to let her know she was not alone.

"Well, seeing as we're talking about husbands," she began, feeling a little nervous. "Tom and I are breaking up."

"*What!*" the girls said together.

"My marriage is over – actually it has been over for a while."

"Jeez, Vivienne, you never said anything," said Helen.

"I know, I know. I didn't want to say anything because Tom doesn't know it, but I am using a solicitor down here in Galway to handle my case. That's why I couldn't say anything, so please, girls, keep it to yourselves."

"Of course," they all said, looking from one to another.

They had not expected this from the glamorous power couple who seemed to have it all.

"Tom has so many friends and family connections with law firms in Dublin that I needed to find someone who Tom didn't know. I didn't know where to look. But then my company had a contract for a law conference in the US and I booked flights for a solicitor down here. I had to deliver his tickets to Dublin airport and when I met him I just knew I wanted him to represent me. So I hope you don't mind but I organised our little trip down here so that I could have meetings with him without being seen in Dublin."

"Jesus, that's very cloak-and-dagger stuff! Are things that acrimonious between you two?" Helen asked.

"Not yet but they will be. He hardly speaks to me at home, and we have slept in different rooms for six months. And it looks like Tom has moved on now. I think he has been with someone else for a while, so it won't come as a complete surprise to him. But when it comes to property and investments Tom won't want to split any of that, so I need a good solicitor to fight my case."

"What about the kids, do they know?" Miriam asked.

"I think they have an idea. Obviously, when I moved out of the main bedroom, Sarah asked me what was going on. I told her and Alex the truth, that Tom and I were not getting on anymore. I told them that we loved them and wanted to continue to have a stable environment for them. Sarah was a bit upset and Alex just asked if we would have to move. Once I assured them that their lives wouldn't change, they were fine. You know teenagers. Sarah is moving to London over the summer. She has a place in the Royal Academy of Dramatic Art and is going with two friends so she will be living an independent life over there. Alex is so busy with school, rugby, and hanging out with his friends that we only see him when he's hungry. I think they'll be fine. It is sad though. It is not what I wanted for them, so I am going to do all I can to make this transition as smooth as possible, for them. I want a different life for myself too. I don't feel like I fit into his life anymore. We are from different backgrounds, and, at the beginning, I just fitted into his, but I don't feel I fit in there anymore. Our differences have become more obvious. I wanted us to go to couples therapy, but he refused. I thought maybe we could find what brought us together in the first place. Anyway, it's complicated as these things often are, but I wish he had just tried, you know. Maybe we could have salvaged something. Now it looks like it could be a bitter and nasty separation. I want to shield the kids from this as much as possible and I really believe Tom does too, but we are definitely done."

The girls were silent. Miriam was the first to speak.

"I'm so sorry you are going through this, Viv."

"You know, it's mad but I spent so long thinking it was me, that I wasn't making enough effort with his friends, didn't get to know the women better but I realised that they never really made the effort with me. Oh, they were nice to me when we were out as couples but because I worked I never made the long lunches or charity coffee mornings, so they stopped asking me. Tom wanted me to stop work, but I love my job and I have worked bloody hard to get to where I am, so I was never going to do that. Now that we are separating and I have got used to the fact, I feel relieved actually. I don't have to keep trying so hard to keep up an image that just wasn't me. I'm becoming more the person I was meant to be. It's easier because I have a successful business and I am financially independent. This is a huge thing, ladies. My grandmother told me before I got married that women should have an account that their husbands didn't know about. She called it 'your running away money'. I thought it was hilarious at the time but apparently my mother and my grandmother put a few bob away in accounts that their husbands knew nothing about. I can tell you it was the best piece of advice ever."

The girls looked stunned.

"Here, let's eat the rest of this before it goes cold," Helen said as she passed around the last of the Chinese food.

Clara passed the last of the rice to Vivienne. "I'm so sorry this has happened to you, Viv. Richard and I are nowhere near breaking up, but I completely understand where you're coming from. I'm changing and I want to change more, and I don't know if Richard will like the changes. It is a worry. I feel like I've been under a cloud, this last year especially, and I want out from under it now. I think being away from the house and kids has given me some breathing space. I didn't even realize I was suffocating, but I was. I can't be of use to everyone else if I am not happy myself. But lying about the contraception is a biggie. Maybe we might need couples therapy to get through this."

"Of course you'll get through it," Miriam said. "It just sounds like a miscommunication."

"Don't let it fester like I did," Vivienne said. "Richard loves you and the last thing he wants is for you to be miserable. You guys will work this out, I know you will. And you look amazing! Doesn't she, girls?"

They all agreed that she was a hot chick now and this made Clara laugh. She was so grateful to be here with this little group of amazing friends.

Miriam turned to Vivienne. "Vivienne, I know you wanted to go to see a therapist with Tom, but can I recommend that you go on your own anyway? I've been seeing a therapist for over a year now and I would highly recommend it."

"Jesus, Miriam, you never said! Did something happen?" Helen asked.

"No, well, yes and no. You don't have to wait for something big to happen, but I felt if I didn't speak to someone I was going to go mad. I was under so much pressure."

"Oh God, Miriam, we never knew. Was it work?" Viv asked.

"No, work is always busy, and I have deadlines that can be stressful, but I do love it. Things went downhill with my mum's health. You know she has dementia, and we were managing fine but now she needs extra supervision. Home help is so expensive, and we tried to manage her care ourselves for a while. I did up a roster for Sharon and Simon, but they have partners and kids, and I don't, so the lion's share of the work fell to me. Mum started to wander around the house at night, so I started to stay with her two nights a week, sleeping in her house. But you can't sleep when she's wandering around the house in case she falls so I was shattered. Mum needs 24-hour care but to do this at home is financially impossible. She needs to be in a nursing home. I found a lovely place for her near her house, but Sharon and Simon wouldn't come to see it. They don't want to hear about it, and we had so many rows over it. Things got too much for me. I had no social life because I was too tired to go out. So I spent my time working, caring for Mum, and then going back to an empty house to sleep. I broke down in my doctor's office one day and she recommended this wonderful therapist."

"Oh God, you poor thing, Miriam. That sounds like huge pressure," Clara said, putting a hand gently on her arm.

"It was. I was shattered and feeling very down. During the first few sessions with the therapist, I cried as soon as I walked into the waiting room! And even though I felt I talked nonstop to her, pouring everything out, she always left me with a thought or view to think about before our next session. Just talking and crying lifted a weight off my shoulders and helped me see things more clearly. The doctor was great too. She organized more home help and also put me in contact with some wonderful people in the Alzheimer's Association who sent someone out to visit Mum one day a week. Anyway, after a few weeks and a bit more sleep for me, the therapist helped me see things from a distance. I had been operating in fifth gear for so long and was too exhausted to change things. Once I could look at things objectively, the clouds cleared and I could see what the future held going down the same road I was on – or, how it could be if I worked out a new pathway for myself, putting my needs first. I have no doubt that I would have had a nervous breakdown if it weren't for my therapist and my doctor."

"God, I wish we could have known, Miriam. Maybe we could have helped somehow," Viv said.

"No, I had to get the help myself and stop being a martyr and learn to speak up for myself."

"So what's the story with your mum now?" asked Helen.

"Well, I've secured a place for her in the lovely nursing home near her house and I know she'll be happy there and looked after very well. And because it is local we can pop in whenever we want, and her friends can visit if they wish to. Sharon and Simon will not agree at first, but I have emailed them the details and the costings. It's half the price of having home carers to look after her at home. I told them that if they want Mum to stay at home they would have to take over my shifts because I am stopping in two weeks due to doctor's orders. Oh, and I told them I was pregnant in the email too!" Miriam laughed. "It will be a shock, to say the least!"

"They didn't know?" Helen asked, amazed.

"No. I wanted to get everything in place for Mum first. She has been my priority. Honestly, I haven't had much time to enjoy my pregnancy because I've been so busy with Mum. But this weekend and my trip to A&E have made me realise how much I want to enjoy this pregnancy as it will probably be my only one. The decision about Mum now is up to Sharon and Simon. I have done all the work and after this weekend I'll be in full baby mode."

"Good for you, Miriam!" said Vivienne, raising her glass to her.

"We are always here for you, okay? Or at the end of the phone," Clara said. "That was so much to carry alone on your shoulders. Please ring one of us the next time things get too much or if you just want to talk. Promise?"

"I promise. Thank you, guys. I really appreciate that. It's just when you're in the middle of it, it sucks so much energy out of you that you just keep putting one foot in front of another. Even calling a friend can seem like too much." Miriam rubbed her tummy. "I'm so glad I got everything sorted before this little one arrives."

"So when did you decide to have a baby? I know you've been talking about it for a few years. Did this whole business with your mum accelerate it?" Viv asked.

"Well, obviously, while looking after my mum I had zero time to meet anyone and, at almost forty, I was running out of time. I mean, I would have had to meet someone and immediately get pregnant. But what guy wants that? When I talked it out with the therapist I realized that it was a baby I wanted, not a relationship. You know, if the right guy comes along then he will have to accept the two of us. It took so much pressure off me when I realized this and then I started planning. The pressure of a relationship is not what I need right now."

"I think you're so brave, Miriam," Vivienne said.

Miriam smiled and shook her head.

"No really," Vivienne insisted. "You have been through so much, but you knew what you wanted and you went for it."

If only you knew, Miriam thought uncomfortably as she looked around the table. She had so much support from these women, and she did not want to give that up.

What happened with Jerry was a once-off and there was no reason to ever see him again. He had helped with difficult jobs around the house over the years but that would have to stop now. She just needed to keep to her donor story and everything would be fine – as long as he kept his mouth shut about their moment of abandonment. Miriam felt her anxiety rising again. These were the only true friends she had, and she didn't want to lose them, and she definitely did not want them to hate her.

Helen sat listening to the women. She felt like such a bitch. Her marriage to Jerry was rock solid. It was she who was causing the problems. Vivienne had tried to save her marriage and Clara was desperate not to lose hers – and here she was with a great husband and wrecking everything with her drinking. She felt like shit. She also felt like shit because she wanted a drink. She was suspicious at first about Viv's suggestion of having a takeout in the apartment, a girls' night in. Was it to stop her from going to the pub? Was she paranoid? Actually, she'd feel very self-conscious drinking in front of the girls after last night's disaster.

She knew Jerry worried about her drinking and she wasn't much fun to be around either. After talking to Grace today it was clear that her menopause was the cause of some of her problems too, like the insomnia, the mood swings. Even Cillian, her eldest, had said recently 'Why are you so cranky all the time? You're always sad or angry'. Helen thought he was a cheeky little pup at the time and had given out to him, but she felt really bad afterward. She blamed her stressful, busy life and her difficulty sleeping as her reason for having a drink at night when in fact it could be the menopause. But she could also see that the drink was just making things worse, not better. She knew she had to change, and she told Jerry she would. He had told her to come back from this weekend with a plan because things could not carry on as they were. What did he even mean by that? She had planned on telling him what he wanted to hear, to get him off her back. But after listening to Clara and Viv, it was clear now that she might have been taking her marriage for granted.

Jerry had been a steady and supportive partner. Her drinking was the only thing that caused rows between them. Never once did she think she was putting her marriage at risk. Was she blind or had she become so selfish? It never crossed her mind that her marriage could be under threat because of her behaviour. Deep down, she knew Jerry would never go off with another woman but maybe she'd been stupid to think that he would put up with her behaviour forever. Helen pushed her plate away. She felt hot, and a bit panicked as she reached for her pint of water.

"Okay, Helen?" Miriam asked.

"Yes, just a hot flush. They're bastards," she said, gulping down the water.

She was too embarrassed to say anything to the girls. She needed to get her act together. She took some deep breaths as the girls were talking. No, everything will be okay, she thought. She had a plan. She would see the menopause expert about her symptoms, she was going to enrol in an Aromatherapy course and get a qualification that would give her a career outside the home that she could work around the family's needs.

Maybe she'd talk to a therapist too. What Miriam said made so much sense. It would be good to talk to someone in total confidentiality with no judgment, to release some of her demons and get some clarity and direction and maybe some help with the drink cravings. Having spent the last two years in a stress bubble she might need help getting her life back on track.

When Helen thought about it, she couldn't remember the last time she wanted to go out or buy new clothes even. Seeing how much a new hairdo and clothes had transformed Clara in just two days, and given her so much confidence, was inspiring. Helen had worn the same clothes for years and, when some extra weight appeared around her waist, she mostly wore leggings all the time now. She and Jerry were always jeans and T-shirt people but maybe she should update her wardrobe a bit. Even a few colourful tops would be a change from her uniform of black and grey.

She felt the urge to ring him, but she didn't want to break up the group. She would talk to him tomorrow when she got home This weekend had been the wake-up call she needed for her mental health and happiness and a stark reminder of how easily couples can drift apart and how easily some marriages can fall apart.

Chapter 30

The girls sat back in their chairs, their tummies full of their feast of Chinese food. Everyone seemed tired now. It had been a night of revelations, some surprising and some shocking.

"I'm completely stuffed," said Helen. "I think I'll call it a night, girls."

"Me too," said Clara. She was so glad she'd told the girls about the phone call. She was worried now about herself and Richard but was determined to create this new path for herself. She only hoped that she and Richard could get over this hump and maybe talk to Miriam's therapist if need be and travel this new road together.

"Let's go back to Nimmo's for breakfast tomorrow. Or do you fancy somewhere different?" Vivienne said.

"Nimmo's was great. I'd be happy to go back there again," said Helen.

"Yes, let's do it. What time have we to check out?" asked Clara.

"Check-out time is normally at ten, but I spoke with the receptionist today and they don't have anyone booked into our rooms, so I paid for an extension until three."

"God, Vivienne, that's brilliant," said Helen. "We'll split the cost. I hate rushing in the morning."

"We can sort it out tomorrow," said Vivienne. "Our train is at three, so we'll have time after breakfast for some last-minute shopping."

"That sounds perfect. See you in the morning so. Night, girls."

Helen and Clara left together to go back to their apartment.

Miriam yawned.

"I'll tidy this up – you go and have a good night's sleep," Vivienne said.

"Are you sure?"

"Yes, of course."

"It was some night, wasn't it?" Miriam said, getting up.

"Yes, it was, but it was so helpful as well. We all have our own stuff going on and it's great that we can support each other."

"It's insane really. This time last year we were all in Budapest and everyone seemed so happy, and we never spoke like this. So much has changed in a year. Is it our age, do you think?"

"I don't know," said Vivienne. "Maybe mid-life crossroads. I'd say it's very common. And a year is a long time too."

Miriam smiled, rubbing her baby bump. "Yes, it is."

"And this time next year you will have a beautiful baby for us to fuss over," said Vivienne, clearing off the table.

"I am so full – I think I will be asleep as soon as my head hits the pillow."

"Good, you need your sleep. Night, see you tomorrow."

"Night, Vivienne, and thank you for everything," said Miriam as she left.

Vivienne gathered up all the empty cartons and squashed them into the bin. She looked at the clock. It was only nine and she was not tired at all.

As if reading her mind, her phone buzzed.

Hi Viv. Sorry to text so late but I have a nice bottle of Beaujolais here and it would be a shame to drink it on my own …

I'm in my jammies but it does sound tempting.

Well, don't change on account of me.

Ha-ha.

I can pick you up in 20 minutes?

Vivienne paused. She shouldn't really. She could see where this was going. But after the talk tonight …

Feck It! My new life has to start sometime, and it may as well start now.

See you in 20, she typed, with butterflies in her stomach as she pressed send.

"*Aw*, you're dressed," Jack said, putting on a disappointed face when Vivienne hopped into his waiting jeep.

"Cheeky!" Vivienne said back, flashing him a smile.

They held each other's gaze. God, he smells good, she thought, dragging her eyes away from his, feeling butterflies in her stomach again.

"But I'm glad you're here," he said as they pulled away from the apartments.

Jack weaved the jeep through the streets of Galway. The town was packed with Christmas party-goers. Groups of people standing outside pubs and clubs, crowds gathered around street buskers singing 'Fairy Tale of New York' badly, but full of Christmas cheer. Overhead strings of fairy lights gave the city a magical feel.

Driving out the road towards Salthill, Vivienne looked out the window at the winter moon reflected on the calm sea and felt so relaxed. She didn't want to think ahead to what might happen tonight, she just wanted to enjoy the here and now. It felt good to know that a good-looking man like Jack Brady found her attractive and enjoyed her company. They were so at ease with each other, yet the sexual attraction was strong and obvious.

Vivienne turned to see Jack was watching her. Her lust for him ran through her body and she wondered how far into the house they would get before they ripped each other's clothes off.

Sunday

Chapter 31

Vivienne smelt coffee and opened her eyes. Looking around the bedroom she took in the luxurious curtains that hung from the floor-to-ceiling windows. They were open, allowing the low winter sunlight to gently ease its way across the floor.

"Good morning, beautiful."

Jack was standing in the doorway barefoot, just wearing a pair of gym shorts.

He came over to the bed and bent down to kiss Vivienne on the nose.

"Sorry to wake you but you said you were meeting the other girls for breakfast, and I was hoping to have you to myself for a little bit before that."

"You are so considerate, Mr. Brady," Vivienne smiled.

She felt wonderful. Last night had been amazing.

They had barely got in the door before their lust took over. They removed each other's clothes while walking towards the bedroom but abandoned that idea and made their way to the couch instead.

Vivienne was so hungry for him. As she had suspected, Jack was very fit under his clothes. As soon as she touched him she wanted more. They made love frantically in the lounge. Every pent-up stress in Vivienne's body was released over and over again. She let herself go completely. Jack was gentle and passionate at the same time. The lust in his eyes made her feel sexy and wild and she loved it. They made love in different positions on Jack's big couch by the light of the moon and wood-burning stove.

There was no awkwardness afterward either. Jack wrapped a luxurious Avoca blanket around her shoulders. He found a robe for himself and returned to the couch with the promised bottle of Beaujolais and poured himself and Vivienne a glass of wine. The dogs were asleep in another part of the house so it was just the two of them. They sat in front of the fire legs entwined, completely comfortable in each other's company, watching the moon over Galway Bay.

They enjoyed the bottle of wine and chatted easily about everything except Tom and Vivienne's marriage problems. Vivienne didn't ask about Jack's private life either. She just wanted to enjoy the night for what it was.

When they finished the bottle of wine, Jack took the glass from Vivienne and placed it on the floor. Holding on to her hand, he kissed her fingers slowly and gently without taking his eyes off her. Slowly he took both her hands and stood up. Without saying anything he led her by the hand to his bedroom.

He stopped at the side of his bed and took the blanket from around her shoulders and threw it on the bed. Vivienne was completely naked but did not feel self-conscious in front of him. She felt strong and sexy and was turned on by his lust as he ran his eyes over her body. His eyes took in the view and this time he took his time.

"You are so beautiful," he whispered as his hands reached for her face and he kissed her gently before lowering her down onto the bed.

This time there was no rush and Jack's breath grew deeper as he explored her body. Vivienne felt every part of her come alive. She embraced his every touch and let herself go. This time they made love slowly and gently. They moved around each other, anticipating each other's needs. Time and place became unimportant. And sometime in the night or early morning, Vivienne fell asleep in his arms.

"I have some coffee on the stove, and I have some almond croissants if you're hungry," Jack said, sitting on the side of the bed and gently brushing her hair back from her face with his fingers.

"*Hmm*, that sounds good but first I need to build up an appetite. Could you help me with that?" she said, flinging the duvet back.

Jack's eyes lit up as he scanned her naked body in full daylight.

"Oh, I'm sure I can help you with that," he said, his eyes returning to hers as he leaned over and placed his mouth over her right breast. Vivienne moaned and Jack's hand massaged her left breast. His mouth moved from one breast to another, flicking her erect nipples with his tongue. Vivienne pulled him on top of her and arched her back to meet his firm body. Looking at him in the daylight just excited her more. Jack made his way around her body, driving her wild with anticipation as he made her wait. She wanted him so much. She couldn't get enough of him and when he entered her, she roared. She wanted him to take charge and do whatever he wanted with her. She was in ecstasy and felt amazing. She let herself go and her body thanked her for it as she came again and again and again.

Chapter 32

Clara and Helen were both awake, having gone to bed early the night before. Clara stood in her pyjamas at the floor-to-ceiling window and looked out as the city of Galway was waking up to prepare for another busy day.

"That was some night last night," Helen said as she made them tea in the kitchen.

"I know," said Clara, turning away from the window and taking a seat at the kitchen table.

"It's incredible that we're all going through something big at this moment, some serious stuff too. It was so good to be able to talk about it so freely though. I would never tell my friends back home the things I tell you girls." Helen brought over two mugs of tea and sat down at the table with Clara.

"I was thinking the same thing last night and I think this friendship works because we don't live beside each other or know each other from school. We have no history, we don't know each other's families and our husbands don't know each other, and I think that's a good thing. It's just about us and we can say things here that we know won't get back to our husbands or friends."

"Yes, that's true. It was great to speak openly and get things off my chest that have been building up for ages. I think the chats last night brought us all closer." Clara sipped her tea. "We will need to be there for Miriam. Bringing up a baby on her own will not be easy, especially with that family of hers. They don't sound supportive at all. I hope they rally around her though."

"And what about Vivienne?" Helen said. "She's going to need us too. It sounds like it's going to be a messy separation. Although if Tom has moved on, maybe he won't be such a bollix."

"Oh, I hope so. Hey, do you fancy a walk before breakfast? It's lovely and sunny out."

"Yeah, why not? I'll just get changed. What time is breakfast again?"

"Eleven at Nimmo's. I'll text Miriam and Viv and tell them we'll meet them there."

"Oh hang on, there's a message in the WhatsApp group from Viv. She is out and will meet us there too. That's grand. I won't disturb Miriam so."

Clara cleared the table and put the mugs in the sink. As she waited for the water to heat up she thought about Richard again. She would message him after breakfast to let him know what time her train was getting in. Maybe he would collect her, maybe not. She didn't want to speak to him over the phone. She wanted to get home and see the kids and unpack and when the kids went to bed they could talk. She only hoped Richard wouldn't create an atmosphere or sulk. The thought of him just made her anxious, so she washed the dishes quickly. A good walk and a big breakfast with the girls would distract her and she could worry about him later.

Helen dressed quickly. Her room was a mess. I really must try to be tidier, she thought as she searched for a matching sock. This room is like my life, she thought, messy and all over the place. Her quilt and bedclothes were tangled up.

She couldn't fall asleep last night between the night sweats and the craving for a drink. She had finished the naggin of vodka before she joined the girls for dinner. She tried to ignore the cravings, but it was too much for her. Her body was used to having alcohol to relax her and help her drift off to sleep. The craving wasn't going to go away just because she stopped drinking. She lay there looking at the ceiling. It was no use. Rome wasn't built in a day, she thought, and it was going to take more than just wanting to stop drinking for her body to get used to her not drinking. She would talk to her doctor when she got home and come up with support mechanisms to help with the cravings. But for now, she needed alcohol to sleep.

Unable to lie there any longer, she had got up and tip-toed into the kitchen to get her bag which was hanging off the back of a kitchen chair. She had carefully gone to Clara's bedroom door and placed her ear against it. Silence. Stepping quietly back to her room, she put on a pair of tracksuit bottoms over her pyjamas and put her hoodie on over her top. Slipping her feet into her trainers, she quietly left the apartment.

The Spar across the road was still open so Helen quickly bought a small bottle of vodka and some Diet Coke. She also bought a pint of milk in case she bumped into one of the girls on her way back.

Putting the bottle of vodka at the bottom of her bag, she carried the milk and Coke back to the apartment. Sneaking back in, she was relieved that all was still quiet. Mission accomplished, she thought giddily as she locked her bedroom door and sat up in bed with her vodka and Coke. She poured the drink into a pint glass and relished the first sip as she felt it run through her veins. By the time she had finished the pint, she felt so relieved and relaxed. Just one more glass, she thought as she filled it up again, feeling in control once more. It had been enough to take away the pain.

But now this morning her head was throbbing. She grabbed her bag and emptied the contents on the bed. There had to be some painkillers in here somewhere. Ah, there you are! At the bottom of the pile stuck to a tissue were two Solpadine. Perfect. Her body ached and she needed something to take the edge off. Dissolving the Solpadine in a glass in the bathroom, she looked at herself in the mirror. She looked so tired. She was so tired. Tired of keeping secrets. Tired of hiding. Tired of pretending to be in control when she was not. Well, enough is enough. It's just too hard to keep it up. She was now ready for the change. Before this weekend she didn't know what that change would be or could be. Now she had a plan and this time she wanted it to work. Listening to Vivienne last night frightened her. She couldn't lose Jerry. She needed to convince him that this time was going to be different. She needed to make him proud to have her as his wife again. Finishing the Solpadine, Helen grabbed her make-up bag and applied as much make-up and concealer as she could to cover the dark rings under her eyes and then headed out with Clara down the town to meet the others for breakfast.

Miriam woke after a very disturbed sleep. What a night of revelations it had been! Her head was spinning when she went to bed.

Here was I, thinking they all had perfect lives, she thought. Well, maybe not perfect but everything I didn't have: husband, kids, busy lives, support. I had no idea how fragile all of that was. Vivienne is really going through it, and it looked like Tom is not going to make this easier for her. Clara, it seemed, was going through some midlife crisis or crisis of identity. Everyone always overlooked Clara because she was so nice and non-confrontational. Nobody knew she was struggling inside. And Helen, well, I thought something was up because she was drinking so much. And obviously, things had not been great at home or else ...

Miriam didn't like to think about it. Of course, she felt bad when it happened and guilty, very guilty. Helen had never been anything but nice to her. It was nothing personal. She didn't feel guilty now, as that one action had given her a new life.

Miriam rolled over on her side and rubbed her tummy, thinking back to that day with Jerry. 'Mum's the word' was the last thing he said when he left.

Mum's the word alright, Miriam thought as she sat up in bed. She had gone through that scene in her head many times and although she really liked Helen, she never felt guilty about what they had done. And now that she was pregnant, she still didn't feel guilty. It was a once-off. She didn't want anyone else's husband and she certainly didn't want to break up any family. She only had good feelings when she thought about that day. The way Jerry smelt. How good he looked in his white T-shirt, his tanned toned arms carrying his toolbox. She was attracted to him, but he was a no-go area. She was happy to relive that day in her mind and leave it at that.

But now that the word was out about her pregnancy and her donor story was completely believed by the women, she needed to come up with some sort of evidence to convince Jerry that she was pregnant by a donor. Miriam could feel a headache coming on just thinking about it, so she pulled the duvet up over her head to rest and see if she could come up with a plan.

Chapter 33

Clara and Helen met Miriam outside Nimmo's. It was a cold crisp morning but thankfully the sun had come out again. Still, nobody wanted to hang around in this weather as the coastal breeze was bitter.

"Hiya, I think Vivienne is out walking so will we go ahead and get a table?" Miriam said.

"Good idea," Clara said.

They were lucky and got a lovely table by the fire.

"This is perfect," said Miriam as the girls sat down, having put their coats on the backs of their chairs. "It is so cold out there." She blew into her hands to heat them. "I can't believe I came out without my gloves."

"I know," said Helen. "It looks lovely and sunny out, but that breeze would cut you. Did you sleep well last night?"

"Yes, I tossed and turned a bit, but I had a bath this morning and went back for another snooze."

"Oh, sounds lovely. I remember when I was pregnant and the tiredness, oh my God! Especially with the first. I used to come in from work and go straight to the couch for a twenty-minute sleep before I could even speak. Poor Jerry, he was so good. He ended up making most of the dinners midweek and became an expert at foot massages."

Miriam turned her head away. She couldn't look Helen in the face, and she certainly didn't want to hear about Jerry.

"I'm so glad we stayed in last night," said Clara. "It was great to talk without judgment. We could never have opened up like that if we were in a restaurant."

"That's true," Helen said. "And if we were in hotel rooms we wouldn't have been able to get a takeaway and sit around together. It really has worked out well coming to the apartments."

"Good morning!"

Vivienne had arrived, looking flushed and windswept.

"Morning! *Wow*, you look fantastic!" Helen said as Vivienne sat down. "That must have been some walk. You're glowing!"

"Well, thank you, but I'm in the same clothes as yesterday so hardly glamorous. It must be the Galway sea air blowing the head off me!" Vivienne laughed and blushed a little, knowing full well why she was glowing. "Have you guys ordered? I'm starving."

"No, but here's the waitress now," Helen said but she was still looking at Vivienne. My eyes are not deceiving me, she thought. She looks so different from the Vivienne who arrived on Friday and, judging by the way Clara is looking at Vivienne, she's noticed this too.

Once again the breakfast was delicious and the range of teas and coffees that accompanied it so refreshing.

"*Mmm*, this breakfast is so good," Vivienne said, tucking into poached eggs on avocado and sourdough bread. "Girls, I've been thinking. We should organise our next meet-up before we leave Galway. So much is happening in our lives at the moment, and it was great to be able to speak freely with you guys last night. I just can't do that with anyone else."

"I agree. It's the same for me. I feel I can say how I feel without judgment and get support from all of you," Clara said.

"How about we meet up in two months?" Vivienne suggested. "Early February, maybe? Christmas will be done and dusted, and the kids will be back at school. We can check in on how we're all doing? The only thing is, we would never have been able to speak so honestly in a restaurant."

"We were just saying that," said Clara.

"Should we go to one of our houses then? Would that be easier? Obviously not mine because we wouldn't get a minute's peace with my lot," said Helen.

"Oh no, we couldn't do that!" Miriam blurted out. "I mean, that would be too much work for you, Helen – sure, you're so busy with the boys."

There was no way that Miriam was ever going to set foot in Helen's house. She didn't want to think about the cosy family life she had built with Jerry. She had separated the two things in her mind. She wanted to think of Jerry as a one-night stand, not Jerry the family man married to her friend with four children. She could live with thinking that way so she would never go to Helen's house. That was way too much for her to handle.

"Miriam's right," Vivienne said. "So I was thinking about it on my walk, and I have an idea. Do you remember me mentioning my parents' cottage in Wexford?"

"In Rosslare?" asked Miriam.

"Yes. How about we go there for a night? It's only two hours from Dublin and if you don't want to drive you can get the train. I was thinking down Saturday back Sunday. We could arrive at about eleven on the Saturday and have a beach walk before lunch and then relax and get a takeaway delivered and stay in for the night. Then have a lazy breakfast on Sunday morning and go home whenever we want. We can catch up with each other without any distractions. It's very quiet, and it would be great to have something to look forward to."

"Oh, that sounds like bliss," said Clara.

"And I will definitely need a break from my family by then," said Miriam.

"Okay, leave it with me and I'll get back to you with a date. The weather won't be great but there's nothing like a windy beach walk to clear the head and I will have the fire lighting for you when you arrive."

"I want to go now!" said Helen, laughing.

"Brilliant," Vivienne said. "We can catch up then and help each other out. The next few months will certainly be stressful for me, and I have no idea how Christmas will go. After I get through all this I will need to get away, that's for sure."

"Well, let's get over Christmas and see how we're fixed – but early February should suit me," said Clara.

"Great, I'll check with my parents, but it should be fine. And if the weather is awful, we can keep the fire lighting all day and lounge around in our jammies again."

"I love that we have a plan for our next meet-up while still on this one," said Clara.

"Great. We have a deal so." Vivienne was pleased. She knew the shit was going to hit the fan when she got home, and she would need a break to get her head together again. "Right. We have to check out at half two and it's only twelve now so that leaves plenty of time for wandering around or shopping. I'm going to go back to the apartment now to shower and pack and then I might pop into TK Maxx to get the kids something."

"I'm heading out to Salthill for a walk," Clara said. "I want to drop into a café I visited yesterday."

Helen felt nervous. She didn't want to tag along with Clara as she clearly had something to do. But if she stayed on her own she would be too tempted to go for a drink. She could feel the anxiety rising already.

"Miriam, could you come shopping with me?" she asked.

"*Ehm*, I'm not sure if I would be any help, I'm not a great shopper." The last person Miriam wanted to be alone with was Helen. She loved Helen but, since Jerry had texted her, she was terrified he would tell Helen what happened. She needed to talk to him properly to throw him completely off the scent. She needed to convince him that there was no way that he was the father of her child.

"Oh, we won't be long. I just need to pick up some rubbish for the boys. We might sneak in some tea and cake somewhere too."

"*Em*, okay," Miriam answered. What else could she say?

The women divided the bill and Vivienne put the cash together for the waitress.

"Clara, will you hang on a minute?" Vivienne said.

"Sure," said Clara, sitting back down. "See you girls later," she said as Miriam and Helen put on their coats and headed off for their shopping.

After the waitress took the bill and the money, Vivienne leaned in to talk to Clara.

"Everything okay?" Clara asked.

"Oh yes, everything's fine. It's just that I have a proposition for you."

"Oh, this sounds interesting," said Clara, intrigued.

"My department in work is expanding. My partner deals with all our domestic travel and public accounts and, as you know, I deal with the corporate section. I have big plans to make the company the largest corporate travel company in the country. This means extra staff and extra training. I have already taken on a few new people, and I will be interviewing for more. The thing is, I need someone with HR experience to deal with this for me. I don't have the time. I want to be out there getting new accounts. I need to create packages and bring them to new companies to get their corporate travel accounts. I need someone I can trust to deal with the staff. From sitting in on interviews, doing up their contracts, organising training, and dealing with staff roster, holidays, and any staff problems that may arise. And I think you would be perfect for the job."

Clara was stunned. "Well I … I don't know what to say. It sounds like an exciting position. I'm just not sure I can commit. Would you not need someone full-time?"

"No, that's the beauty of it and why I think it would suit you. You could create a HR manual and training manual from home. We could work your office hours around your schedule. You could log your work-at-home hours, and I would pay you for those of course. Once we are up and running, you could decide when you need to be in the office for face-to-face issues. This way you could create your own hours."

"That sounds amazing, Viv. You're describing my dream job. I just need to think it over. I don't want to commit and then not be able for it. I would hate to let you down."

"Clara, you could never let me down. I think we could work well together but I don't want to put you under pressure either. Think about it. See how it would work at home and, when you have considered all options, let me know. If you start with me and after a few months it turns out that it is not what you want, that's fine too. It's not like I'll never talk to you again!" Vivienne laughed.

"Thank you. When do you need an answer?"

"I have a planning meeting in a week. If I could know by the middle of next week, I could add it to the agenda and include you in our company's plans for moving forward."

"Great. I'll definitely let you know by then," Clara said.

"Okay, let's get out of here. I'm sure they need this table back, judging by the queue outside. I'll see you back at the apartment."

"Yes, see you back there and thanks, Vivienne, I really appreciate your offer."

"Hey, no problem. We're friends and that's what we do, help each other out. Enjoy your walk."

Clara headed over the bridge towards Salthill. People rushed by over the bridge with their hoods up, trying to protect themselves from the biting wind coming from the River Corrib. But Clara didn't mind the cold. She felt alive again. She was walking on air. Vivienne's job offer was perfect. Daunting, yes, but exciting too. This could be her way out of the life she wanted to change. This could be her way back to herself. She smiled from ear to ear. It just felt right. The right job at the right time. She had just under a week to get back to Vivienne with her answer. She didn't need a week. She was taking the job. It was now or never. She just needed the time to convince Richard. This weekend had been life-changing. If she just stayed confident and strong, she could have the life she wanted because with or without Richard's approval, she was taking this job.

Chapter 34

The girls did their own thing for the rest of the morning and then met back at the apartments as arranged. They packed their bags, double-checked they hadn't forgotten anything and checked out of the Western City Point Apartments. It was a short walk down the side of Eyre Square to the train station, so they arrived in plenty of time.

As Vivienne had booked first-class tickets for everyone, they could board the train immediately and get comfortable. Vivienne and Miriam sat beside each other, and Clara and Helen sat in the row across from them. There would be no champagne and treats on the train going home. Everyone had a lot to think about after their revealing weekend.

Miriam took the window seat as she wanted to lean against it and take a little nap. This suited Vivienne as she wanted to get her laptop out and get herself set up for the coming week.

"Do you want me to get you a cup of tea if the trolley comes around?" Vivienne asked.

"Oh yes, please," said Miriam. "I'm just going to doze a bit. I need to get my head clear for when I get home."

Miriam leaned her head back against the headrest and watched the stone walls and green fields fly by. She had been tempted to turn on her phone to see how her brother and sister had reacted to her email, but she knew it would only cause her to worry and she couldn't reply to them properly on the train. Instead, she had emailed them to say she would be going straight from the train station to their mother's house and if they wanted to meet to discuss the email, that's where she would be from six.

I made myself very clear in the email, she thought, and this weekend has given me the focus and strength to deal with any objections they might have.

This was going to be her new life and she was proud of it. Okay, maybe not proud of sleeping with her friend's husband, but she was going to sort that out with Jerry and hopefully never have to deal with that issue again. She reckoned she could easily convince him she was having a donor's baby, as it would be what he would want to hear. No, her main job was to get him to promise to never tell Helen what happened between them. It was clear Helen had no doubts about Jerry's loyalty and that's the way it should stay. There was no reason to tell her. It could ruin their marriage and what was the point in that?

She folded up her jacket and placed it against the windowpane and closed her eyes. She would talk to her brother and sister tonight and then she would try to contact Jerry tomorrow to get all the awkward conversations over with. The next few weeks needed to go to plan so that she could relax and enjoy her pregnancy and get ready for her baby to arrive.

Vivienne pulled down the tray table in the seat in front of her and opened up her laptop. While she was waiting for it to power up, her phone buzzed. It was a text from Jack. She glanced over at Miriam sitting beside her before she opened the message, and thankfully she was asleep.

Molly and Milly miss you

Vivienne smiled and answered.

Aw that's so sweet. I miss them too

They were wondering when they would see you again

Well, my dashing solicitor is based in Galway, and he may have forms that I have to sign in person, so it depends on him really

I see, well, I can guarantee you that he will work hard to get the paperwork ready ASAP

That is wonderful news. I will await his instructions

Until then X

Until then X

Vivienne felt herself blush. She looked around to see if any of the other girls noticed but Helen and Clara were chatting away. She knew, in theory, that what had happened between herself and Jack probably wasn't the wisest thing to happen. But the reality was that she hadn't felt so alive and happy and attractive in years. This confidence boost was exactly what she needed. The separation wasn't going to be easy. But it was clear that Tom had moved on and, in some way, although it was sad, it made things a lot easier.

He probably thinks I want to fleece him for every penny he has, but that is not the case, she thought. If I sit him down and tell him what I want, he might be pleasantly surprised. Hopefully, when he sees that I just want the house, and the kid's college funds reinstated, he will realise he's getting a good deal and won't fight it. He's probably worried that I want a share in his family's rental properties, but I want none of it.

Jack had pointed out that Vivienne could go after Tom for much more, but she didn't want to. If they could do this amicably, that would be the greatest gift. The least amount of disruption to the kids the better.

Vivienne couldn't think much further than that at the moment. She needed to get Tom to agree to that and then she could give her full attention to her company. She was a partner now and had great plans for the expansion of their corporate accounts. That would keep her very busy over the next few months. She really hoped that Clara would come on board. She would be perfect for the role. She was kind and approachable but also very skilled in this area.

Vivienne closed her laptop and rested her head on the headrest. Everything could work out fine, she thought as she watched the fields go by. For the first time in ages, she could see how her future could be and, as for seeing Jack again. well, that was something she was happy to explore too.

Clara was quietly flicking through a magazine that she bought just before boarding the train. The girls were quiet. It had been a revealing weekend, and everyone had things they needed to change or resolve.

Clara felt a tightness in her stomach when she thought of Richard. They would have to sit down tonight and have a heart-to-heart. Very often, she was the one to compromise if she and Richard had different views on things. Of course, he would hear her out and sometimes they would both compromise, but if she added up all the times she compromised it would definitely be more times than Richard. So she expected some conflict tonight.

She understood how hurt he must feel finding out she was

secretly on the Pill, but she had avoided talking to him about it before because she didn't have a definite idea of what she wanted or how she saw her life in the future. She had needed to figure that out herself. And now she knew. She wanted a different image and a different life from the one she left behind on Friday. Nothing too dramatic, although she wasn't sure Richard would like her hair. But she was going to take Vivienne up on her job offer – that was one thing she was sure of. This time she would lead the conversation with Richard and get all her points across. Hopefully, he would support her.

She looked over at the girls. They meant a lot to her. They listened to her and understood her and would support her. This friendship was important in her new life, and she wanted to protect it. She was looking forward to meeting up with them in February. A lot would have happened in that time for all of them. Clara was both nervous and excited about what lay ahead but she felt clearer than she had in a long while and she planned on drawing strength from that.

Helen closed her eyes and tried to sleep on the train but just couldn't. She didn't want to talk either, so she put her head back and closed her eyes so that Clara didn't feel like she had to speak to her. So many plans were going through her head. The new course to check out, the therapist to call, the menopause consultant to contact. But, mostly, all she could think about was how much she wanted a drink. Her longing for a drink was a physical pain. There was no bar on this train, and it was just as well really. She had to meet Jerry with a smile on her face and new plans to save their marriage. She knew he would be pleased with her plans, and she knew she would have to go through with them.

Of course, it was what she wanted too. She wanted to be that person, the person with her shit together. She needed to be. And the only person who would fuck this up was herself. The path was there in front of her and she knew what to do. But the longing to just buy some drink and go home and relax on the couch and drink all night was so strong. How was she going to do this? Was she fooling herself? Could she really be that person? The girls seemed to think so, but they didn't know the half of it.

She tried to get comfortable in her seat. Her insides were crying out for just one drink to ease her anxiety. Oh great, a hot flush!

She sat up and rooted in her bag for some painkillers.

"Are you okay?" Clara asked.

"Yes, just a bit of a headache," Helen answered, rummaging around in her handbag.

"I have some Solpadine if you want."

"Oh god, yes, that would be perfect," Helen said, relieved.

"Here you are."

"Thanks, I'll just go and find the tea trolley and get some water."

Helen found the tea cart in the next carriage and bought a bottle of water. She stood in between the carriages, leaning against the door as she dissolved the Solpadine into the water bottle.

Oh God, can I really do this? And what will I destroy if I can't? As she watched the fields pass by as the train crossed through county lines, she felt panicked. She just wanted these feelings to go away.

Chapter 35

The train conductor announced the arrival of the train at Heuston Station, Dublin. The girls gathered up all their belongings, each lost in her thoughts. They queued up and got off the train and stood on the platform together.

"Well, ladies, this is it. Thank you for such an amazing weekend. I'm so happy I have you guys," Vivienne said. "Come on in for a group hug."

The girls smiled and hugged each other on the platform.

"Right, enough of that," Helen said, laughing. "I'll see you all in Wexford in February!"

"I am so looking forward to that already," Clara said.

"Me too," said Miriam.

"Guys, stay strong," said Vivienne. "And let's call each other if we need each other, okay? I'll organise the cottage with my folks and confirm during the week. Make sure you look after yourselves!"

"We will," said Helen.

The girls made their way down the platform towards the exit.

"Is that your Jerry, Helen?" Clara said.

Helen looked up to see Jerry standing at the exit gate.

"I wonder why he's here? He must have forgotten I had my car with me," Helen said, puzzled.

Miriam felt sick. *Fuck, fuck, fuck,* she thought. I can't do this. I can't face him.

"Oh, I think I left my scarf on the train," she said, stopping and pretending to look for it in her bag.

"Will I check for you?" Helen said.

"No, no, you ladies go ahead. I'll talk to you soon," Miriam said, turning and heading back for the train.

"Are you sure, Miriam? We can wait!" Clara called after her.

"No, not at all. Go ahead. We'll talk soon, yeah?" Miriam said over her shoulder, trying to get back on the train as soon as possible.

Once on the train, Miriam ducked down in one of the seats and sneaked a look out the window to where Jerry was standing.

Jesus Christ, what the hell was he doing here? Had he really forgotten that Helen had taken her car? Did he just want to see her reaction? Maybe I should have brazened it out? Oh shit, have I made it more suspicious now? *Calm down, Miriam. Take control.* Yes, I will see him when I want to, if I want to, and I will sit here until they have all gone.

She sat back and exhaled deeply. Her heart was racing. I am going to have to deal with this, she thought. I can't have this reaction every time I see him. I need to sort this once and for all.

The Irish Rail cleaners came into the carriage, looking curiously at her, so she had to get up and leave.

Chapter 36

Vivienne was relieved when she got in the door from Galway to hear that Tom was out. The kids were happy to see her and loved their TK Maxx tops. She caught up with their news, cooked them a meal and the three of them sat down to watch a Netflix comedy together. Vivienne had unpacking to do and could do with having a shower, but she didn't want to move. It wasn't often that they watched something together anymore and it was a lovely welcome home. Alex made microwave popcorn and the three of them munched it all from the same big bowl on the couch. Sarah got some throws from the blanket box and, although they didn't snuggle, they all sat together under the blankets. It was bliss.

After the movie, the kids hugged her before they went up to bed and Vivienne tackled the huge baskets of washing that had piled up while she was away. She fell into bed just before midnight. Tom hadn't come home, and no one asked about him. The kids had got used to him coming and going so much that the whereabouts of their dad was of no interest to them.

The following evening, Tom was home when Vivienne got in

from work. She heard his voice as soon as she opened the front door and she stiffened. He was talking to Alex about a game, so Vivienne took a big breath, put a fake smile on, and entered the kitchen.

"Hi, everyone!"

"Hi, Mum," Alex answered.

Tom said nothing, kept his head down and scrolled on his phone.

"Dinner will be ready in about thirty minutes," Vivienne said, taking off her coat and putting the oven on. She had taken a pasta bake out of the freezer that morning and now set about heating it.

"Okay, Mum," said Alex.

"Can we talk after dinner, Tom?" Vivienne asked quietly as she passed by him.

"If we have to," he said, not looking at her.

They all ate dinner together. Vivienne and Tom didn't look at each other but were civil and let the kids do the talking at the kitchen table. Luckily, Alex had a hilarious story from school, and it was good to see everyone laugh at his impression of his maths teacher.

When the kids went off to their rooms to do their homework, Tom stood up and began to clear the plates.

"We need to talk, Tom."

"Okay, talk," Tom answered without looking around.

"Can you sit down?"

He sighed as he pulled out a chair, sat and looked straight at Vivienne.

"So?" he said.

"It's about the separation."

"Go on."

"I have a solicitor."

"Anyone I know?"

"No, you wouldn't know him. He isn't based in Dublin."

"Clever. Did you think it could influence things if I knew him?"

"You and your pals know every law firm in Dublin, so yeah, maybe that was part of it, but I just wanted someone who didn't know either of us and could deal with this objectively. I think we can come to a separation agreement without going down the judicial route. It will be easier and quicker and less public for the kids."

"Well, that depends on your demands, dear."

Vivienne hated it when he sneeringly called her *dear*, but she had to let it slide and stay calm.

"I can tell you now what I want. It's very straightforward. I want the fifty-grand put back into the kid's college fund, I want you to give the kids a weekly allowance and I want this house signed over to me."

"The kids' account and allowance I can do but do you honestly expect me to just sign over this house to you?" Tom's eyes were so cold.

"I want nothing for me, no alimony, no share of your pension, no share of your investments or family properties, just this house. You know I could ask for a lot more."

Tom moved uncomfortably in his seat. He knew this was a good deal. Over the years he had seen his friends fleeced by their wives in separation cases and some had very public grievances aired in court. Viv knew Tom would hate that.

"I will think about that and discuss my options with Bob. Are you being straight with me? You won't come after me for more later?"

"No, this is it. This is all I want. You have my word. I want to do what is easiest for the kids. Despite how we feel now, we made two amazing kids. Can we set aside our grievances and make this as easy a transition as we can?"

Tom's eyes met Vivienne's and softened. "Yes, I don't want to make it any more difficult for the kids either. I promise to play nice if you do," he said with a half-smile.

"I would like us to be civil and I hope we can be friends. I mean that."

Tom got up and poured two glasses of wine, bringing them back to the table.

"I don't want a war either, Viv," he said, handing her a glass. "When do you want to tell the kids?"

"Alex has a big match on Saturday so maybe Sunday night?"

"Okay. I suppose you want me gone then?" asked Tom.

"Don't say it like that." Despite her suspicions that he'd spent the weekend with another woman, she still felt sad about it all.

"There's no rush," she said softly. "It's only two weeks until Christmas. Why don't you stay until the 27th?"

"Actually, my dad has an apartment coming empty in a week. It's in Cherrywood so the kids can walk or cycle there. It's a three-bed so the kids can have their own rooms. I'll move in there and we can talk about Christmas nearer the time."

What the fuck! Vivienne was taken aback. The bastard had already been planning his move. He knew she would get the house, he just wanted her to ask for it. She felt her blood boil but bit her tongue. She had to stay calm and play the game to get what she wanted. How handy to have a wealthy landlord father to bail you out again, she thought while putting on her best fake smile.

"We will need to have a plan for Christmas, so the kids know where they stand," she said.

"They're not kids anymore, Viv, they'll be fine. I'll check my plans and get back to you."

Vivienne wanted to scream. He was trying to have the upper hand, as usual, to keep control. But there was nothing she could do. She had to play the game if she wanted him to go quietly so she had to sip her wine and say nothing.

Chapter 37

When Clara arrived in the door from Galway, Richard met her in the hall. You could cut the atmosphere with a knife.

"We need to talk," he said as she stood there with her bags.

"Well, I need to see the kids first and give them their presents," Clara had answered, walking past him into the living room.

The kids ran to meet her, and she took her time, enjoying their hugs. Seán squealed with delight from his playpen. She picked him up and gave him a squeeze, inhaling his gorgeous baby scent. She listened to their news and told them all about Galway as she gave them their presents. She took her time. She was in no rush to go talk to her husband.

"I love your hair, Mommy. You look so cool!" Jessica said, smiling and hugging her. "And your clothes are lovely."

Clara was delighted.

"Thanks, Mum," James said as he opened his present.

"Soft," Seán said, rubbing her dress against his cheek.

Richard hadn't even come into the living room or mentioned her hair. This hasn't got off to a good start, she thought.

After the kids had settled and were distracted playing with their new toys, she put Seán back in his playpen and went into the kitchen to make a cup of tea.

Richard was sitting upright and stiff at the kitchen table.

"Tea?" she asked.

"No, thank you," he said, without looking at her.

Clara sighed. He was sulking. She knew he was annoyed, but this was ridiculous. At the same time, she didn't want a row, so she made her tea and sat down opposite him.

"I know you are annoyed about me being on the Pill and I apologize for not telling you."

"I feel like a fool. Why are you taking it?"

"I'm taking it because I don't want another child."

"But we agreed – I thought we were trying for a baby."

"No, Richard, I said I didn't want another baby, but you pushed me into saying I'd think about it and I was just too exhausted to argue any further with you."

"So you went on the Pill behind my back?"

"I went on the Pill to buy me some time to think about what I do want, that's all. And the more I thought about it, the more definite I am now that I don't want another baby. I have enough on my plate with Seán and I want to give all the kids what energy I have. I also want to return to work part-time or flexible hours because I need something for me."

"Well, if you don't have energy for another baby how will you have energy for a job?"

"Because meeting people energizes me. I loved working. I need something outside the home even for a few hours a week and the perfect opportunity has come up."

"Oh, so now you've been going to interviews behind my back too!"

"No, of course not. This just fell into my lap. Vivienne's company has expanded, and she has taken on extra staff and is looking for someone with HR experience to look after all that for her. She doesn't need anyone full time and I don't want to work full-time, so she said the job is mine if I want it."

"Okay okay, one thing at a time. Jesus!" Richard said, rubbing a hand through his hair and smirking.

"Is something funny?"

"No, it's just you go away for a weekend and come back all guns blazing. I don't know about the job, Clara. I'll have to think about it."

"What do you mean *you'll* have to think about it? I'm taking the job, Richard."

"Oh, so no discussion?"

"We're discussing it now."

"It sounds like you are telling me you are taking it, not discussing it."

"Well, it sounds like you think I should ask you if I can work or not."

Clara and Richard glared at each other, both of them angry.

"Where did all this come from? You're like a different person!" Richard said.

"I have felt like I've been going around in a fog and now, with Vivienne's job offer, I feel excited about something."

"What about Seán?"

"Well, that's the beauty of working for Viv. I can work whatever hours suit me so I can work it around the hospital appointments and school runs."

"It looks like you have it all figured out."

"Yes, I do, because it is always down to me to figure everything out, isn't it? You go out to work every day and meet new people, have a chat over coffee, and have the craic with clients and everything here falls to me to organize. So, yes, I do have it all figured out and I can make this work." Clara held his gaze. Her heart was racing, but she was not backing down.

Richard sighed. "It's all a bit much at once. I need to get my head around it. I'm a bit confused. Have you been hiding all these plans from me, or do you think I am that unapproachable that you couldn't have talked to me about this?"

Clara sighed. "Look, I just felt stuck, rudderless and I didn't say anything because I was so busy with day-to-day life that I couldn't see the wood from the trees. The weekend away gave me the headspace to really think about what I want and about the person I want to be."

"Well, it seems you have it all figured out and of course I want you to be happy, but I would have thought we could talk and think about these things together and then decide together."

Clara said nothing because she knew if she had discussed it with him he might have fobbed her off. If something didn't suit Richard, he pushed it down the line until she got tired of asking about it. But not this time.

"So, I hear what you're saying," Richard said, "and I would never force you to have another child if you don't want to. So just to be clear about everything, are we really ruling out having another baby?"

Oh for *fuck's* sake, she thought. He's still not listening to me.

"*One hundred percent, Richard.* I do not want another baby. My mind is made up."

"Okay," he said, getting up from the table. "Sure, give the job a try and let's see how things go," he said, patting her hand.

What the fuck does that mean, Clara wanted to shout at him, but she didn't. She didn't want to talk about it anymore. She was never having another baby and she had already accepted Vivienne's job offer. She was doing this whether he liked it or not. And the bastard didn't say anything about her hair either. Didn't he even see her anymore? *Fuck him!*

Chapter 38

Helen had been surprised to see Jerry at the train station, but she had taken it as a good sign. She was confused though because he knew she had her car with her. But he said he had been called out to a job and was passing the train station so he decided to pop in. He looked very well so Helen was happy to show him off to Vivienne and Clara.

"Only the three of you?" he had asked.

"No, Miriam is with us, but she left something on the train," Helen said.

With the introductions done, Vivienne and Clara headed off and Helen headed back to the car park with Jerry.

"Can we talk later, Jerry, when the kids go to bed?"

"Eh, sure," he answered, distracted.

"It's just that I've had loads of time to think, and I have loads I want to tell you."

"Sure, yeah, great, let's do that. I'll see you at home," he said, kissing her on the cheek.

How nice of him to meet me, Helen thought as she put her bag in the boot of her car. But then she wondered, did he show up to make sure I wasn't going to drive with a drink on me? That has to be it, she thought, deflated. Okay, well, I'd better show him that I am going to change because I am so lucky to have him, and we have such a good marriage. I don't want to become like Viv and Tom.

She got in the car and drove out of the station.

At home that evening, after the boys finally went to bed, Helen sat down in the kitchen to tell Jerry her plans as he was washing the pots.

"Do you want to sit down, and we can talk?"

"It's okay, I can hear you from here and I don't want to leave these," Jerry said, scrubbing away.

"Okay then, I had a fantastic weekend, and I had a lot of time to think about everything you said."

"About your drinking, you mean?"

"*Em*, well, yes, amongst other things." That was a bit blunt, Helen thought, but maybe I deserved that. "Part of the reason for my drinking is that I have been feeling crap, you know, physically. The night sweats, hot flushes, mood swings, and no libido are all menopause symptoms as well as low mood, and low energy. I was worn out with the kids, and I had no energy to get up and change things, so it was easier to just sit down on the couch and have a few drinks and ..."

"A few bottles, you mean," Jerry said without looking around.

"Yeah, okay, maybe sometimes." Why is he being so tetchy? "Well, anyway, I met this lovely massage therapist, and we got talking and she said all my symptoms were classic menopause and she recommended a specialist place in Dublin. So, first thing tomorrow I am going to get an appointment to sort that out."

Jerry said nothing and continued washing the pots.

"Can you sit down? I don't like talking to your back."

Jerry finished what he was doing, dried his hands on a tea towel and sat down.

"Okay," he said, "what's next?"

"Well, I mentioned to this therapist that I had done an aromatherapy course and I had loved it and, so, I decided there and then that I want to get qualified. I need something for me outside the house. It doesn't suit me to be here all day. I need something for myself, and we could do with the extra few bob coming in although it won't be much at first. It is also a job that I could work around the kids and term time, when I get my own clients."

"That's great news. It sounds very doable. How much will it cost? To get qualified?"

"I don't know exactly, but I can do a six-month course part-time which will be cheaper and that will bring me up to scratch. Then I can get some work experience and then apply for jobs or expand my skills."

"Okay, well, that all sounds great," Jerry said, fidgeting with the placemat.

"Are you okay?"

"Me? Yeah, why?"

"You just sound very flat. I thought you might be more enthusiastic, that's all."

"I am happy for you. It sounds like a step in the right direction. But doing a course isn't going to fix everything, you know. You can plan all you like but you need to tackle the drinking first, or it will all go pear-shaped."

Helen looked down at the table. This was not going how she thought it would go.

"Look, I'm not getting on your case. It's hard to stop drinking and I'm just a little nervous that you'll slip back if you don't have outside help, and you haven't said anything about that."

"I have stopped, Jerry, and I won't slip back, I promise. I finally have a plan and I really want it to work. I'm going to get rid of any drink out of the house now."

"It's already done. I emptied anything I found open, and the rest have gone up to my mum's."

"Oh …. great," Helen said but her heart sank a bit.

"So, is that it?" Jerry said, getting up from the table.

"*Um*, well, I have the name of a therapist from Miriam too that I might call if I need to."

"Miriam has a therapist?"

"Yes. Poor thing has been through the wringer the past year. But you're tired so I won't bore you."

"No, no, I'm intrigued, tell me what's going on there," Jerry said, sitting back down at the table.

"Well, her mother has dementia, very bad, and poor Miriam was left doing all the care until she was completely worn out. Her brother and sister are fighting with her because Miriam has suggested putting their mother in a home. It's very stressful."

"*Hmm*, but you said she was pregnant."

"Yes, by a donor, can you imagine? Sure, she had no time to meet anyone, and she's not getting any younger so …"

"So, she went to a donor clinic? I didn't even know we had them here."

"Oh yes, well, it's very interesting actually. She told us all about it. It's a very stressful process and – "

"When is she due?"

"Early April, I think. You're very curious, Jerry. I hope you're not getting clucky, because that is a road I am definitely not going down again!" Helen laughed but Jerry seemed to be miles away. "I'm going to bed – are you coming?"

"*Em* no, I'm staying up for a bit. You go ahead."

Helen left him in the kitchen. She had hoped he would be more enthusiastic about her plans but maybe his belief in her was too low for him to get excited. I'll just have to prove to myself and Jerry that I can change. And with that she went off to bed, thankful for such a wonderful husband and determined to make him proud of her.

Meanwhile, in the kitchen, Jerry sat with his head in his hands, trying to work out the dates. He felt sick. By his calculations, Miriam could be pregnant with his baby. The day he was there she got the letter saying that she was not pregnant, so it had to have happened after that. Could she really have had another round of donor sperm and all the tests that went with that after they had sex and got pregnant immediately? It seemed too much of a coincidence.

But the possibility that he was the father of her baby wasn't the only problem. He had gone to the station to see Miriam, even for a minute. At the time, in her house he'd felt sure that it had been a mistake and he felt terrible for cheating on Helen. But since then, he could not stop thinking of Miriam. He had replayed their lovemaking over and over in his mind. Her touch, her smell, how she felt, how wild and free she had looked. He just could not stop thinking about her. She had seemed so lost, and he felt so protective of her. She made him feel alive again. And now with a baby coming, possibly his baby, he just had to see her.

Chapter 39

Seeing Jerry turn up at the train station had shaken Miriam. Was he there for her or was he there for Helen? She knew she would have to see him and convince him the baby was not his and put an end to this. Then he started texting her. She ignored his first text but, as he knew where she lived, she didn't want him turning up on her doorstep, so she texted him and asked him to call over later that week, after she had spoken to Sharon and Simon.

As soon as she got home to her house, she rooted out an old appointment letter from the donor clinic. With a little copying and editing, she managed to produce a letter confirming that her donor implantation had been successful and congratulating her on a positive pregnancy test. She would show it to Jerry when he arrived, but she wouldn't let him keep it as she didn't want him ringing the clinic. As a dad of four already, Miriam reckoned he would be relieved and then they'd have no reason to contact each other again.

Since returning from Galway refreshed and rested, she'd had nothing but conflict and confrontation from her brother and sister over the care of her mother. She had taken a taxi straight from the train station to her mother's house where Simon and Sharon were waiting for her. Sharon's face was priceless when she saw Miriam's bump. Since telling the girls over the weekend and deciding not to hide her pregnancy anymore, her bump seemed to have grown or maybe her muscles had relaxed. Either way, there was no denying she was pregnant now.

Sharon was furious, of course, that she had not told them sooner and accused her of dumping them in this situation with their mum. Simon was kinder though. Seeing his younger sister pregnant and on her own seemed to soften him a bit and this time, for the first time, he sided with Miriam about the future care of their mother.

Predictably Sharon lost the plot, but Miriam didn't care anymore.

"Sharon, I can't do this anymore," she had said.

"And what about the baby's father? Can't he help out or has he legged it?" she snarled.

"I told you in the email that I went to a donor clinic. I will be raising this baby myself," Miriam had said, putting her hand on her bump, feeling protective of the little one.

"Some life that child will have," Sharon said under her breath.

"Sharon, that's enough!" Simon said. "We are here to deal with Mum's care and that is all!"

Sharon glared at him.

"I know I have taken your side in the past," he went on, "but I stayed here with Mum for two nights while Miriam was away, and it was a nightmare. We can't do it anymore. She needs full-time care."

"Well, I don't agree," Sharon said, folding her arms defiantly.

"*You weren't here!*" Simon shouted at her. "*You are never here!*"

"*I was here on Saturday!*" Sharon shouted back.

"For two hours, Sharon! Try twelve hours and see how you feel then!"

"The kids had stuff on. I'm here when I can be!"

"Exactly," said Simon, lowering his voice. "Your kids have stuff on, I want to do more with my family and Miriam has a baby on the way. We can't do it anymore."

Miriam sat back and said nothing. She had said all she wanted to say in the email.

"I need time to think about this," Sharon said and then, out of the blue, she started to cry. "I hate this! I hate that we have to do this!"

"We all do," Miriam said, reaching over and squeezing her sister's hand. "I wish we could keep on looking after Mum here, but we can't. I wish things were different, but they are not."

"Okay," Simon said, "we need a plan. Why don't we set up a meeting with the woman from the Alzheimer's Association and let's take the tour of the nursing home and see how we feel then? We can't afford to keep paying for all this private home care, Sharon – you've seen the figures Miriam did up. Something has to change."

Just then, as if to prove Simon's point, Annie came into the kitchen with her swim bag looking for a bucket and spade to take to the beach even though it was 8 pm on a winter's night in December. Miriam smiled and brought her into the living room while Simon and Sharon stayed in the kitchen to talk it out.

By the time Miriam had got their mother to bed, Sharon had agreed to meet for the nursing-home tour as soon as possible. Miriam could have seen it as a victory but there were no winners in this situation. She just wanted her mother safe and cared for and, despite their differences, she knew Sharon wanted this too.

They arranged to visit the local nursing home. Miriam had been there before, of course, and she was delighted and relieved to see how impressed Simon and Sharon were with the place. It was the week before Christmas and the nursing home was decorated so nicely.

The day they were there, a local man was providing entertainment, treating the residents to a Christmas sing-along. The nursing home manager brought them into the big hall where the concert was taking place, and it was a joy to see the residents sing along to all their favourite carols. Some were up dancing with the nurses and carers.

Miriam was very moved by the scene and when the wonderful entertainer sang "Silent Night", tears rolled down her cheeks.

"I think we'll move on now," the manager said, offering Miriam a tissue as they left.

The rooms were lovely too and the three siblings, over a cup of tea in the canteen, agreed to put their mother's name down that day. It was the first time they had agreed on anything in over twenty years.

There was a place available immediately, but they decided to spend one last Christmas Eve and Christmas Day together in their mum's house where they all grew up.

It turned out to be one of the best Christmases ever. Annie was delighted, and more than a little confused, at having everyone there. She kept wandering around asking where her mother was and why she hadn't made dinner for their guests.

On Christmas Eve Miriam and Simon stayed and watched an old movie on the couch with Annie. Then Simon helped Miriam get her to bed before he headed home to do Santa for his daughter.

Christmas morning Simon, his wife and daughter, and Sharon,

her husband, and all her kids with their toys filled the house with noise and laughter. There were some tears too, but the younger children kept everything light with their joy of Christmas and the gifts they received. The three siblings cooked most of the food at home and brought it to the house for a great Christmas Day feast.

Then on St Stephen's Day they packed a bag for their mum and walked from the house to the nursing home.

Annie was delighted with her room and she thought she was on holiday in a hotel. They all had a little cry when they left but they knew she was in the best place for her now, to keep her safe and happy. As it was so close to the family home, they could bring her favourite ornaments and photo albums to her over the coming weeks. They agreed to visit her one night a week each and then one of them on a Saturday or a Sunday. They also decided to hang on to their mother's house for the moment. Sometime in the new year they would figure out if they would sell it to pay for her nursing-home care or rent it out. Those decisions could wait a bit. Their main concern was settling Annie into her new home. Her old neighbours were also able to visit as it was close by for them too. All in all, it couldn't be better.

Sharon dropped in a bag of baby clothes and baby blankets to Miriam and offered to help out the first few days after the baby came home. Miriam was more than delighted at the gesture and it also made the birth seem very real. She actually hadn't thought as far as the birth or birth partners. She should ask Vivienne this weekend if she would be her birthing partner. Although they weren't super close, she liked Vivienne's no-nonsense approach whereas Clara might be too emotional, and she couldn't ask Helen for obvious reasons. She was so looking forward to meeting her baby now.

Jerry arrived later that week as arranged. Miriam had left work early to go home and have a rest before he arrived.

After an hour's sleep, she had a long hot shower and was massaging in moisturizer when the doorbell rang. She went to the window to see Jerry's work van outside. *Shit*, he was an hour early. Cursing him, she grabbed her silk kimono and went downstairs to answer the door.

"You're an hour early," she said as she opened the door.

"I'm sorry, I couldn't wait, so when I drove by and saw your car, I had to call in."

"Come in then," Miriam said, standing aside to let him pass. Oh god, that cologne again, he smells so good, she thought as he turned sideways towards her to get by her in her narrow hallway.

Her eyes took in his broad shoulders as he walked ahead of her into the kitchen. She couldn't deny he looked good but tried to push this from her mind. Be professional, she thought, closing her kimono tighter over her chest while realising she was completely naked underneath it.

"Would you like a cup of –"

"Miriam, I have been going mad. I have to know, is the baby mine?"

"No, Jerry, it's not."

Jerry sat down at the kitchen table and put his head in his hands.

"The father is a sperm donor."

"But the dates, it's very close to when you and me ... you know."

"*Fucked?* Is that the word you're looking for?"

"Ah, don't say it like that."

"You can relax, Jerry," Miriam said, still standing up, leaning against the worktop with her arms crossed over her chest.

"I'm sorry, I'm all over the place. It's all I have been thinking about."

"I have the letter here from the clinic," she said, opening the kitchen drawer. "Have a look at it while I make you a cuppa. You look like you need one."

When she handed him the letter he looked into her eyes and the chemistry between them filled the room. It was like an electric shock. Miriam blushed and turned away quickly, taking mugs out of the press and switching the kettle on to distract herself.

She heard him open the letter and sigh.

"Tea or coffee," she said, trying to sound cheery.

"I don't want a drink," he said, standing up and coming around the table to where she was. She felt his presence behind her and was so aroused she could not turn around.

"Miriam, look at me."

"Jerry, I don't think ..."

"No, listen," he said, touching her gently on the shoulder.

Her head spun and her legs felt weak as she turned around to face him. There was less than a foot between them. She steadied herself by holding on to the worktop.

"When I said it's all I've been thinking about, I meant you."

"Jerry, don't," Miriam said, but she didn't mean it.

"I can't stop thinking about you. I know it's unfair. Helen and the boys, well ... I can't offer you anything but all I can think about is you and the last time I was here."

"I'm pregnant," Miriam said, standing straight now and meeting his eye.

"You're beautiful," he whispered, stroking her jawline with his finger.

Miriam knew it was wrong, but her body felt differently. She was incredibly aroused, and she could feel her nipples harden under her silk kimono.

Keeping eye contact with Jerry, she loosened the belt of the kimono, allowing the silk to slide down her naked body to the floor. She had given him his answer. She watched as his eyes slowly scanned her body. He looked up, his eyes wild with lust for her. She felt powerful and sexy as she pulled him to her, bringing his head down to her mouth. He kissed her hungrily. She pulled back and then guided his head to her enlarged breasts. He threw his jacket off and knelt before her, moving his mouth down her body. One hand massaged her breast and the other moved down between her legs, making her moan and cling on to the worktop. He gently spread her legs with both hands and allowed his mouth to follow where his hand had been. He raised her leg over his shoulder and, with his head between her legs, Miriam arched her back as her body shuddered in ecstasy.

And so, without discussion or negotiation, Jerry started making twice-weekly calls to see Miriam. In her head, she separated the Jerry who came and made love to her twice a week, and the Jerry who was married to her friend and father of four children. That was not her concern. She had stood by and seen friends get married or set up homes with their partners. But she hadn't met someone to do that with. She always felt like the spare friend left out of that cosy picture, so why shouldn't she enjoy this? She was single and had no responsibilities yet and she had never met a man who could arouse her like Jerry could. She wasn't going to give this up any time soon.

Chapter 40

Helen looked at the piece of paper in her hand as she stood outside a redbrick Georgian house on Dublin's Merrion Square. She was in the right place. A plaque on the wall told her the therapist's office was in the basement. Her stomach churned and she had to fight the urge to walk away. She could walk away, nobody would know, except the therapist of course, because she hadn't told anybody that she was coming here. She had typed the therapist's name into her phone when Miriam had mentioned her in Galway and had contacted the secretary the week she returned.

Things had been going well since she got back from Galway. She had seen the menopause expert who had been so understanding that Helen had cried with relief when she said that her symptoms were typical menopause symptoms and that she was not clinically depressed. She started on HRT patches straight away and noticed a difference within two weeks. The night sweats and hot flushes were gone, she slept so much better and her bad and dark mood had lifted. The HRT was working and making life less stressful and the house calmer. The aromatherapy course had started after

Christmas and Helen loved getting out of the house to attend her classes every week. The course involved online work and modules to be completed at home so that kept her busy too. But two things were not working for her. Jerry was very distant. He didn't seem interested when she told him what she was doing on the course. She was not falling asleep on the couch with a bottle of wine anymore but, if he was happy about this, he didn't show it. He wouldn't come near her in bed either. He made excuses about being tired but then stayed up until the early hours watching programmes on Netflix. Helen knew he was avoiding her. She felt so bad about this. Clearly, it was her fault, having been such a lush before, and it was going to take time to rebuild their connection. Helen hoped the therapist would help her with this and try to fix her past behaviours so that Jerry could trust her again. Maybe he might even come for some couples counselling further down the line.

The other reason she was here was that in fact she had not stopped drinking and found it hard to stop. She was secretly drinking now. She was sure Jerry had no idea, but she wanted to stop. She totally discounted going to AA as that was for real alcoholics, not for people like her. Helen was sure the therapist would see this and just give her some coping tricks maybe. Taking a deep breath, she went down the basement steps and pushed the buzzer.

An older lady took her name and payment before directing her to a consulting room. The room was calm and quiet. The walls were beige, and the comfortable chairs were brown with a soft cream throw on the arm rest. There were boxes of tissues on a small table beside the chair and on the coffee table in front of her. Helen sat down and waited. There seemed to be two consulting rooms that the therapist worked between. That makes sense, thought Helen, as this meant the 'clients' never saw each other.

I mean, imagine if Miriam and I were sitting in the same waiting room ready to bare our souls, Helen thought and laughed.

Just then the door opened and a woman in her forties entered and introduced herself.

"I'm Cathy Doherty. Pleased to meet you, Helen."

Helen stood up and shook her hand. She wasn't sure what she had been expecting but Cathy Doherty was very relaxed-looking in black trousers and a black turtleneck jumper. Her hair was loosely tied back with a hair brooch, and she had lovely soft brown eyes. She could easily have been one of the mums at the school gate.

"I *um* ... I've never been to a therapist before, so I don't know what it entails. Do I just tell you about my present situation? Or about my previous life? My family history?"

"Yes, tell me all about yourself so I can get a full picture. Take your time," said Cathy, sitting in a chair opposite Helen. She crossed her legs and opened a notebook.

Helen took a deep breath and began to talk. Eventually she reached her life and its difficulties leading up to the Galway weekend. Then she told Cathy about the changes she had implemented since then and that she was getting her life in order and just needed some advice about her marriage and help with her drinking.

"Okay, well, we have a lot to unpack there, Helen. There have been a lot of changes in a short space of time. Let's talk about the drinking first. There is some resistance in you to stop drinking altogether. So can we go back to when you first started drinking?"

"Do you mean, drinking to sleep? I think that was just stress."

"No, I mean the very first time you ever drank, why you started, and what you thought of it."

"The very first time? Like when I was a teenager?"

"Yes, please."

"Oh well, okay," Helen said hesitantly.

This is going to take up the whole hour, she thought, slightly irritated.

"I was a late starter when it came to drinking. All my friends started drinking around sixteen years of age. Not often, of course, because we had very little money but when a few of us got paid for our summer jobs, we would buy some cans of beer or cider, usually on a Saturday night and head off to the local park to drink them. I hated the smell and taste of the drink. When the cans were passed around my way, I would pretend to drink some and then pass the can on. The smell of drink repulsed me because it reminded me of my grandfather. My grandfather was an alcoholic, a drunk. Back then people would say he 'liked a drink'. He was a quiet man who said very little. He was a quiet drinker but a daily drinker. He always smelt of whiskey or Guinness and his clothes smelt of rolled cigarettes. My mother never said much about Grandad's drinking, but she did say that money was tight and that her mother used to have to hide money around the house because if Grandad got his hands on it, he would take it and go off to the pub. Every Saturday my mum used to take us to visit Grandma and Grandad and I would be forced to hug him. The smell of drink from him would make me gag. He just sat there in his chair. He looked so old when, in fact, he was only in his fifties. He may have had his own reasons for drinking, as he had a tough upbringing, but whatever the reasons he kept them locked away in his head. It is sad really that the only memories I have of him are of an old man sitting in a chair smelling of stale booze. So, I vowed back then that I would never drink because I didn't want to look or smell like Grandad. Instead, I faked the drinking and pretended to be drunk sometimes but mostly I took on the role of minder, making sure that my friends were okay. I always brought a packet of mints with me to help them cover up the smell of drink."

Helen patted her pocket at this memory and felt the old familiar bulge of a packet of mints in her pocket. She blushed when she realised she never left home without them now. She put her head in her hands.

The therapist said nothing, allowing the silence to stay between them as Helen gathered her thoughts.

"I haven't thought about Grandad in years," she said, not raising her head, not wanting to meet the therapist's eye. "In fact, I don't think I have ever told anyone about Grandad and his drinking. I have never associated my drinking with his drinking. He was an embarrassment. Repulsive." Helen felt ill saying that word.

"What is it, Helen?"

Helen felt embarrassed. "I just wonder if that's how Jerry, my husband, feels about me. If he finds me repulsive or an embarrassment." She thought back to the times he found her on the couch surrounded by empty wine bottles, unable to drive the kids to school. "Oh god, I feel sick just thinking about it."

"Has your husband said anything to you to make you believe this?"

"No, not exactly, but he did say things needed to change and they have. I have cut down a lot and neither he nor the kids see me drinking now."

"Do you drink alone?"

"Yes, I hide it. I know that sounds bad, but it's just until I can sort myself out."

"What about the rest of your family? Have they ever said anything about your drinking?"

"No. Well ... yes, my mother, but she was overreacting."

Helen looked away. These memories were painful as they came forward. How many times had her mother remarked on her drinking? She had told Helen she knew that look and had begged her to get help. Helen had told her she was being ridiculous. She had been so angry with her mother for bringing it up but, of course, her mother had seen it all before.

"Okay, well, I think we will leave it there for today, Helen."

"Oh I see," Helen said looking at her watch. She couldn't believe how fast the time had gone.

"There is a lot to think about and pick through. Over the week, I would like you to think about what makes you drink now. What are the triggers, how do you feel when you don't drink? Notice the urges and see if you can distract yourself instead. Get yourself a notebook or a jotter and write down anything that comes up. Don't think about it too much, just write whatever comes into your head and bring the notebook when you come back to see me. I would like to see you back here at this time next week if that's okay and we can go through how the exercise went for you."

"*Em*, okay," Helen said, getting to her feet.

She felt shaky as she left. This is not how she thought things would go at all. How did they spend the whole hour talking about her drinking? She had a lot more she wanted to talk about. Still, where did those memories come from? She hadn't thought about her grandad in years.

Helen let herself out and climbed the steps to the street. Pausing, she took a deep breath. Holding onto the wall, she felt lightheaded and drained. I am nothing like him, she thought, nothing like that sad man smelling of drink and despair. Then Helen realised she had replaced her wine-drinking with vodka. Vodka had no smell. Helen shuddered and walked towards her car, patting her pocket, making sure she hadn't forgotten her mints.

Wexford

Chapter 41

Vivienne emailed the girls the directions to her mum and dad's cottage and the plan was for everyone to meet there for elevenses on Saturday morning. From Vivienne's house on Dublin's southside, the cottage was just under a two-hour drive. As it was February and nobody had been to the cottage since November, Vivienne took a half-day from work on the Friday to arrive early and get the cottage ready for the girls. She was looking forward to having some headspace Friday afternoon before everyone arrived on Saturday. The cottage would be freezing so she wanted to switch on all the electric heaters and keep the fire lighting to warm it for their arrival. She popped into Marks and Spencer's in Blackrock and picked up a lasagne, some garlic bread, and some salads for dinner that night. She also got some breakfast items, some snacks, sweet treats, six bottles of wine, a bottle of gin, a bottle of rum, some tonic, and a tray of Diet Coke. She was very sure they would get through all of it.

Her parents bought the holiday cottage twenty years before and from March to November spent at least one weekend a month down there. Every summer when the kids were younger Vivienne spent at least two weeks in the cottage during the kids' school holidays. She also tried to get down for a few days over Easter and midterm breaks. Sometimes Tom would come for all of it or, if he was busy with work, he would join them at the weekends. Over the years Vivienne's kids had made friends with other kids who came down at the same time every year. The older the kids got, the less they needed Vivienne. They would run out and play in the communal playground for all the holiday cottages in the estate, coming in only when they were hungry or tired. This allowed Vivienne to completely relax and read books she never had time to read when she was working so hard in Dublin.

She also loved spending time down here with her parents. Everybody relaxed here, and the quiet and fresh air was a tonic and a gift that Vivienne treasured. The beach was a fifteen-minute walk away and Vivienne loved to take long beach walks all year round.

Arriving at the cottage, all the summer memories came back to her. She was so thankful that this was her parents' cottage and that it had nothing to do with Tom, therefore it was not a consideration in the legal separation and couldn't be touched by Tom or his solicitors. It would be a place that Vivienne and her kids could come to for many years to come.

Vivienne pulled into the little driveway at the front of the cottage. It was raining lightly but the cottage looked very welcoming. The dormer had a black slate roof with a bedroom window in it. The walls were whitewashed, and the small cottage window frames were painted bright-red to match the red wooden front door. A withered creeper was attached to the wall and trained over the door and when the early summer arrived it would bloom with white roses, giving off a beautiful scent. Her parents kept the cottage in great order. They put a lot of work into its upkeep and Vivienne was forever grateful to them for that.

Turning the key in the door, Vivienne smiled as she carried her bags into the narrow hallway. Her walking boots were on a shelf beside her parents' and children's boots. Hanging over them were an array of walking jackets, rain jackets, and fleeces. A shelf over the coats held different types of hats, from sun hats to rain hats to baseball hats. It felt good to be back. The short hallway opened up to the open-plan sitting room.

She turned to the left and put her bags down on the kitchen table. The kitchen was small, a fraction the size of her own at home but it still had everything you needed. There was a twin bedroom and a bathroom downstairs and another bigger twin and a huge double room upstairs as well as a full-sized family bathroom.

Downstairs a conservatory had been added by her parents, adding light and extra space so although it looked like a little cottage with small windows at the front, it opened up to a bright airy open-plan area inside. As soon as Vivienne arrived and unpacked, she could feel the stresses of her Dublin life disappear. After putting the food away, she put all the heaters on and lit the fire. Putting the fireguard up, she wrapped up and headed out for a walk on the beach. It was cold and windy but the perfect weather to clear her head. The beach was deserted except for a woman walking her dog. Vivienne nodded as she passed her, wrapping her scarf tighter around her as she walked against the wind. She loved the wildness of the beach in winter. The wind whipped up the waves and they crashed noisily on the beach shore. There was no time today to stand and look out at the waves, so she walked as far as she could and then turned back as the clouds got darker.

The weather forecast was for wind and heavy rain tonight, but a lovely crisp sunny start was forecast for the morning when the girls would be arriving. Vivienne was really looking forward to seeing them all again. They had become closer over that weekend in Galway. Vivienne had gone with her own agenda but each of them had had something big happening in their lives. They had kept in touch via their WhatsApp group and so many changes had taken place since then.

Vivienne had seen Clara of course, as she was now working in the office. She was an absolute godsend. The staff loved her. She managed to be very organised while keeping everyone happy in her gentle way. It took a weight off Vivienne's shoulders having her on board, and it freed her up to pursue other projects. But the job suited Clara too, and behind that sweet smile was a steely determination to do this job right. Vivienne could see that Clara was changing things in all aspects of her life and she was glad to help with that. It would be nice to sit around with the girls and see what else had happened since they last met. And Miriam was more than seven months pregnant now so she definitely would look different.

Vivienne walked faster now as the wind swirled around her and the rain started to spit. When she got back to the cottage, it was warm and cosy. She topped up the fire with some more briquettes and a little coal. There was plenty of hot water, so she ran a bath and added relaxation oils that she had brought with her. When the bath was ready she put the lasagne in the oven, poured herself a glass of red wine and took it upstairs to the bathroom with her. Soaking in the bath and listening to the wind outside, all Vivienne's stresses melted away. This was exactly what she needed after a very difficult eight weeks.

Stepping out of the bath, she applied the luxury moisturizer she had brought with her as she watched the water go down the plughole. She applied a hair product to her hair and shook it to let her hair air dry. She used to be so particular about her hair, applying products and straightening it and spraying it so no hair would move. But now she wasn't that fussed. She had relaxed her image and felt more like herself. Of course, she tied it up to look professional in work but, apart from that, her naturally wavy hair fell around her shoulders as it used to before she was married.

The wind was howling outside now, and the rain was beating against the windows. The storm they predicted was currently over the southeast. Vivienne changed into a pair of leggings, put on a cute tea dress over them and pulled on a chunky oversized cardigan over the dress. She finished her look off with a big pair of fleecy socks and headed downstairs to put another log on the fire.

She put some music on from her Spotify playlist and checked the lasagne and turn the oven down. As she topped up her wine glass, she heard a car outside and saw the reflection of car headlights on the kitchen window. She heard the car door shut and then the knock on her door. Looking at her watch, she smiled as she got up to answer the door.

"Well, well, Mr. Brady, right on time," she said as she opened the door for him.

"I hate to keep a lady waiting," Jack said as he stepped in, dropped his bag, and scooped her into his arms. He kissed her long and hard while shutting the door with his foot. The timer on the cooker went off to say that the lasagne was ready but neither of them cared.

Chapter 42

Clara drove down the dark country lanes of County Wexford, listening attentively to her satnav. It was a rainy Friday afternoon and getting dark already at only four o'clock and a stormy night was forecast. She was a little nervous when she turned off the N11 and drove down the many winding roads, wanting to get there as soon as she could. She was relieved when she saw the sign for Monart Hotel and Spa. The electric gates opened and before her, lit up in the dark, was the 18th century Georgian Manor which was the 5-star Monart Hotel. Set in over one hundred acres of woodland, Monart Destination Spa was one of the top spas in Ireland if not the world.

Clara pulled up outside the main door and a young man came out to greet her.

"Good evening, Ms. Byrne. If I may, I would like to park your car for you and bring your bags inside. You go ahead to reception."

"Thank you, that would be lovely, my bag is in the boot," Clara said, giving him the keys.

Another staff member was waiting at the door to direct her to reception. The service here was second to none. The walk from the main door to reception was lined with candles. Relaxing spa music was piped through the system and the air was filled with the scent of various aromatherapy oils. It was a refuge from the wind and rain that was making its way across the country.

"Good afternoon, Ms. Byrne, you are very welcome to Monart," the friendly girl behind the reception greeted her. She looked like a Scandinavian model. Her blonde hair was tied back neatly and her piercingly bright-blue eyes were beautiful. "Your room is ready for you. And your massage is booked for 6 pm so I took the liberty of ordering a tray of refreshments to your room for you while you unpack. Would you like me to book a table for dinner later?"

"No, thank you. I was hoping to have my meal in my room if that's okay?"

"Of course, I will have menus delivered to your room. Marina will take you to your room now. Enjoy your stay."

Clara followed another lovely girl, Marina, to her room, and oh what a room it was! It was the biggest hotel room she had ever stayed in. Marina showed her around. The king-size bed took up only a third of the room. Clara glanced into the bathroom where a free-standing bath and footstool took centre stage. A dressing table ran along a wall of muted earthy colours and a round table with two chairs in the centre of the room had some arrival chocolate strawberries on it.

She followed Marina over to a luxury couch that looked out onto a balcony. Marina explained that the garden was an award-winning holistic garden. Out past the garden Clara could see the property's dark woods with mature trees that had been there for generations. She felt like she could look out into those dark trees for hours.

A gentle tap on the door heralded the arrival of a tray of refreshments and treats – a selection of miniature sandwiches and mixed fruit carved as flowers, arranged beautifully.

"Thank you so much, this looks delicious."

"You're welcome," the girl said as she placed the tray on the sideboard table.

"The spa is on the ground floor and your therapist will meet you there at six. Enjoy your stay," Marina said as she left and closed the door quietly behind her.

Clara threw her coat on the bed and kicked off her shoes. She poured herself a tall glass of herbal tea and took the plate of chocolate-covered strawberries with her, to sit on the couch. Although it was pitch dark outside now, the specially located lighting in the grounds showed off the grasses and various specialty trees. She could see a babbling brook and a small Japanese bridge lit up too.

She sipped her tea and took a deep breath.

She would love to ring Richard and tell him about the room, but Richard didn't know she was here. He thought she was in Vivienne's cottage. She didn't feel guilty about lying to him. She needed a night away by herself. She told him she was going to the cottage for two nights and there was no way he would find out differently. Things had been strained between them since she returned from Galway, and she didn't need the hassle of explaining why she wanted a night away on her own. He wouldn't understand and his questioning would only irritate her. Clara shuddered and brushed the thoughts away. I am tired of analyzing the situation, she thought as she got up and started to unpack her overnight bag.

She hung up her clothes for tomorrow then undressed and put

on the beautiful white fluffy robe that lay across the bed. Finishing off her peppermint tea, she removed her make-up, slipped on the complimentary slippers, and picked up her room key. I will not waste any time thinking about Richard, she thought as she looked around her beautiful room. This time is for me, and I bloody deserve it. She closed the door behind her and headed down to the spa.

Chapter 43

Helen threw a few things in a holdall. These eight weeks had come around very quickly. She thought that she would feel more together and have her life on the right track, but she still felt a little chaotic. Some things had improved though. Her aromatherapy massage course was going well, and she had some work experience coming up. She was looking forward to practising what she had learned so far.

She had visited her GP for a checkup, and she had been so kind that Helen felt comfortable mentioning that she had been relying on a few drinks a night to help her sleep and to lower her stress levels. The doctor explained how the sugar in alcohol increased the night sweats, which in turn woke you up, so she suggested that Helen try to cut the evening drinking out and see if that helped. She also gave Helen leaflets about the cancer link for women who drank more than the recommended amount, and a separate leaflet on women and drinking that had helplines and a list of AA meetings in the area. She was kind and not judgemental at all and Helen felt so much better for speaking to her.

Not everything was perfect: she still got tired and craved a drink. Sometimes the craving was so strong it manifested as real physical pain. Helen tried not to give in but some days it was just too hard. She had a small bottle of vodka in her backpack that she kept upstairs in the back of her wardrobe, and she always kept Diet Coke in the fridge. Once the kids were fed in the evening and she didn't have to go out or drive the kids anywhere she sneaked upstairs and had a small drink of vodka and Coke to ease her pain. This didn't happen every night.

Normally she used anything she could to distract her from wanting a drink. She went for a walk most nights. Sometimes one of the kids came on their bike and Helen looked forward to these little one-on-ones now. She felt guilty when the kids noticed she was singing or dancing and said, 'Mum, you are so happy today'. It reminded her that she must have been so hard to live with and cranky and tired all the time. She knew things weren't perfect and she felt so guilty when she sneaked upstairs for a drink, but it was way better than all the bottles of wine she used to consume a week. And no more hiding the bottles around the house so Jerry couldn't see how much she was drinking. No, Helen was feeling proud and just trying to take every week as it came.

"I have to get going," Miriam said, sitting up in bed. It was ten o'clock already and she was supposed to meet the girls in Wexford at half-eleven. Being organised, her overnight bag was packed just waiting for her toiletries.

"Can't you stay a little longer?"

"No, Jerry," Miriam said with a laugh, "and you need to get back to those kids. You farmed them out to other parents for the football training today, but they'll be back soon!"

"You're right," he said, sitting up and kissing Miriam's bare shoulder.

She turned to him and gave him a long slow kiss and then got out of bed.

"*Aw*, come on, you can't leave me like this!" he said, pulling back the sheets and exposing his erection.

"I will take a mental picture of that and carry it around in my head, until the next time," Miriam said, smiled coyly.

"*Hmm*, the next time, and when might that be?" Jerry said, leaning back on the pillows with his arms behind his head, watching Miriam dress.

"You text me when you're free, and I will consider your request," Miriam said, flinging his socks at him. "Now get up and get out, I'm running late."

"You're such a romantic!" he said, jumping up and wrapping his arms around her from behind.

Miriam giggled but then moaned as he sucked on her neck and his hands cupped her bare breasts. She held on to the wardrobe to steady herself as one of his hands reached down between her legs. She moaned louder and opened her legs wider. His breath got heavier as he licked her ear.

"We can … can't …" Miriam panted but when Jerry moved his hand away she pushed it back and bent over, spreading her legs as much as she could so he could enter her. Let them wait, she thought as her jewellery and hairbrushes fell from the dressing table to the floor from the rocking of the wardrobe.

Clara woke and stretched out in a star shape in the big king-sized hotel bed. Every muscle in her body felt relaxed. Lying there enjoying the silence, a thought occurred to her. When was the last time she had had such a refreshing night's sleep? Had she been tense sleeping beside Richard since returning from Galway without realising it? They weren't exactly fighting but they weren't exactly getting along either.

She had done everything she could to make going back to work as easy as possible for everyone. She went into the office every morning after dropping the kids to school and Seán to creche. She made sure to leave in time to collect the kids when school was finished and did whatever housework needed to be done in the afternoon. When Richard came home from work his dinner was ready and things were the same as they had always been, for him anyway. Clara was tired but she made it work because she loved being back at work. It was so wonderful to be out of the house, meeting new people. The chats with the staff over coffee gave her life. Most of the staff were young, so there was no talk about kids which was great. Clara loved joining in on the chat about the latest celebrity gossip or new Netflix series gripping everyone. She even joined Twitter so she could see what topics were trending without having to know too much about them.

She felt like she was getting her energy and her life back. On the days when the schools were closed, she could work from home. Vivienne had given her a brand-new company laptop and she set up a little space in the corner of the dining room to work from. She gave all the staff her mobile number so that anyone could contact her at home if they needed to. Everything was working out so well on the work front but at home things were not so great.

Richard had no interest in her work. Occasionally he asked how work was going but when she started to go into the details his eyes would glaze over, or he would pick up his newspaper and start glancing over it. It was clear he did not want to know.

Last week, she started to tell him about Jo, a girl in the office who booked a client to Dayton in Ohio instead of Daytona in Florida, and the panic that ensued to exchange the wrong tickets for the right tickets.

"Why are you telling me a story about people I don't know?" he'd asked.

"Because it's a funny story and they are my work friends," Clara had answered, trying to keep the irritation out of her voice.

"Work friends? Clara, you have only been there a few weeks, they are hardly your friends, now are they?" he'd said.

"Yes, they are my friends, Richard. I see them every day. You could at least show some interest."

"This was all your idea, not mine, so forgive me for not caring what Jo did or didn't do today. I'm glad you are enjoying your little job, but I won't pretend that I'm interested in people I don't know."

Clara had been furious. "*I can't believe how unsupportive you are!*" she shouted at him. "*I do everything around here! Nothing has changed for you! I have not asked you for a thing. Or maybe that's your problem, is it?*"

"What are you talking about?"

"I'm working, earning money, and not asking you for anything. Is that why you don't like it? Because I am more independent now?"

"You are being ridiculous. All this because I don't want to hear about your work stories? I don't understand you, Clara."

"No, I don't think you do," she had said and left the room.

Her hands were shaking. Shaking with anger and also with fear,

fear for the future of her marriage. She had gone to her handbag and had taken out the phone number of the therapist Miriam had recommended. She rang to make her first appointment.

Clara wiped a single tear away. Things weren't great but she really hoped they would work through this. Her sessions with the therapist had been enlightening. They had spoken a lot about the past but mostly about the present and the changes that Clara was making in her life that Richard was so resistant to.

The therapist had said that she would exhaust herself physically and mentally trying to do everything herself, trying to keep things the way they had been just for Richard's sake. The fact was that things were not as they were before. Richard's resistance might be because change can be hard for some people and all these changes had come at once. He needed time to adjust and accept them. Clara needed to talk to him when neither of them were tired.

This overnight break by herself had given her the space to look at her situation now from a distance. She was happy with her work – it energized her. She loved her new funky look and she had cut out all the chocolate and had started to eat less of the bad food and think about what she was eating now. She found that she no longer needed the sweets and chocolate because she was busy and happy getting up each morning for work. Her clothes were getting a little looser and she had started taking a walk in the evening to get a bit fitter and to clear her head.

She did love Richard, but she just didn't like him much at the moment. The therapist suggested that they have a date night soon. She suggested going to a movie and then getting a bite to eat or a drink afterward. By going to a movie, you couldn't argue in the cinema, and it gave you something to talk about afterward. Clara was going to suggest this to Richard next week. She really wanted to get that connection back between them. Their relationship was definitely worth fighting for.

Clara yawned and then pushed back the covers. Her breakfast was being delivered at nine-thirty and she wanted to get a swim in beforehand. She was looking forward to seeing the girls later and catching up. So much had happened since the Galway trip and she was dying to hear everyone's news.

Helen put her hood up and walked quickly from the service station to her car. God, it is freezing, she thought as she struggled to open her car door without spilling her coffee or dropping her doughnut. Safely inside, she placed the coffee securely in the cup-holder and dragged her big shoulder bag up from the passenger-seat floor onto the seat. Opening the bag wide, she removed the three almost full bottles of Coke she had brought from home. Reaching into the inside pocket of her jacket she took out the half bottle of vodka she had just purchased. She had deliberately chosen this service station on the N11 as it was the largest and the smaller ones didn't have off-licenses. She unscrewed the vodka and the Coke bottles and carefully poured some vodka into each of them. She then put the lids back on the bottles tightly and put the vodka bottle under her seat and the Coke bottles back in her bag. Now, she thought zipping up the bag, I can relax knowing that they are there when I need them

Taking a bite from her doughnut she felt pretty good about her progress. She was feeling much happier about her life since returning from Galway but Jerry was still being distant from her. When she tried to get close to rekindle their love life, he complained about being tired from early starts and long days. She understood that he worked hard but his mind just seemed to be elsewhere these days.

I have to make more of an effort, she thought as she looked at her face in the rear-view mirror. Maybe I can get some make-up tips from Vivienne this weekend. I just have to remind him that the old Helen he fell in love with is still here.

Starting the car, she took a sip of her coffee, finished her donut, and got back on the motorway to Wexford.

Chapter 44

The sweet fragrance of flowers reached Vivienne's nose before she opened her eyes. Waking up, her eyes focused on a beautiful bouquet of white roses lying beside her head on her pillow.

"What …?" Vivienne rubbed her eyes and pushed herself up in the bed. She picked them up and inhaled their scent. Turning her head, she saw Jack lying beside her, his head propped up with pillows. He had a big grin on his face.

"Oh Jack, these are beautiful! But where did they come from?"

"Honestly? The back seat of my car. I brought them with me last night, but my passionate companion didn't give me any time to go back out to get them."

"Thank you, I love them."

Vivienne leaned over and kissed him slowly.

"How can I ever thank you?" she said coyly.

"I will leave that up to you, darling," he said, his blue eyes twinkling.

Vivienne was so turned on. Placing the flowers gently on the bedside table she then turned back, pushed back the duvet, threw her long leg across his torso and straddled him, sitting up straight and arching her back.

"Now that is some view," Jack said, reaching his hands up to cup her breasts.

Vivienne moaned and arched her back more, feeling his arousal beneath her thighs. She leaned over him, their mouths meeting as his hands moved from her breasts to glide gently over her buttocks. They moved in time with each other's bodies. Jack had a way of making her feel wild and free. She was never self-conscious when she was in bed with him, and this just aroused him more. They moved into different positions without speaking, matching each other's rhythm and passion until they both came loudly together and crashed back on the bed.

"That was amazing," Jack said, panting and resting his hand on her ass.

"The things you do to me, Jack Brady," Vivienne said when she found her breath. "Okay, now move it, my friends are coming soon."

"Charming! You've had your way with me and now you're kicking me out?"

"Yes, sir, I am," Vivienne said, laughing, "but don't worry – I'll feed you first."

"Actually I'm starving," said Jack, rubbing his stomach.

"Well, there is a whole lasagne downstairs that we never got to last night."

"And why was that?" Jack said, smiling and gently biting her shoulder.

"I guess we were too busy?" Vivienne smiled back.

"I can't wait for Chicago when we won't have to sneak around. Did you get your flights sorted?"

"Oh yes, and I've told the kids and Tom about Mummy's extra-long business trip to source clients."

"It's going to be great. I know some great restaurants and jazz bars that I can't wait to take you to."

Vivienne could hardly believe her luck that this gorgeous man was still interested in her. She had hoped that Galway wasn't a once-off fling but didn't feel she was in a position to expect much more as she was still officially married. But the multiple bouquets that greeted her when she returned to the office after the Galway weekend confirmed that Jack Brady did want to see her again. She had travelled to Galway twice since then and Jack had travelled here to be with her. He was attending a three-day conference in Chicago and Vivienne was flying out when it finished to spend a whole five days with him. She got butterflies in her stomach when she thought about it. When she told the kids that she would be away for five days they didn't bat an eye. They were used to her going away for work and they would stay with Tom for the five days. Vivienne was surprised at how easy it was to get away and how easily everyone accepted it. The reality was that the kids were older now and did not need her so much anymore. This was her time now and she was going to enjoy every minute of it.

"Come on, time to get up. I will make you breakfast after my shower," Vivienne said, standing up.

"Does that shower fit two?"

"No, it's tiny."

"Well, we'll just have to get as close as possible then," Jack said as he chased her out of the bedroom.

Chapter 45

Miriam checked her watch as she clenched the steering wheel, waiting for the lights to change on the dual carriageway. I'm so late, she thought, crinkling her forehead and biting her lip. She had texted Vivienne to say she had got delayed and would not get there until dinner time. That was not the plan of course. She should have been there by now walking on the beach but, with Helen already down there, Jerry was in no hurry to leave her bed.

She knew it was wrong but usually he could only stay for an hour before having to pick up the kids or rush home for dinnertime, but today neither of them was in any rush. Miriam could not believe she was having an affair with the father of her child. It had not been her intention. She placed a hand on her bump and felt her baby move. She felt so alive. How Jerry found her attractive with this big bump was a mystery to her, but the bump did not put him off in any way. Sometimes after sex, he lay beside her rubbing her bump and something in his eyes made her suspect that maybe he knew the baby was his. Maybe she was imagining it as he never once asked, so hopefully he would never bring it up. Bizarre as it sounded, she was going to ask Jerry to help her paint the nursery and put a cot together as she couldn't do it all by herself. Was she mad to ask him? It didn't feel mad. It felt completely natural.

The sound of a car horn beeping from the car behind her jolted her. The lights had turned green. She took off, ignoring the other driver as he passed her at speed. It was raining heavily now, and she was going to take her time. She was in such a good mood now and no cranky driver was going to change that. She couldn't believe how well things were going actually.

Chapter 46

"Welcome!" Vivienne greeted Clara at the door of the cottage and hugged her friend.

"Oh, it's beautiful here!" Clara said, stepping into the cottage and feeling the heat from the open fire.

"Helen should be here any minute. She just rang me for directions. Let me show you to your room. You are here first so you can have the downstairs room to yourself if you like and Helen and Miriam can share the room upstairs."

"That sounds good to me," said Clara, picking up her overnight bag and following Vivienne to the downstairs bedroom. It had two single beds. The orange duvet covers matched the curtains. A shelf in the bedroom had framed photos of Vivienne and her kids, at different ages, playing on the beach.

"This is a lovely room," Clara said, putting her bag on the spare bed.

Just then Helen pulled up in her car and Vivienne went to open the door for her.

"*I made it!*" Helen called from the driveway. "*I'm so happy to be here!*"

"Come in, come in!" said Vivienne and she opened the door wide for her.

"Vivienne, this place is amazing. The cottages are so cute. How did you ever find somewhere like this?"

"Oh, nothing to do with me. My dad's golf club took a day trip to play a golf tournament down here against the local golf club. He took a wrong turn when he was leaving and ended up driving into this estate and that's when he saw this cottage for sale. It was in the winter, so it hadn't had many viewings. A few days later he took my mum down and they bought it immediately. And it has been the best investment ever. We have had some great times down here and the kids have had great summers here. But I love it in winter too. The quiet is so restful, and the beach is only fifteen minutes' walk away."

"I just love it," Helen said, looking around and wondering if she and Jerry could ever have a holiday home like this one day.

"Let me show you to your room," Vivienne said, taking Helen's bag.

"Oh, I'll carry that," Helen said quickly in case Vivienne saw the Coke bottles in her holdall.

"You're sharing with Miriam if that's okay?"

"Of course! I can't wait to see her. I'd say she's huge since we saw her last."

"Here we go," Vivienne said, leading Helen into a blue room decorated in a nautical theme. The blue striped duvets matched the curtains and pictures of the beach hung on the wall. There was a double bed and a single bed in the room.

"I'll give Miriam the double bed. This will do me fine," Helen said, putting her bag on the bed.

"Okay. Well, come down when you're ready and we might head out," Vivienne said.

"Great, I'll come with you now. I'd love a walk."

Clara was standing in front of the fire when they came downstairs.

"Clara, you look so well!" said Helen as they hugged. Clara looked so relaxed since the last time she saw her, and her clothes definitely looked looser.

"I've lost a few pounds, not much, but I'm trying to stay away from the chocolate and the biscuits." She was about to tell the girls about her night in Monart but stopped herself. She might tell them later or maybe she would keep it to herself, she wasn't sure yet.

"I thought we might go for a walk on the beach before Miriam gets here," Vivienne said. "She messaged me to say she had got delayed in Dublin, so she won't be here until later."

"A walk sounds great. I don't think the weather forecast is too good later."

"No. It's lovely now but there is rain and strong winds on the way. It's already raining in Dublin, so it's best to go out now and then we can settle down for the night. We can pick up a few things for dinner too. I have a lasagne and there's some wine here, so maybe we'll get a salad and some bread in the village. We can stay in tonight and relax in our jammies and have a great catch-up. It's lovely down here by the fire when it's stormy outside."

"That all sounds good to me," Clara said, putting on her coat.

"Vivienne, you wouldn't have a spare jacket, would you? I don't think my jacket is warm enough," said Helen.

"Again, Helen?" Clara said, laughing.

"There's no TK Maxx down here, babe," smiled Vivienne, "but

I always leave a few jackets here. Let me get you one."

"I'm such an eejit. I was so happy to be coming here that I just rushed out the door and didn't think," said Helen with a shrug.

Vivienne handed Helen a big wax jacket she usually used for standing in the cold watching Alex play rugby.

"Thanks a mil," Helen said, putting on the huge jacket, and they all headed out the door.

"This is a beautiful beach," Clara said as they stood by the lifeguard hut, looking out at the rough sea. Fishing boats could be seen in the distance and the big Irish Ferries ship that sailed to France daily could be seen in Rosslare harbour.

"I remember sailing on that boat for our first campsite holiday in France," said Helen. "The kids absolutely loved it."

"I would have loved to have done a campsite holiday with the kids, but Tom wouldn't hear of it. It's not his style at all," Vivienne said, looking over at the harbour. "Let's keep moving."

She led the way down onto the sand towards the shoreline. The sun was breaking out from behind the clouds, but the wind was getting up a bit and the sea was very choppy. They walked along the beach past Kelly's Hotel, but the dark clouds over Wexford town looked like they were heading their way.

"Right, let's turn back," said Vivienne. "This wind is bitter."

Her phone vibrated in her pocket.

"Oh, it's a text from Miriam. She's halfway here. That's good. She should be here by five so we can have dinner when she gets here."

"Great," said Clara.

"I just need one or two things. We'll pop into the shop and then head home," Vivienne said, leading the way.

Chapter 47

Miriam put her phone into a phone holder on her windscreen so she could follow the directions to Vivienne's place. She had texted Vivienne from a service station to get the address again. Damn pregnancy bladder, she thought as she left the ladies'. This was the second garage she had had to stop at to use the bathroom. Picking up a bottle of wine and some pastries, she paid for her items and then ran to her car. The wind was getting stronger, and the rain was getting heavier, but she was almost in Wexford now. She was looking forward to relaxing and having the chats when she got there. Vivienne had mentioned an open fire and Miriam planned to plonk herself beside it and put her feet up. Maybe Jerry could take out my gas fire and put a real one in, she wondered. I shouldn't be thinking of him. He'll probably stop visiting when the baby comes, she sighed. Best not to think too far ahead, she thought as she typed Vivienne's address into her phone. She did not want to waste any more time getting there.

Pulling out onto the motorway, google maps told her it was forty minutes to her destination. Brilliant, she thought, I'll be there in no time. Pressing start on the app, she set off again.

The traffic wasn't heavy but there were a lot of trucks on the road. Miriam tried to avoid driving behind them as the wet roads caused the trucks to spray dirt up onto her windscreen when they passed her. She just took her time and let them pass. It was getting dark now and visibility would not be great if this rain got any heavier.

Just then a text popped up on her phone. It was from Jerry.

Hey, gorgeous, let me know when you get there

Keeping her left hand on the wheel, Miriam typed a reply with her right hand.

So, sweet, are you worried about me?

Well, you are carrying special cargo

So, you're not worried about me at all then? Miriam typed, keeping her eyes on the road in between each word.

Of course, but I know, Miriam

Know what? That I'm special? Miriam typed, smiling at his cryptic texts.

I know the baby is mine

Miriam gasped. A truck blew its horn at her.

"*Shit!*" she shouted, grabbing the steering wheel with both hands. *Shit! Shit! Shit!* He knows. How could he know? It must be just a hunch.

Miriam could feel her heart racing. She took deep breaths. Oh God, what am I going to reply? She needed to pull over. She couldn't concentrate. Seeing a garage up ahead, she indicated. The rain was getting heavier, and her heart was pounding.

Babe? Are you okay? Jerry's message flashed back at her from her phone.

She glanced at it and then pulled in left to the garage. But she wasn't concentrating and did not slow down enough for the turn. And as she looked at Jerry's message again, she didn't see the truck pulling out of the garage and, when she did, she tried to jam on her brakes.

But it was too late.

Chapter 48

"I think I'll put the lasagne on now," Vivienne said as she took it out of the fridge. "Miriam should be here in twenty minutes or so."

"I hope she's okay driving. It's gone very dark out there and the rain is belting it down now," Clara said, looking out the window.

"She should be grand. There wouldn't be much traffic on the road except for the trucks heading for the Euro port."

Helen's phone buzzed as she received a message from Jerry.

"*Aw*, that's so sweet. Jerry says hi and was just checking we all got here safely. It's lashing in Dublin too."

He doesn't normally message me, she thought, but it is nice to know he's thinking about me.

Clara wondered if she should text her husband. She didn't really want to but felt now that she should make an effort. She took her phone out and sent him a quick text: **Arrived safe and well, lashing here, hope all okay at home.**

She had to add that last bit, but he was well able to look after everything when she was away and needed to pull his weight a bit more.

Helen read out her reply to Jerry's text: "*All here except Miriam. Raining here. Staying in for the night. Hx.*" She sent the message. "Sounds wild out there, doesn't it?"

"It does, rather," Vivienne replied. "Will I open a bottle of wine?"

"Oh yes, please!" said Clara.

"I'm fine. I have some Coke upstairs," Helen said, standing up.

"Oh, my phone is ringing," said Vivienne. "I hope Miriam isn't lost. No, that's not her number." Vivienne looked quizzically at her phone. "Hello? Yes?"

Vivienne's face turned white.

The two women looked at her as the atmosphere changed from jovial to alarmed.

"Viv! What is it?" Clara said.

"Okay, yes, thank you, we're on our way," Vivienne said shakily and closed her phone.

"Viv?" Helen said.

"That was Wexford General Hospital. There's been an accident. Miriam … My number was the last one she called … so they redialled. We have to get there."

Vivienne grabbed her coat and bag.

"Is she okay?" Helen said, feeling panicked.

"I don't know. They said a very serious accident. Should I ring back?" Vivienne teared up, looking at her friends' shocked faces.

"No, let's just get there. Vivienne, are you okay to drive?"

"Yes, I am."

"Okay, let's take your car – do you know the way?" Clara said, trying to pull her friends together.

"Yes, we had to take Alex there years ago. Oh God, I feel sick. She's going to be okay, isn't she?"

"Let's just go," Clara said, grabbing the car keys and pushing her friends towards the door.

They closed the door of the cottage, locked it, and ran to Vivienne's car.

They drove in silence, not knowing what they were about to face at the hospital.

Chapter 49

"I think you might want to sit down," a young nurse said as she motioned them toward four seats in an overly bright room that said *Family Room* on the door.

The ladies had been led to this side room when they arrived at the hospital reception in the Accident and Emergency Department. The hospital was busy and noisy with staff rushing around and the sound of machines beeping in the background.

Clara looked around the small room and felt scared. She had a really bad feeling about this.

A doctor quietly entered the room.

"I am Doctor Rasheed – myself and my team are looking after your friend, Miriam," he said solemnly, looking from one face to another.

Vivienne felt her heart beat loudly as she looked into the doctor's eyes, terrified of what he was going to say next. The women looked from one to another. A tear ran down Helen's face as the fear of what they were about to be told took hold.

"May I ask, what relation are you to Miriam?" the doctor asked.

Clara spoke first. "We're her friends. We're staying at my friend's cottage," she said, pointing to Vivienne, "and we were waiting for Miriam to arrive. Can you tell us what has happened, please? Is she okay?"

The doctor looked up from his notes.

"I'm afraid it's not good news. Miriam was in a serious car accident. We couldn't ascertain who her family were on the contacts list on her phone, so we called the last person she spoke to and that was Vivienne?"

"Yes, that's me," Vivienne nodded.

"Do you ladies have the name or phone numbers of her next of kin?"

"*Oh, God!*" Helen started crying.

Clara moved to put her arm around her, and the nurse came over with a box of tissues.

"I can try to get her brother or sister's number from her phone if you like, but how serious is this?" said Vivienne, gripping the sides of her seat.

The nurse and doctor looked at one another.

"Miriam was involved in a collision with a truck on the M11. She was very seriously injured and is on a life-support machine at the moment."

"Oh my God," Clara whispered. "And the baby?"

"Miriam is very far along in her pregnancy and as her injuries are mostly head injuries, the baby seems unaffected by the accident. However, there could be delayed shock, so we need to deliver the baby by caesarean section as soon as possible. She is being taken to theatre as we speak."

"And Miriam?"

"I'm very sorry but Miriam's injuries are too great, and I'm afraid she will not recover. She was resuscitated at the scene and the paramedics kept her alive until we could put her on life support, but our tests show no vital signs. I'm so sorry."

Clara quietly sobbed.

"Delivering her baby safely is our main concern now. I will come back to you when we have done that and update you then. Sonya here will go through Miriam's phone with you and hopefully we can contact her family. We don't have time to wait, I'm afraid. Once again, I am so very sorry."

"Thank you, doctor," Helen said in a whisper.

Vivienne was in shock, staring into space.

The doctor turned and left the room, closing the door quietly behind him.

Silence.

"I – I –" Clara stuttered.

"You have all had a terrible shock. Take a moment and then we can go through the phone together," the nurse said, rubbing Clara's back as she sobbed.

The sounds of her sobs echoed around the small room.

Vivienne felt suffocated. "Can I open a window?"

"Yes, of course, I'll do that for you." The nurse pulled up the blind and opened the window. It was dark outside now and the wind and rain were adding to the chill factor. The freezing air blew in, rustling the papers on the noticeboard.

Vivienne stood at the window, closed her eyes, and let the icy air pinch her face like pins and needles. She wanted to feel something. She wanted the cold air to slap her in the face and wake her from this nightmare.

A tap on the door was followed by a catering staff member with a tray of tea and biscuits.

"Just let reception know if you need more," she said quietly and nodded as she left. It was clear that she had delivered tea to this room many times to grieving and shocked family members whose lives had been changed forever.

The nurse stood up and poured the tea. "Milk or sugar?" she asked Clara.

Clara blew her nose and stood up to get her tea. "Just milk, thanks."

"And your friend?" she said, motioning to Vivienne.

"Eh, a little milk too," said Clara.

The nurse poured the milk in and went to Vivienne who was still standing at the open window.

"Come and sit down and drink some tea," she said gently, taking Vivienne's elbow and leading her to the seat. She handed Vivienne the cup and saucer, went and pulled the window in, leaving it slightly ajar, then returned. "When you're ready we'll go through the phone if that's okay."

"I can do that now," said Helen and the nurse pulled up a seat beside her and took out a notebook and pen.

"Okay, well, there was no lock on the phone so we can just switch it on," she said, taking the phone out of her pocket.

Helen gasped when she saw how broken and cracked the screen was from the crash.

"I'm so sorry," the nurse said, looking from the phone to Helen, registering her shock.

Helen wiped a single tear away and took a deep breath. "Okay, let's do this."

"We can go to her contacts list," said the nurse, "but there are twelve missed calls from this one number and a few texts from it too. Can you take a look and see if you recognise it? Maybe it is one of your numbers?"

Helen took the phone. "I don't think any of us rang her today except for ..."

Helen stopped mid-sentence.

"Wait. Sorry. I need to check something," she said, shaking her head. Taking her own phone out of her jeans pocket, she hit her own contacts list. "This doesn't make sense. It couldn't be ..." Helen looked from her phone back to Miriam's in disbelief.

"What is it?" Vivienne said, getting up and walking over to look over Helen's shoulder.

"It's ... it's Jerry's number."

"*Your* Jerry?" Clara said, putting down her cup and saucer on the coffee table.

Helen scrolled through Miriam's phone. "They're all from Jerry."

"Is Jerry a family member?" the nurse said, looking around at the girls' obvious shock.

"No," Helen said, staring at the phone. "Jerry is my husband."

"But why would he be ..." Clara started but then stopped when she saw Vivienne shake her head, signalling for her to stop talking. Clara's hand flew to her mouth in shock.

Helen looked from Miriam's phone back to the girls.

"*What the actual fuck!*"

"Helen, let me check the phone," said Vivienne. "There might be a reasonable explanation."

"No! I need to read them," Helen said calmly as she scrolled down the list of texts from her husband to her friend.

"I don't think now is the time … we need to find her brother's number or Sharon's number," Vivienne said, putting her hand out for the phone.

"Back off, Viv," Helen said firmly but calmly as she read the texts that Jerry had sent to Miriam.

The atmosphere in the room changed as Helen's eyes widened at what she was reading.

"Is there something wrong?" the nurse said, looking confused.

Vivienne placed her hand on her shoulder to signal that they needed to wait until Helen was finished.

"Here," Helen said, handing the phone to Vivienne. "I have seen all I need to see. Sorry," she said to the nurse. "I can't help you with this."

With that, she stood up and walked to the window.

Clara nodded to Vivienne to carry on with the nurse and went to stand beside Helen. She said nothing, just stood there. Whatever was in those texts, she didn't need to know about it right now – she just needed to let her friend know that she was standing with her, supporting her.

"Okay, I found it," Vivienne said to the nurse. "I have her brother's number here." She pointed to it and the nurse took down the number. "And this is her sister Sharon."

"Great, thanks, I'll go and get the doctor to call them." She hesitated, glancing over at Helen. "Is she okay?"

"Yes. Yes, you go – we'll look after things here."

The nurse left and Vivienne went and stood on the other side of Helen and the three friends stood in silence looking out into the dark of the night, trying to make sense of what had just happened.

Chapter 50

The next hour or two went by in a blur of confusion and shock. Helen had taken a walk to clear her head, refusing Vivienne and Clara's offers to go with her. They were both glad when she returned but she refused to speak to them. A staff member brought more tea and biscuits, but Helen couldn't sit still and chose to stand by the window as she tried to make sense of everything.

The three women were deep in their own thoughts when the door opened. Vivienne turned around first.

"Oh ... oh dear," she said as Jerry entered the room.

Clara and Helen turned to look at him in disbelief.

"What are you doing here, Jerry?" Helen said calmly and slowly as she approached him.

"*Em*," Jerry said, moving towards her, looking nervously from one woman to another. "Well, when you said in your text that Miriam had not arrived and it was getting late and it's such an awful night out there, I ... well, I had her number from a job I did for her ... so I rang to check that she was okay, you know, being pregnant and everything."

Jerry was shuffling awkwardly from foot to foot. He kept running his fingers through his hair which he always did when he was nervous. Helen knew this, of course, because she knew Jerry or at least she thought she did up to now.

"So why are you here?" Helen asked, looking directly at him.

"Well, I tried your phone and then I just had a bad feeling, so I rang the hospital, and they told me about the accident. And, oh my God, I just felt I should come and support you and … what happened? Do you know? Have they spoken to you yet?"

"Incredible," Helen said, shaking her head.

Jerry ran his fingers through his hair again.

"Yes, I suppose it is. I just had this feeling, and …"

Helen turned away from him and sat down.

"Just shut the fuck up, Jerry, you're pathetic," she said.

"*What!* What are you talking about?" he said nervously.

Before she could answer him, Nurse Sonya came into the room.

"Oh hello," she said, looking at Jerry.

"Is there any news?" Vivienne said, coming forward.

"Yes, yes, there is. The doctors delivered a baby girl. She's a bit on the small side, not being full-term, but all tests at the moment show that she survived the crash intact. She has been taken to ICU, but at the moment it looks like she'll be fine."

"Oh, that's wonderful news," Clara said, crying again.

"And Miriam?" Jerry said.

The nurse looked confused. "Are you a relative?"

"No, I'm Helen's husband," he said, looking over at Helen.

"We haven't had time to tell him," Vivienne said, turning to Jerry. "Jerry, Miriam didn't make it. The doctors kept her on life support long enough to deliver the baby."

Jerry almost stumbled backward with the shock.

"*No, that can't be, oh my god!*" he said, running his two hands through his hair and steadying himself against the wall.

"I'm so sorry," the nurse said, putting her hand on Jerry's shoulder.

Helen looked at him and felt nothing.

"Are you okay?" the nurse asked Jerry. "Do you need a seat?"

Jerry shook his head.

The nurse turned to speak to the women.

"We are still waiting on Miriam's next of kin to arrive, but I can let one of you down to see the baby if you wish."

"Thank you, that would be lovely," Clara said.

"Jerry will go," Helen said.

"What? Me?" Jerry said.

"Yes, *you*, Jerry. I know everything. I saw all your texts on Miriam's phone. I know."

The room was silent as the women looked at each other, not knowing what was going to happen next.

"Nurse, this is my husband Jerry, but it seems he is also the father of Miriam's baby," Helen said, standing up.

The nurse's jaw dropped open for a second and then she just nodded. "Okay, I see."

"Helen, please, I need to talk to you," said Jerry.

"Well, I don't want to talk to you, Jerry. And this is certainly not the time. I am going back to Vivienne's cottage." She picked up her coat and bag.

"But Helen ..." Jerry said, taking her arm.

"*Don't you dare touch me!*" she said, pulling her arm away from him. "Go and see your daughter." Turning to the nurse, she said, "I'm leaving but Jerry will stay here until Miriam's brother and sister arrive. They have things to talk about."

The nurse was trying to process all that she had heard. "Yes, of course, come with me then," she said to Jerry.

"Helen, we need to talk, just five minutes."

"Get out, Jerry," Helen said and turned her back on him.

He turned and left with the nurse.

"Jesus Christ! Are you okay, Helen?" Vivienne came and put her arm around her.

"No, I'm not. It's all too much to take in, I don't know how I feel. What a bloody nightmare."

"Oh, darling," Clara said, hugging her.

"I need to get out of here. Is it okay if I get a taxi to the cottage?"

Clara glanced at Vivienne and gave her a nod.

"I'll drive," said Vivienne, picking up her bag.

"You don't have to, Viv. If you want to stay, do."

"No, I don't think there is anything we can do here."

"Well, I don't mind staying until Miriam's brother and sister get here," said Clara.

"Are you sure?" asked Vivienne.

"Yes, I'd like to."

"Okay then. You can keep us up to date then if there are any further developments."

"I will, of course."

"Do you have the address for a taxi later?"

"I do, yeah. You two go home and get some rest and I'll ring you if there is any news. Otherwise I will see you both in the morning."

Vivienne linked Helen's arm as she led her out of the room. She had a feeling that nobody would get any sleep tonight.

Three Months Later

Chapter 51

"Hi!" Vivienne waved at Clara as she entered the restaurant.

Clara looked so well. She had lost a stone in weight and had kept the funky hairstyle that she had got in Galway. She looked so cool and happy in herself.

"How are you? How was your trip?" Clara asked as she embraced her friend before sitting down.

"Great. Everything went really well, and I think all our clients were impressed. You picked the perfect venue for the conference."

"Oh that's great. This place is lovely," Clara said, looking around. The small café was beautifully decorated in the blue and lilac tones of the south of France and the walls bore pictures of café scenes and lavender fields. French doors at the back opened out onto a lovely garden.

"I went ahead and ordered a selection of their scones for us because they are divine and get sold out quickly if it's busy. They come with fresh cream and locally made jam."

"Sounds perfect," Clara said, taking her jacket off.

Clara had been made permanent in Vivienne's company and

Vivienne had given her the official title of HR manager and increased her wages. The truth was that Clara did way more than just HR. She looked after everybody and had become Vivienne's right-hand woman. Vivienne could go away on business happy, knowing that Clara would keep everything on track back at the office. Although they never spoke about him, Vivienne knew that Clara knew about her relationship with Jack Brady. Clara could keep secrets and Jack would remain a secret for the time being. Vivienne wanted to wait until the kids had well and truly got used to the new situation of having separated parents and living between two houses before even approaching the idea that their mother might be seeing someone.

She had put the house up for sale and when she had her new place, she might feel more comfortable about Jack being there. He understood this. She just couldn't have him in what was their family home. Sarah had moved to London and was about to start her college course. Vivienne had waited until she was settled in college before putting the house on the market. Alex didn't care as long as he could stay in the area and that their new place would have an extra bedroom so he could have his friends stay over. The family home would sell for a good price as there was always demand for family homes in their area, so Vivienne would have the money for a big three-bedroomed apartment or a townhouse. She had heard through the grapevine that Gareth had lost his job and that there was a big enquiry going on at the bank, but Tom had said nothing to her about it and she didn't think he would either.

Her relationship with Jack was going from strength to strength. They'd had a few trips away together and she stayed in Galway with him when the kids went to stay with Tom.

"Did you get a new colour in your hair?" Vivienne asked Clara.

"Yes, a subtle purple stripe. Do you like it?" Clara said, swishing her hair.

"I love it!"

Just then a commotion at the door made them both turn around. It was Helen, struggling to get a buggy through the restaurant's narrow doorway.

Vivienne waved over, smiling, as two members of staff helped Helen through the door and carried her bags to their table.

"Hey, Helen! Great to see you!" Clara said, standing up and hugging her friend tightly.

" You look great!" Vivienne stood up and hugged her friend.

"Well, I don't know how, seeing as I've been up all night with this one," she said, smiling.

"Okay, take her out. Where's our Miriam?" Clara said.

Helen pushed back the hood of the buggy.

"Here she is!" Helen gently lifted Baby Miriam out of the buggy and handed her to Clara.

"Oh she is so light," said Clara, cradling the baby, "but she has changed a bit since we saw her in your house."

Clara and Vivienne had arrived with baby clothes, nappies and a brand-new buggy when Baby Miriam was finally released from Wexford General Hospital and had been regular visitors ever since.

"Well, she is still tiny. Technically she is twelve weeks old but if she was a full-term baby she would only be two weeks old now. But she is putting on weight. Thanks again for all the baby things. You forget how much you need with these little ones." She ran her finger gently down the side of Baby Miriam's face.

"You must have had a path worn to Wexford," said Vivienne.

"Oh God, yes. It's a relief to have her home here in Dublin. And thank God we had your cottage to stay in. It made a world of a difference. And the boys loved it too. They thought they were going on holidays every time we went down to see her."

"I don't know who she looks like," Clara said, rocking her on her knee.

"You don't have to be polite, Clara – she's the bloody image of Jerry. The DNA test proved it but sure he couldn't deny her, could he?"

"God, Helen, you are just amazing," Vivienne said.

"Regular Wonder Woman, me!" Helen laughed as she took off her cardigan and put it on top of the buggy before moving it to the side out of the way.

Just then the waiter arrived with a selection of scones on a tray with three different jams, some butter, and freshly whipped cream. Another waiter arrived with pots of tea and coffee.

"Oh, I am so looking forward to this!" Helen said. "Will I put her back in the buggy?"

"Not at all. You go ahead and eat. I want to hang on to this little beauty for a while longer," said Clara, smiling at Miriam.

Vivienne poured herself some tea and Helen buttered her scone.

"So, Helen, tell us, how has it really been?" Vivienne asked.

Helen was spreading jam and cream on her scone. "If I look at the whole situation then obviously it has been horrendous, and three months on I still don't know how this will all work out. When I walked out of that hospital, the night of the crash, I didn't want to have anything to do with Jerry or the baby or any of it. I thought my head was going to explode with all the questions, the lies, the betrayal. I just couldn't believe it. But, like I told you, only for the fact I had agreed to meet Sharon and Simon at the hospital the next day I might have walked away."

Clara and Vivienne exchanged glances. Helen had told them about that meeting and how, after seeing Miriam's tiny baby in the incubator fighting for her life, neither Simon nor Sharon stepped up and offered to look after her. Helen couldn't believe it. Despite the shock of Jerry being the father, there was a fragile vulnerable baby here and none of this mess was her fault.

"I wish you could have seen the look on Sharon and Simon's faces when I suggested we keep her. The relief! I knew then that she would have a better home with us. You know, they haven't rung me once to see how we're getting on?"

"Unbelievable," sighed Clara. "And how have the boys reacted to having a sister?"

"Honestly, the kids are great. We told the older ones that Daddy had a baby with a woman who died in a terrible car accident and that they had a sister now. And that if anyone asked them, to just say that they have a new sister and that's it. The younger ones were just delighted to have a sister now and they never questioned it. It helped that we brought them to the hospital to see her, so they got used to the idea before she came home. I know people will probably gossip about it, but life goes on. Of course my mother thinks I'm nuts!" She laughed. "And I get that. What Miriam did was horrible – she slept with my husband and continued to do so and part of me will never forgive her for that. But she was single, and Jerry was not. And Miriam is not around to be angry at."

"Is it not a constant reminder, though, Helen?" Vivienne said tentatively. "And the name? You could have called her anything."

"Yes, but I insisted that she be called Miriam as a reminder to Jerry of what he did and also out of respect for Miriam. She was flawed just like the rest of us, and she betrayed me, but I still can't hate her, and she did not deserve to never see this little one." Helen leant over and tickled Baby Miriam under the chin. "And, as well as all that, I am madly in love with her. She took my heart. I have cleaned up my act and stopped drinking. I want to be the best mum to her. It just feels natural and right that she is part of our family now."

"You are fecking amazing, Helen – I don't think I could have done what you have done," Clara said. "How are things with you and Jerry now?"

"Different. He says he is sorry a hundred times a day, and he wants us to stay together and for everything to work out."

"And what do you want?"

"I don't know yet. He is certainly making an effort to keep the family together, so we'll see how it goes. Before Miriam came home, he converted the garage into two rooms – a bedroom and games room for the older two – and they moved down there. So Jerry is in their old room, and I am in the main bedroom."

"*Wow!* The sacrifices you have made, Helen," said Clara.

"Yes, it's mad and I have no idea how it will play out for me and Jerry. I'm not sure we're even ready for therapy yet. At the moment we are just getting on with it."

Baby Miriam opened her eyes and looked around

"Miriam would be so thankful and proud of you, Helen," said Vivienne. "There's not many women who would do what you are doing."

"Yes, but you ladies saved me. We have such a strong bond, and I did not want to break that. Hurt and anger could easily have broken this group up, but I need you girls. And now look at us here today. The four of us – Helen, Clara, Vivienne and Baby Miriam.

We will stay connected through this beautiful baby and we will keep Miriam alive for her and tell her about her. Miriam will always be with us now."

"We are here for you, Helen, and we will help out. And anytime it gets too much for you, you just call us, and we will be there," said Vivienne.

"We mean it, Helen, any time night or day we are here for you," Clara said, leaning across and squeezing her hand.

"Thanks, guys, I couldn't do this without you," Helen said, welling up and reaching out for Vivienne's hand too.

And with that, Baby Miriam waved her hands in the air, making the women laugh and the circle of friends was complete once more.

THE END

Made in United States
Troutdale, OR
04/25/2024

19418375R00206